After spending 35 years of his life in international business, British author Malcolm Roscow has no shortage of material from which to create absorbing stories. And after writing for 22 years, before finally being published, he feels he has earned his stripes and is now justified in calling himself a writer.

Also by this author, **'Another Boring Day in Paradise'**.

To Adrian, Heather and Laura.

Malcolm J. Roscow

THE KIPLOCK AFFAIR

To Rachel

AUSTIN MACAULEY
PUBLISHERS LTD.

A CIP catalogue record for this title is available from the British Library.

ISBN 9781786129819 (Paperback)
ISBN 9781786129826 (Hardback)
ISBN 9781786129833 (eBook)
www.austinmacauley.com

First Published (2017)
Austin Macauley Publishers Ltd.
25 Canada Square
Canary Wharf
London
E14 5LQ

Acknowledgments

First, I should like to thank my partner, Hil, for her patience while I was writing the book, her unswerving support, and for going through my work with a fine-tooth comb prior to my submitting it to Austin Macauley.

At Austin Macauley, I should like to thank Senior Editor, Hayley Knight, for her hand in taking on my book; Sophie Chamings, for the work she has done on the manuscript; Vinh Tran, for his kind words and constructive comments, and Ellie Johnson, who is my daily contact and who responds promptly to my emails, gives me advice when I need it, and champions my work in the marketplace. And last, but by no means least, all those behind the scenes who have made a contribution towards the publication of my book.

Chapter 1

Lake Buena Vista, Florida. Early August 1982

It was just after 1.30am and Angela was watching the old black and white movie Casablanca with Humphrey Bogart and Ingrid Bergman on the TV in Kiplock's hotel room. Bogart had just asked the pianist to Play it again, Sam, when a voice in the darkness growled, "If it's an apartment in the best part of town you want, now's the time to start earning it."

He sounded wide-awake, and Angela had the uneasy feeling he had been laying there watching her.

He sat up and switched on a bedside lamp.

Angela clicked the on/off switch on the remote to switch the TV off. "All right, Gerry," she said. "But I need to use the bathroom first."

He lurched over and grabbed her breasts. She made no effort to remove his hands, even though he was hurting her. "Take your clothes off." His voice was thick.

"Don't be ridiculous, Gerry. If I need to use the bathroom, I need to use the bathroom."

He let go of her. "All right, but be quick about it. And don't try to leave."

"Why would I try to leave when I've been sitting here waiting for you to wake up?" She had left her clutch bag on the nightstand beside her. She picked it up, rolled off the bed and headed for the bathroom, where she switched on the light and locked the door.

Kiplock yelled, "Don't lock the door."

"Shut up, you stupid man," she muttered.

In her clutch bag was a slim plastic container of about three inches' diameter. In it was a diaphragm. She took out the diaphragm, lifted her dress, fitted the diaphragm, and pulled her dress down again. Her dress had become badly creased after lying on the bed for four and a half hours, and she tried, unsuccessfully, to smooth out the creases. She took a quick look in the mirror, unlocked the door, switched off the bathroom light, and walked back into the bedroom.

She almost burst out laughing, because Kiplock was standing in the middle of the bedroom naked, not to mention fully erect, and he was trying to take a condom out of its foil package. He was clearly still very drunk because he was making a complete hash of it. And when she saw the size of the protuberance between his legs, she knew it was not only his millions that Maureen was interested in.

She took the foil package from him. "I think we can dispense with that," she said, tossing it in the waste paper basket. "I didn't come all this way to have one of those get in the way."

A thoughtful look crossed Kiplock's face. "It seems I might have underestimated Bill. He evidently knew what he was doing when he married you."

Angela said, "Gerry, can we please stop talking about Bill. It's you I came to see." She pressed herself against him.

Kiplock threw his arms around her and tried to undo the zipper on her dress.

She let him fumble with it for a moment or two, and then she backed away from him and looked him in the eye. "Are you going to take all night?"

"The zipper's stuck."

"The zipper is not stuck, Gerry. There's a little hook you have to undo first."

He tried to find the hook.

She backed away from him again. "For God's sake, Gerry" she tut-tutted. "Are you going to take all night?"

"I can't find the hook."

"Then rip my dress off."

This time it was he who backed away; suspicion written all over his face. "What are you up to, Angela? I know an expensive dress when I see one."

"Gerry, haven't you figured out yet that it's the rough stuff I like? Just stop talking, and rip it off."

"Anything to oblige a lady," Kiplock said. He grabbed the front of Angela's dress and ripped it off. It fell in a heap on the floor. "Now what?" he said. "You seem to be in charge here."

"I'll tell you what, Gerry, Bill isn't half as slow on the uptake as you are."

Kiplock's eyes narrowed. He ripped off her bra and threw her on the bed. He ripped off her panties and climbed on to the bed. He forced his knee between her legs.

As he prepared to enter her, Angela looked deep into his eyes. "You're not going to disappoint me, Gerry, are you?"

Chapter 2

Welwyn Garden City, Hertfordshire, England. Eight Months Earlier.

The phone on Bill Smith's desk rang. He picked it up. "Yes, Maureen?"

"There's a call from New York for you."

"Who is it?"

"Marcia something or other. She says she's Gerry Kiplock's PA."

Bill's pulse quickened. He had never met Gerry Kiplock, but he knew him to be the head of a very successful New York outfit, and he wasn't the sort of man to call just to pass the time of day. "Put her through."

A female voice with a nasal Brooklyn twang said, "Mr. Smith?"

"Speaking."

"Hold for Gerry Kiplock, please."

Bill had to smile. She had made it sound as if she were introducing the President of the United States.

"Bill?"

"Yes, hello, Gerry?"

"How are you?"

"I'm fine, thank you. And you?"

"I'm good."

"To what do I owe the pleasure?"

"Jacques Peterson suggested I call you."

"That's kind of him. How is the old devil? I haven't seen him since Canadian Pulp and Paper Week in Montreal last year."

"He's good. Drinking too much, like the rest of us. I guess you know he runs my French operation?"

"Yes, I'm aware of that."

"Bill, I'm calling because I'm setting up a network of offices around the world and Jacques recommended you for the UK. What do you say?"

Bill knew that Kiplock's company had sources from an extensive number of American paper and board mills and he could certainly use the business, but it depended on what the American had in mind.

"It depends what you're offering, Gerry," he said carefully. "I've been running my own business for three years now, and if you're offering me a job, I wouldn't be interested. I like my independence."

"I'm not offering you a job, Bill. Let me ask you a question; are you making as much money as you would like to be?"

That was an easy one to answer. What businessman worth his salt was ever making as much money as he would like to make? Money was the only reason businessmen were in business. "No, of course not," he said.

"How about if I offered you the opportunity to make let's say twice what you're making now?"

Bill was long enough in the tooth not to be taken in by unsubstantiated grandiose offers, but the American now had his full attention. "I'm listening," he said.

"Bill, I have a plane to catch, but I'll be in London next week. Can we meet? Preferably for dinner, to give us time to talk?"

"I don't see why not, Gerry. But it will have to be later in the week. I have to be in Finland on Monday and Tuesday."

"Look, Bill, I gotta go. I'm gonna miss my plane. Let me get back to you when I have my schedule worked out."

After Bill had hung up, he spun his high-backed black leather chair round and gazed through a pair of French windows that provided natural light to the desk end of his long rectangular office.

His office suite comprised three adjoining rooms, two of which were interconnected, over a row of shops on the first floor of a two-storey building on a shopping street that ran parallel to the main London to Edinburgh railway line in Welwyn Garden City, Hertfordshire. His landlord was the local council.

Welwyn Garden City was a small, but prosperous town, with an even mix of shops, offices and restaurants arranged around beautifully kept gardens. One of three garden cities built in the 1960s; the town's architecture was mock Georgian. Connected by the A1(M) motorway to the M25 motorway and London to the south, and Leeds, Manchester and Edinburgh to the north, the town was located about twenty-five miles due north of London. Because Bill did business with paper and board mills all over England, Scotland, and, to a lesser degree, Wales, motorways were his lifeline.

It was late afternoon on what had been a dull, grey January day and drivers were switching their lights on. The supermarket across the street seemed to be doing good business, and Bill recognised a pair of well-heeled women with early-teenage children in tow. The children were wearing the uniform of the private school that Jason, thirteen, and Melanie, eleven, attended. This meant that, by now, Angela would have picked the children up and taken them home.

Angela came in five days a week. She came in after dropping the children off at school in the morning, and she left again when it was time to pick them up in the afternoon. Her duties in the office included administration, invoicing, payment of bills, and whatever else she could take off Bill's hands to free him up and allow him to do what he was supposed to do: build the business.

Within the hour, trains from London would be disgorging floods of commuters at the station, which lay a walking distance of no more than three hundred yards from the office. If Bill happened to be looking in that direction, he was able to see the rooves of the trains, and when the weather was good, and his French windows were open, he would hear the whine of the inter-city expresses as they whistled past at speeds well in excess of a hundred miles an hour.

Being on the main rail line into London was another reason Bill had chosen Welwyn Garden City from which to run his business. He often had meetings with customers and overseas visitors in London, and many of these included lunch, or dinner. Heavy drinking was endemic in the industry, and whenever a meal was involved, copious amounts of alcohol would be consumed. For this reason, he would take the train into London. The last thing he needed was to lose his driving licence.

The door connecting his office to his secretary's office opened and Maureen, his secretary/PA, walked in. She handed him a blue and white folder containing the ticket for his Finnair flight to Helsinki. "You're booked into the Intercontinental Hotel, as usual," she said.

Maureen was not what Bill considered to be particularly good-looking, but her figure made up for what she lacked in the looks department. She had a figure to die for. In fact, when she had left after her interview, Angela, who was a director of Bill's company, had given him an emphatic no.

Unfortunately for the tall, slim, blonde, and very beautiful Angela, Maureen was better qualified than any of the other applicants, and Bill had hired her. He rarely overruled Angela, but with only three people in the business, he needed the best secretary/PA he could get.

Maureen had now been with the company for just over a year, and Bill had never had cause to regret his decision. Even Angela had to admit she was doing a good job.

Maureen was twenty-eight, and she was married to a man more than twice her age. Bill had met Ted, her husband, three or four times, and he had never been able to figure out what Maureen saw in him. To him, Ted could only be described as average; average height, average build, average looks and average in the way he dressed. He was the sort of man you would fail to notice even if you bumped into him in the street. But evidently Maureen saw something in him, because they had been married for over ten years and whenever Bill saw them together, she was either laughing at something Ted had said, or was clinging to his arm as if her life depended on it.

A couple of months ago, Maureen had let slip that she and Ted were trying for a baby and, as she stood there in front of Bill's desk waiting to see if he needed her for anything else, he asked her how things were going in the family department.

She pulled a face. "Nothing's happening. I think Ted's firing blanks."

Bill's mind flitted back to the conversation he had had with Gerry Kiplock. "Right," he said, absent-mindedly. "Let me know if I can help."

Maureen walked out with a thoughtful look on her face.

Chapter 3

On the Monday evening, it was after 10pm when Bill and Heikki Pentilla walked out of the four-star Palace Hotel, Helsinki.

Heikki, or at least the Finnish company he worked for, had stood Bill a slap-up dinner, starting with gravlax with mustard sauce, and the inevitable aquavit to wash it down with, a reindeer steak for the main course, complete with red wine, and cloudberries for dessert, washed down with two glasses of a very expensive dessert wine.

The hotel stood immediately across the street from the harbour. Backing on to the harbour, and standing slightly to the right of the hotel, was the old food hall where locals came to buy their perishables: bread, meat, fish and vegetables. At this time of the year, walking into the unheated Food Hall was like walking into a refrigerator.

The outside air temperature was registering minus 30°C, and Bill was wearing shoes with leather soles. He was stepping extremely carefully, as one slip on the icy pavement could have resulted in him finding himself in the back of an ambulance. He had seen it happen. The good news was that, considering how much alcohol he had drunk, if he had fallen it was unlikely he would have felt any pain.

A stiff wind blowing off the Baltic meant that the chill factor was several degrees lower than the actual air temperature, and Bill pulled the collar of his overcoat up around his ears to try and protect them from the icy and quite painful blast. He blew on his hands in a futile attempt to warm them, berating himself for his stupidity in forgetting to bring gloves. He should have known better. He had been here in the winter often enough.

On the far side of the harbour, a ferry of the Swedish Silja Line was preparing to ease away from its slip to begin its overnight crossing to Stockholm. The lights on the vessel's superstructure sparkled like stars in the freezing night air. On this side of the harbour, a ferry of the Finnish Viking Line was also preparing to leave its slip.

Seven nights a week, the two ferries crossed the Baltic, side-by-side. They left Helsinki together, and they arrived in Stockholm together. They left their slips in Helsinki at 10pm, negotiating their way to the Baltic through the maze of islands constituting the Finnish archipelago, and they arrived in Stockholm after negotiating the islands of the Swedish archipelago, eight hours later. The vessels had perfectly acceptable restaurants, and dancing, on board.

Bill did business in both Finland and Sweden and he had once been talked into taking the ferry, rather than flying to Stockholm. And once had been enough. The vessel had run into a force-eight gale in the middle of the Baltic and he had spent the night throwing up in the toilet in his cabin. To him, a one-hour flight against an eight-hour sail was a no-brainer.

As they climbed over piles of frozen snow en-route to the taxi rank, Heikki slapped Bill on the back and said, "Okay, my friend, dinner was on me, so the nightcap's on you."

Bill knew only too well that a nightcap to a Finn didn't just mean a drink, it meant a trip to a nightclub, of which Helsinki had many, and Bill knew from experience how expensive Helsinki nightclubs could be. But he didn't mind. He had secured the business he had come for. "You're on," he said. "Where would you like to go?"

"We go to Hesperia," Heikki said.

"Hesperia it is," Bill said.

All Bill's contacts in Helsinki were married, or had been, since some, thanks to their philandering, were now divorced, but most of them strayed if and when they got the opportunity. Their wives were well aware of what went on when their husbands went out for their so-called 'dinner meetings' and, in exchange for not making a fuss, they were allowed out themselves one night a week. Over time, the wives had settled on the Thursday night, and Thursday night in Helsinki had become known as wives' night, when the nightclubs were full of married women.

As they approached the taxi rank, Bill said, "So how is Ulla, Heikki?"

"Better than nothing," the Finn replied.

It was an old joke between them and, while it had long since ceased to be funny, Bill responded with the obligatory polite chuckle.

Bill had met Ulla on a couple of occasions. A Swedish-speaking Finn, she was absolutely stunning, and Bill knew that if he lived in Helsinki and he was married to Ulla, there would be no way she would be going out on a Thursday evening, unless it was with him.

They found a taxi and climbed in. Heikki gave the driver instructions as to where to take them, in Finnish.

Bill knew the odd word in Finnish: please, thank you, good day, that sort of thing, but otherwise the language was a mystery to him, as it was to most visitors. But it didn't matter because all the Finns he came into contact with were well educated and spoke excellent English.

As the driver eased the vehicle away from the curb, frozen snow crunched loudly under the vehicle's tyres.

Heikki slapped Bill on the thigh and said, "So, my friend, we give you a year, and we see how it goes."

The material to which he was referring was off-grade paperboard from a huge board mill in Karelia, the Finnish province lying next to the Russian border. In fact, it was possible to see the smoke stack of a Russia pulp mill from the windows on the eastern side of the Finnish mill. It was the best material of its kind on the market, and Bill had been trying to get his hands on it for at least two years. The material was to be sold for repulping, and he knew of five UK paper mills that could, and would, use it if he got his hands on it. And now he had. Since he did not have the means to buy and resell the material, his function would be to act as agent for Heikki's company. If he sold all the tonnage Heikki had told him was available, his commission on the business would exceed £100,000 a year, which, to Bill, was serious money.

The taxi crunched to a stop outside the five-star Hesperia Hotel, which was a mere hop, skip and a jump from the Intercontinental Hotel where Bill was staying.

They walked down a set of wide carpeted stairs, and handed in their coats.

In the basement nightclub, the lights were dim and a trio comprising piano, double bass and drums, was playing *If It Takes Forever I Will Wait For You*. On a small dance floor, men in business suits were dancing with much younger women. About half the tables were unoccupied, which was hardly surprising considering that today was a Monday. Young unattached women occupied some of the other tables. Candles flickered in sparkling glass holders on white linen tablecloths.

Bill and Heikki were shown to a table alongside the dance floor and a waitress appeared and asked, in English, what they would like to drink. Heikki ordered a Dewars and soda, Bill a Remy Martin. "And make them large ones," Bill said, feeling magnanimous as a result of the success of his trip.

Letting his eyes acclimatise to the gloom, Heikki looked around the room until he spotted who he was looking for. He raised his hand and one of two young women sitting at a table on the other side of the dance floor smiled and returned his greeting. It was clear she had been expecting him. "I'll be right back," he said, getting to his feet. He strode around the dance floor, and Bill watched in amusement as he bent and kissed the young woman full on the mouth.

The young woman introduced Heikki to her companion, and Bill watched Heikki shake hands with her. Heikki then nodded in Bill's direction, and said something, and the two women picked up their handbags and followed him to where Bill was sitting.

Bill got to his feet. "I see you haven't lost your touch, Heikki," he said, grinning.

Heikki introduced them, and then said, "Erva's mine, Bill. Harriett's yours."

Harriett looked to be in her early to mid-thirties. In typical Scandinavian fashion, she was tall, blue-eyed and blonde, and she spoke English as if she had been born and raised in England.

24

When they had all sat down, Bill raised a hand to summon the waitress. They ordered and made small talk until the drinks arrived. Then, to impress them with a Finnish toast someone had once taught him, Bill raised his glass, and said, "A toast."

They looked at him expectantly.

"Ettyhampartravistussi," he said.

Heikki and the two women burst into peals of laughter.

Finally, wiping the tears from his eyes, Heikki said, "Who taught you that, Bill?"

Bill eyed him suspiciously. "Someone I met at one of the mills. He said it had something to do with drinking enough to keep the teeth from going soft."

"That's not what it means where I come from," Erva said, still laughing.

"Looks like I've been had," Bill said ruefully.

The band ended the number they had been playing and began to play a slow modern ballad. Heikki got to his feet and put out his hand. "Erva, they're playing our tune." Erva smiled at him and got to her feet. They stepped on to the dance floor hand-in-hand.

Harriett shifted her chair closer to Bill's and pressed her thigh against his. Her perfume was light and intoxicating. She glanced at his wedding ring. "I see you're married, Bill," she said.

He nodded. "Yes, I'm married."

"Yes, but are you happily married?"

Bill knew what she was up to, but he went along with it. No sense ruining what was actually a very pleasant atmosphere. He shrugged. "Like any other married couple we have our ups and downs, but on the whole I'd say we are very happy."

"Do you have children?"

"Yes, two. A boy and a girl." Bill noticed she wasn't wearing a wedding ring and he asked her if she had ever been married.

"Once," she said, wistfully, "a long time ago. I married too young."

"Perhaps, when the right man comes along," Bill said encouragingly.

"Perhaps the right man already has come along," Harriett said, stroking the back of his hand.

Bill was well aware that in Finland there were a lot more men than women. This was partly because a large number of Finnish men of marriageable age had died in wars with Russia, and partly because there were a lot more girls being born today, than boys. The current imbalance was sixty-forty, the sixty percent being women, which explained why a lot of women of marriageable age would never be lucky enough to find a husband. And Bill knew that this was why perfectly respectable women went to nightclubs. There was always the chance they could persuade a visiting businessman he would be better off with them than the woman looking after his children back home. Two of Bill's friends in the industry had succumbed to such women and were now married to Finnish women. Once, he had almost succumbed himself, and he wasn't about to let that happen again which was why he was on his guard now.

He moved his hand and took a sip of his cognac.

Heikki and Erva were dancing cheek-to-cheek. They were covering less than a square metre of the dance floor, as were most of the other couples.

"What business are you in?" Harriett asked.

"The same as Heikki," he said. "Pulp and paper. What do you do for a living?"

"Perhaps I tell you later," she said coyly. She took his hand. "Dance with me."

Bill had no objection to dancing with her. It wasn't going to go any further. He stood six foot one, and she was almost as tall, although she was wearing heels. She pressed herself against him. His jacket was unbuttoned and he could feel her hard, erect nipples through his shirt.

The band was playing The Shadow of Your Smile and she murmured the words to the song in his ear. Her voice was husky.

He felt himself becoming aroused and tried to pull away from her.

She must have been aware of what was happening because she tightened his grip on him." Don't fight it, Bill," she murmured. "Just let it happen."

The memories of this happening to him some years ago flooded back. The conditions were exactly the same: the soft music, the dim lights, the nearness of a woman who would be available later if he wanted her, the intoxicating perfume. Also came the recollections of the four months it had taken for Angela to let him back in the house, and the two years it had taken before she would trust him again.

He pulled away. "I can't do this."

She relaxed her grip on his arm. "All right," she said, reluctantly. "Do you want to go back to the table?"

He needed to get himself under control first. "Yes," he said, "but give me a minute to compose myself."

When they got back to the table, Heikki had a drink in one hand, and Erva's hand in the other.

After they had sat down, Harriett took Bill's hand and rested it on her knee. It was more the gesture of a friend, than a provocateur, and it seemed to indicate she realised she had crossed the line, and was agreeing not to cross it again.

Heikki said, "Bill, ask Erva what she thinks of Gerry Kiplock."

Bill had told Heikki about his phone call from Gerry Kiplock over dinner, because he wanted Heikki's opinion of the American. Heikki had said at the time that he had only met Gerry Kiplock once, and didn't feel he knew him well enough to comment, except to say he certainly knew what he was talking about when it came to matters of business. Bill had not given Gerry Kiplock any thought since they had left the restaurant, and Heikki's comment took him by surprise.

This must have registered on his face, because Heikki said, "He was here two months ago. He was trying to get his hands on the material I've given you. We had dinner, and then I brought him here. I was with Erva, Gerry was with a friend of hers."

Erva took up the story. "Gerry did not like my friend, so Heikki asked me to dance with him. As we danced, he asked me to go back to his hotel with him. When I refused, he became abusive."

Heikki confirmed this, explaining, "He was very drunk. In fact, he almost got us thrown out of here."

Bill was not unduly concerned with how Gerry Kiplock behaved when he was drunk. It was the business side of the man he was concerned with, and on that score, from what he had known before and what Heikki had told him over dinner, he had nothing to worry about.

The party broke up just before 1am.

When Bill was handed the bill, he blanched.

They got their coats and walked up the stairs together, Harriett slipping her arm through Bill's and pressing his arm against her breast.

"By the way," he said, "you never did tell me what you did for a living."

Harriett fished a business card out of her handbag, and handed it to him. "Call me next time you're coming to Helsinki."

Bill slipped the card into his jacket pocket without looking at it.

Heikki and Erva left in a taxi, together.

Bill, who had only a short walk to his hotel, saw Harriett into a taxi. Before he closed the vehicle's door, she asked him if he was sure he wouldn't change his mind and come home with her.

He smiled and shook his head. "It's a nice thought, Harriett, but I don't think so."

When he emptied the pockets of his jacket in his hotel room, he read her card. Printed on the back was what she did for a living: *I Please Men*. He tore the card up and dropped the pieces in the wastepaper basket.

Bill had come to Finland primarily to see Heikki, but he would never make an expensive international trip without seeing what else he could come up with while he was there, and for the following morning he had arranged meetings with two Helsinki waste paper dealers, and for the afternoon a meeting with a paper mill in Lappeenranta on the southern tip of the Saimaa Lake system.

The meetings with the waste paper dealers yielded nothing, other than adding two more names to his already extensive list of Finnish contacts.

He had rented a car at the airport when he had arrived, and it was a two hundred-kilometre drive to Lappeenranta, made worse by the fact that he encountered heavy snow on the way. With only four

29

hours of daylight, and having to drive in heavily falling now with his headlights on, meant that driving conditions were hazardous at best. There was a possibility of some business with the mill at some point in the future, but nothing for the moment. After the meeting, Bill climbed back into the car and headed for the airport, getting snarled up in more snow on the way. It was already pitch dark when he left the mill.

At the airport, he turned in the rented car and headed for the check-in desk, where he learned that the inbound aircraft for his 9pm flight to Heathrow had been delayed by two hours due to inclement weather. He had dinner in the airport restaurant, and spent the rest of the time waiting for his flight in the Executive Club lounge where, because he was travelling Business Class, he could get free drinks.

He, Angela and the children lived in a large detached four-bedroom house with half an acre of land in a village on the edge of the Hertfordshire countryside about six miles from Welwyn Garden City, and when he drove into the semi-circular drive at the front of the house at just after 1.30am he was surprised to see a light on in the living room. He had expected everybody to be in bed and the house in darkness.

He stopped the Jaguar outside the front door, switched off the lights and killed the engine. He climbed out of the car, closing the door as quietly as possible, and collected his suitcase and briefcase from the boot.

A pony living in a field across the lane whinnied softly, as if welcoming him home. In the stillness of the night, an owl hooted.

The front door opened and Angela appeared, in her dressing gown. "Where on earth have you been?" she asked, clearly worried, but keeping her voice down. "You should have been home hours ago."

Bill put his luggage down and hugged her. Her hair smelt of shampoo. "I'm sorry," he said. "Bad weather delayed the incoming aircraft. I spent five hours in Helsinki airport."

"You could have called me. I'm sure they have pay phones in the airport."

"They do," he said. "And I'm sorry, I should have. I will do next time."

"And you've been drinking again. You know what the doctor said."

Bill picked up his luggage and followed her into the house. "Why are you up so late, Angie? I thought you would have been in bed ages ago."

Instead of answering him, she turned and walked into the kitchen.

He put his luggage down in the hall and closed the front door. He followed her into the kitchen. He could tell from the set of her shoulders that something was wrong.

She asked him if he would like some tea. She said she was having some.

"Yes, tea would be nice." He sat on one of the stools at the breakfast bar and waited for her to tell him what was wrong.

"I wasn't going to tell you until you'd had a good night's sleep," she said, filling the kettle from the tap. "But I might as well tell you, now." She put the kettle on its base unit, switched it on, and then turned and faced him. "I had a call from the bank today. They're calling in the company's overdraft. We might have to sell the house."

Chapter 4

The next morning, Bill was uncharacteristically quiet over breakfast, hardly even noticing the children squabbling about which of them should sit in the front seat on their way to school.

Melanie was arguing that it was her turn today.

"No, it was your turn yesterday," Jason said.

"No, it should have been my turn yesterday, but I let you sit in the front yesterday."

"Yes, but that doesn't count, because ..."

Angela silenced the children with a terse, "If you two don't shut up, neither of you will sit in the front. You'll both sit in the back. For a week. Now be quiet the pair of you. How do you plan to play it with the bank today, Bill?"

"I'm not sure," Bill said. "That's what I've been sitting here thinking about. The one thing I'm not going to do is show weakness. If I do, they'll crawl all over me. As a matter of interest, Angie, when did Bob call you?"

"He called on Monday afternoon, just before I left to pick the children up from school. I called you that evening to tell you, but you weren't in your room."

"I was having dinner with Heikki. I didn't get back until late. I think what I'll do is wait until you get to the office, and then get Bob on the speakerphone. Then you can hear both sides of the conversation."

Bill was in the office by 8.30am. He read the mail, the messages Maureen had left for him, and the faxes that had come in over the two days he had been away.

Maureen came in a 9am. Angela arrived ten minutes later, when Maureen made them coffee.

At 9.45a.m. Bill looked at Angela, who was sitting on the other side of his desk. "Ready?"

She nodded. "As I'll ever be."

Bill took a deep breath and picked up the phone. He dialled the bank's number and asked to speak to Bob Cummings, the manager. He switched on the speakerphone, and replaced the receiver.

"So you're back from Finland, then." The bank manager's voice came through loud and clear. So loud in fact that Bill turned the volume down so Maureen wouldn't hear what he said through the interconnecting door.

"Yes, I'm back. I got back early this morning. My flight was delayed due to bad weather."

"Good trip?"

"It was until I walked into the house early this morning and Angela told me you guys were talking about pulling the plug. What's this all about, Bob?"

"Yes, I'm sorry about that, Bill. Head office think …"

"How long have we banked with you, Bob?"

"Bill, it's not a question of how long you've banked with us. It's a question of …"

"It's been seven years. We've banked with you since we came to live in Hertfordshire. You have my account, you have Angela's account, you hold the mortgage on our house, and you have the company's account. We couldn't give you any more business if we tried. My account is in the black, Angela's account is in the black,

33

and the company is within the agreed overdraft limit. So what's the problem?"

"Bill, if it were my decision …"

"I've had personal loans from you, and never missed a payment. I've never missed a payment on my car, or Angie's car, and we've never missed a payment on our mortgage. I would be surprised if you had a better customer than me."

"Bill …"

"Doesn't all the business Angela and I have put your way count for something, Bob? Doesn't it at least count for some loyalty on your part?"

"Bill, it's not a question of loyalty."

"You were only too willing to take us on when we didn't need you, and now, when we do need you, you talk of pulling the plug."

"Bill, head office feel …"

"Bob, when Angela and I opened these accounts with you, you promised to be our complete bankers. Those were your exact words."

"I know, Bill, but …"

"Bob, I don't know anyone who has started an international business without a little help from a bank."

"But you've been at it for three years, Bill. It's not as if you've only just started the business. Head office think …"

"Do you have any idea how expensive international travel is? Flights, hotels in foreign countries, entertaining customers."

"Yes, I do know how expensive international travel is. I get a set of your accounts every year. But the fact remains, Bill, that …"

"Well I think you should give me another year before you start talking about pulling the plug. Do you not think I have enough to worry about without having you breathing down my neck as well?"

"Things change, Bill," Cummings sighed. "Banking isn't what it used to be."

"You can say that again. And things can change for me too. There are other banks, you know."

"Bill, we need to get together. Can you drop in this afternoon? At say four o'clock?"

Bill glanced at Angela, who nodded and, keeping her voice low so the banker would not hear her, told him she would get Betty to pick the children up. "All right, Bob. We'll be there."

"I take it you were referring to Angela when you said we. But that won't be necessary. She doesn't need to be here."

"Oh yes she does," Angela said, now speaking loudly.

"Oh," the banker said. "Am I on the speakerphone?"

"Yes, you are," Angela said.

"I didn't realise. Hello, Angela. I'm sorry, I didn't mean to …"

"We'll see you at four o'clock," Bill said.

"And that means both of us," Angela said.

Bill switched the phone off before the banker had a chance to respond. He sat back in his chair. "You know something, Angie, I would rather sell the house than have to kowtow to a bloody bank." He got to his feet, and winced.

"Is it that pain in your lower back again?" Angela said.

"It's nothing," he said, not prepared to admit that the pain was quite sharp. He walked up and down the room and then tried to touch his toes, failing to get within twelve inches of them. He straightened up again, wincing. "I'm probably not getting enough exercise."

"Come off it, Bill. We both know what it is. It's your drinking. You'll go to bed one night and your liver will pack up and you won't wake up in the morning."

Bill tried to touch his toes again. He got closer than last time, and his exertion cost him another sharp pain.

"Are you listening to me, Bill?" Angela said, as he walked back to his desk and sat down. "If you don't at least moderate your drinking, one of these days I'll be a widow and the children will have no father."

"Well at least you won't be short of money. With all the life insurance I carry, I'm worth a lot more dead than alive."

Angela frowned. "That's not even remotely funny, Bill. It's you I want, not a cheque from some insurance company." Annoyed with him, she got to her feet. "I'm going to my office. I have work to do."

Bill waited until the door had closed behind her, and then picked up the phone and called Jacques Peterson, in Paris.

"Well, perfidious albion," the Frenchman said, using the insult the French had used against the English during and after World War II, "this is an unexpected pleasure. Ça va?"

The two of them had been friends for a long time, meeting each year at paper trade events in London, New York and Montreal. They always started a conversation by insulting each other. Bill grinned. "Ça va bien, merci, froggy. And how is the lovely Janine? I still don't know what she sees in you."

"She sees I am ze most 'andsome man in all of France."

Bill laughed.

"And 'ow is ze lovely Angela? What I would give to 'old 'er in my arms."

"In your dreams. She prefers Englishmen to Frenchmen." It was time to get serious. "Jacques, I had a call from Gerry Kiplock last week."

"Oui, so 'e told me."

"Well first of all, thank you for suggesting he call me. I really appreciate it."

"Pas de problem, mon ami. You would do ze same for me. You have dinner wiz 'im tomorrow evening in London, non?"

"Correct. Jacques, I'm calling because I'm having a problem with the bank. Would you mind faxing me the details of the commission you made on Gerry's business last year. The prospect of me getting a lot of new business by getting involved with him might help get them off my back."

"You will 'ave ze figures within ze hour."

"Thank you, my friend. Probably better if you didn't let Gerry know I'm having a problem with the bank. It could weaken my negotiating position with him."

"My lips, zey are sealed."

"By the way, Jacques, how much business did you do with Gerry last year? I know you do very well out of him, but I've no idea how well."

"Last year, he paid me $240,000."

Bill whistled. "Wow, I'd no idea you were making that much with him. How is he to work with?"

The Frenchman paused. "'ow shall I put zis? If you do as you are told and you work 'ard, you will 'ave no problem wiz Gerry."

"Okay."

"When do you bring ze lovely Angela over to Paris, again?"

"I have no immediate plans to come to Paris, but when I do come, I'll bring her with me."

"We go to ze Crazy Horse Saloon again, oui?"

"Oh, my God, anywhere but there. My liver has only just recovered from the last time we went there."

When Bill and Angela got to the bank that afternoon, there was another man sitting in the manager's office, a man neither of them had met before. He was short, middle-aged, and stout, and he had a distinctly officious air about him. He got to his feet and Bob Cummings introduced him as Mr McKenzie, from head office.

Oh great, Bill thought.

"Don't mind me," McKenzie said, shaking hands with them. "I'm merely here as an observer."

I'll bet you are, Bill thought.

Cummings offered coffee, which they declined.

After they had all sat down, Bob Cummings, who had a certain sympathy for Bill's position, although he couldn't admit it, and certainly not in front of the man from head office, got things started by asking Bill how his trip to Finland had gone.

"It went very well, as it happens," Bill said. "I picked up a source of material I've been after for two years. It's reject reels from a bleached board mill, referred to in the industry as a pulp substitute. It can be used as a direct replacement for bleached hardwood pulp, and at a significantly lower price."

"But we've heard it all before, haven't we?" McKenzie said. "You've been all enthusiastic about new sources you've come up with, and nothing's ever come of them. How do we know it's going to be any different this time?"

"Because I know what the UK mills are looking for. I know of five mills that can use it. It's the best material of its kind on the market, bar none."

"That's no guarantee the mills will buy it."

"And there's no guarantee I won't get hit by a bus the minute I step out of here, is there?" Bill snapped. "You'll just have to take my word for it, won't you?" He handed Cummings a set of figures he had spent the day putting together. "These are my projections for the rest of this year, and I've added some of the Finnish tonnage for the third and fourth quarters. If I sold everything they have available, I would generate $100,000 a year in commission. But that won't happen this year. These things take time."

McKenzie put his hand out for the figures and Cummings handed them to him. "And when could we expect to see some of this commission showing up in the company account?" he asked, as he studied them.

"I would say it would be showing up by late third quarter," Bill said. "And once I've got the business, there's no reason why I shouldn't keep it."

"Does that mean you'll be signing a contract with the Finnish company?" McKenzie asked.

"The industry doesn't sign contracts on sources of waste," Bill said. "We've shaken hands on it. We have a gentleman's agreement."

McKenzie looked at Bill as if he were mad. "And you seriously expect us to extend your overdraft facility on the basis of a handshake?" He ran his finger slowly down the list, making mental calculations.

Angela was staring at McKenzie, her posture rigid. She looked like a pressure cooker about to blow.

Cummings noticed. He had seen what could happen when Angela was feeling pressurised and he was anxious to diffuse the situation. "Children all right, Angela?"

"They're fine." Angela folded her arms across her chest.

"Are they still doing well at school?"

"They're doing just fine at school, thank you."

McKenzie finished reading Bill's notes and looked up, "Quite frankly, Mr Smith, from what I've seen so far, I'm still inclined to withdraw the facility."

"Then you need to see this." Bill handed him the fax he had received from Jacques Peterson.

"And what might this be?" McKenzie said.

Bill felt his anger rising. He wanted to say 'if you read the effing thing you'd know what it was'. He forced himself to calm down. He explained about the phone call he had received from Gerry Kiplock the previous week.

"And what do you think he has in mind?" McKenzie asked.

"He told me he wanted to set up an office in the UK and he asked me if I was interested. He had a plane to catch and he didn't elucidate, except to say he wasn't offering me a job. He said he would be coming to the UK this week and he asked me if I would join him for dinner so we could talk. We're having dinner together tomorrow evening and I'll know more about what he has in mind then. I suspect he's going to offer me his agency here. That fax is from his agent in France. Jacques is an old friend of mine and, as you can see, he made $240,000 in commission on his business with Gerry last year. As to prospects, all I will say is that the UK is a bigger market than France."

"And what do you know about Mr Kiplock's company?" McKenzie asked.

"I haven't seen the figures, but I've been told that his retained earnings for last year amounted to $21million. He has offices in North America, South America, Mexico and the Far East. And France. He told me he wants offices all over the world, starting with the UK."

"I'm still not convinced."

Bill sighed. "Well, if you're still not convinced, Mr McKenzie, I'm wasting my time sitting here talking to you. Angie, I think we should go and find ourselves another bank. These people clearly don't want our business."

"I think you're right," Angela said.

"Let's not be too hasty," Cummings said, checking his desk diary. "Why don't we talk again after your dinner meeting? How about we meet here the day after tomorrow, Friday? Shall we say the same time, 4pm?"

"How's my diary looking for Friday, Angie?" Bill said.

"It's clear for Friday," Angela said.

"Good." Cummings made a note in his desk diary. "There won't be any need for you to come next time, Angela."

"You're probably right," Angela said. "Since you haven't asked my opinion on anything except how the children are doing at school, it was a waste of time me coming today."

"You seem annoyed, Mrs Smith," McKenzie said. "Was there something you wanted to say?"

"Since you ask," Angela said, "yes, there was. I wanted to say that I've been married to Bill for over fifteen years, and in all that time I've never known him fail in anything he set out to do. Neither have I ever known anyone work as hard as he does. He's always travelling, and he hasn't had a holiday in two years. He was right when he told Bob you should give him another year. He will succeed. That's what I wanted to say."

"And that's very commendable," McKenzie said. "And you're obviously a loyal and supportive wife, but …"

Angela's eyes flashed. "Don't you dare patronise me."

"Why don't we leave it at that for the moment?" Cummings said hastily.

"Yes," Bill said, getting to his feet. "I think we'd better."

Chapter 5

For his dinner meeting with Gerry Kiplock at London's Savoy Hotel, Bill decided to take the train from Knebworth. The station was no more than a two-mile drive through open country lanes from the house. He knew beyond a shadow of a doubt that a fair amount of alcohol would be consumed, and if he drank too much he could always leave his car at the station and walk home.

It was dark and the weather was cold and crisp when he left home for the 6.20pm train to King's Cross. Before he left, Angela implored him, "Please, Bill, don't drink too much tonight. Think of your health."

"I won't, and I will," he promised, smiling at his little joke and kissing her on the cheek. "Don't wait up. I'm sure I'm going to be late."

"I won't. Good luck with your meeting."

Bill had to park at the far end of the long thin car park at the station. A lot of people commuted into London from here, and the car park was invariably full during the week. Probably, his car would be the only vehicle in the car park when he got back.

He bought a first-class return ticket and stepped on to the deserted platform. It was cold and he stepped into the waiting room, thinking it would be warmer than standing on the platform. The waiting room, which was as deserted as the platform, was a rectangular room of perhaps fourteen feet by ten, with poor lighting, wooden bench seats, and a fireplace in which no fire was burning. It was colder in than out, so he stepped back out on to the platform.

As he waited for his train, an express whistled through the station, heading north. The draught it created forced him to button up his overcoat and put on the gloves he had been carrying.

Five minutes later, his train pulled in. He looked for a pair of yellow lines, to indicate a first-class carriage, and opened the door into a compartment with a no-smoking sign on the window. When he opened the door and stepped inside, he was met by a fog of choking cigarette smoke.

A youth in his mid-to-late teens was lounging in the far left corner of the compartment with his feet on the seat opposite. His head was shaved and he wore a scarred leather jacket and jeans torn at the knees. His boots, which had stainless steel toecaps with a fleur-de-lys motif engraved in them, looked better suited to kicking the hell out of someone than walking the streets. He wore an earring in the shape of a cross in his right ear, and he held a lit cigarette in his hand. Since there was ash all over the seat beside him, but none on the floor, he had clearly been using the seat as an ashtray. He looked like the archetypal football hooligan, and Bill knew there was no way on God's earth he was carrying a first-class ticket.

Bill debated as to whether he should move to another compartment, but he didn't see why he should. Someone had to stand up to people like this and he was not one to walk away from something he felt strongly about, so he slammed the door behind, and stood there looking at the youth.

"Can't you read?" he said, pointing to the no-smoking sign on the window. "This is a no-smoking compartment."

"Your point being?" the youth said arrogantly.

"My point being put the cigarette out. And while you're at it, take your feet off the seat. People have to sit on that."

"And if I don't?"

Bill felt his anger rising. He forced himself to keep it in check. "I assume you can read, so you'll know this is a first-class compartment."

"Your point being?" the youth repeated.

"My point being, do you have a first-class ticket?"

"In that fancy overcoat of yours, you don't look like you work for the railway, so why should that be any business of yours?"

"I'm making it my business," Bill said. The train started with a lurch and he was thrown off balance. He sat down heavily.

The youth sniggered.

Bill got to his feet again. The youth's legs were between him and the door to the corridor. "Shift your legs."

"And if I don't?"

"I'll shift them for you."

The youth lifted his legs. Once Bill had passed him, he put his feet back on the seat.

Bill needed to find someone in authority. It was an inter-city train, which meant there should be a ticket inspector on board. The question was; where in the eight-coach train would he find him? He took a chance and turned right and headed towards the rear of the train. He found the guard inspecting tickets half way down the next carriage. Bill waited for him by the door.

"Good evening, sir." The guard touched his cap respectfully.

"Good evening," Bill said. "Do you have a minute?"

"Do we have a problem, sir?"

"Yes, I believe we do. It's in the next carriage."

"Right, sir. You lead, I'll follow."

Bill led the way. When they got to the compartment, he said, "I pointed out it was a non-smoking compartment, and I told him to take his feet off the seat. And, as you can see, a fat lot of good it did me." He stood back to let the guard take over.

The cigarette now hung from the corner of the youth's mouth, and the soles of his boots were now on the edge of the seat opposite.

"Right," the guard said, "we'll start with you taking your feet off the seat, and then you can put the cigarette out."

The youth took his feet off the seat and sat up. He dropped the cigarette on to the carpet and waited until there was a burning smell before grinding it out with the heel of one of his boots.

"That will cost you a day in court for damaging railway property," the guard said. He put out his hand. "Let me see your ticket."

"And what if I don't have one?"

"Then you have two choices. You either pay me, and I issue you with a ticket, or I take your name and address and report you to the railway police. Then you'll find yourself having another day in court."

The youth dug into the pocket of his jeans and took out a ticket. He handed it to the guard.

"I thought you said you didn't have a ticket," the guard said.

"I didn't say that," the youth said. "What I said was, …"

"I don't have time for games," the guard said. He glanced at the ticket. "This is a second-class ticket."

"Is it? Well fancy that. I must have got into first-class by mistake. Well silly me."

The guard was having none of it. "You either pay the difference, or you travel in a second-class compartment. You're not travelling in here."

The youth got to his feet. He was tall, almost as tall as James. And he was even more threatening on his feet. He stepped out into the corridor and then turned and looked Bill in the eye. "You haven't heard the last of this," he said, and set off towards the front of the train.

"Where do you think you're going?" the ticket inspector said, setting off after him and grabbing his arm. "You're not going anywhere until you've given me your name and address."

Bill slid the door closed and left them to it. Before sitting down, he opened a window to let some of the smoke out and some fresh air in.

When the train stopped at Welwyn Garden City, Bill was sitting by the window, facing forward, when the youth walked along the platform and up to the window of his compartment. "I'll remember you," he said, loudly enough for Bill to hear his words through the glass, and pointing his finger at Bill. He stared at Bill for a moment, and then walked on.

When the train got to King's Cross, he decided to walk to the Savoy rather than take the tube, or a taxi. He had plenty of time and he needed the exercise, not to mention it would give him a chance to get some fresh air into his lungs. He would have moved into another compartment on the train, to get away from the stink of cigarette smoke, but he had noticed when he went to find the guard that all the other first-class compartments were full. And it was only a fifty-minute ride.

At the Savoy, the American bar was crowded, but Bill had no difficulty finding Gerry Kiplock because the New Yorker spotted him when he walked in and stood up and raised his hand.

As they shook hands, Bill asked him how he had known who he was.

"Just as you've probably been doing your due diligence on me, I've been doing my due diligence on you," Kiplock said. "And I've seen your picture in a recent trade magazine."

Bill followed Kiplock's lead and sat down.

On the table stood an ice bucket in which an upturned bottle of champagne resided in water that had once been ice. On the table stood a flute with about a half-inch of champagne in it.

"Champagne, Bill?"

"That would be nice."

Kiplock raised a hand and a waiter hurried over. "Yes, sir, Mr Kiplock, sir."

Kiplock tapped the bottom of the upturned bottle with a fingernail. "Another of the same, Sam."

"Right away, sir." The waiter hurried away.

From his investigations into Kiplock and his company, Bill knew the American to be forty-five years of age. He was a good-looking man with sandy-coloured hair, freckles and pale blue eyes. He was a couple of inches shorter than Bill, and much slimmer. Bill envied him his flat stomach. It had been a long time since he had had a flat stomach, and he doubted his would ever be flat again. He knew Kiplock to be a regular runner of the New York marathon, and it showed. There didn't look to be an ounce of fat on him. Bill wondered how he managed to look so good, while drinking as much as he was reputed to drink. Perhaps the stories of his capacity for alcohol had been exaggerated, although not if what Heikki Pentilla had said about it was anything to go by. In his double-breasted blazer and grey slacks, the American could have been mistaken for an Englishman, although the Harvard tie and tasselled loafers gave the game away. Not to mention the American accent.

"So how was your trip to Finland, Bill?" he said.

"It was good. I got what I was looking for."

"I know you did," Kiplock said. "I've been after that material myself."

"I know you have," Bill said, grinning.

The New Yorker's eyes twinkled. "No flies on you, I see."

The champagne arrived. The waiter removed the cork, poured and left. Kiplock raised his glass. "Absent friends."

Bill raised his glass and repeated the toast.

They touched glasses and drank.

Kiplock put his glass down and sat back in his chair.

"So tell me something about yourself, Bill."

"Where do you want me to start?"

"Start with when you joined your family paper mill. Did you know my father knew your uncle, by the way?"

Bill shook his head. "No, I didn't. It was probably before my time."

"Before mine too. He supplied your uncle with wood pulp from British Columbia, and apparently for quite some time. I understand they got to know each other quite well."

"I had no idea."

"Did your family own the mill outright?"

49

Bill shook his head. "No, but they had controlling interest."

"Smart thinking. How long were you there?"

"Nine years."

"How did your uncle react to your leaving?"

"Better than I expected. My father hit the roof. He called me an ungrateful bastard. All he could see was me breaking a line of four generations. He wasn't thinking about what I might want to do."

"Sometimes our fathers don't realise we've grown up and have minds of our own."

Bill nodded his agreement. "Do you have children, Gerry?"

"Yeah, same as you, a boy and a girl. Tell me about your connection with Finland."

"Well, without appearing to sound flip, I suppose I could say I've been to Finland more times than I care to remember. Over the years, I've done a huge amount of business with the Finns. I know a lot of people there."

"I know you do. And you're highly regarded there."

"Am I?" Bill said, surprised. No one had ever told him that before.

Kiplock shrugged. "I believe in passing on compliments when they're due. Tell me about your move to the good ol' US of A."

A stunning blonde in a figure-hugging red dress walked past and Kiplock's eyes locked on to her like iron-filings on to a magnet. She walked to the bar, hitched up her skirt and sat on one of the high barstools. She took out a cigarette and the barman lit it for her. It looked like a well-rehearsed procedure, as if she were a regular.

Kiplock raised a hand and the waiter hurried over. "Sam, ask the lady in the red dress what she's drinking."

"I can tell you that without asking, Mr Kiplock. She drinks kir royale. That's all she ever drinks."

"Sounds like she's one of your regulars."

"Yes, sir. She is."

Kiplock took a twenty-pound note from his wallet and handed it to the waiter. "You know what to do, Sam."

"Leave it to me, Mr Kiplock, sir." Sam walked back to the bar, the banknote vanishing into his trouser pocket.

Kiplock turned his attention back to Bill. "Right, where were we?"

"You were asking me about my move to the States."

"So I was." He paused, watching what was going on at the bar. "Hang on a second, Bill."

The barman had just poured Cassis into a champagne flute and he was topping it up with champagne. He put it in front of the girl, and said something to her. She turned. Kiplock raised his glass to her. She raised hers to him, and smiled.

Kiplock turned his attention back to Bill. "You were saying, Bill?"

Some Russian businessmen on the next table were getting rowdy. They were drinking vodka, and lots of it. They were making toast after toast, and banging their glasses on the table.

"Goddamn Russians," Kiplock growled. "I can't hear myself goddamn think. Let's go to my suite. We can talk without being interrupted there. Smoked salmon sandwiches okay, Bill? Or did you want something more substantial."

Bill had no doubt that the reason they would not be having a proper sit-down meal, which is what he had expected, had a lot to do with the girl in the red dress.

But he could always eat later. "Smoked salmon sandwiches would be fine," he said.

"Right, back in a sec." Kiplock got to his feet and walked to the bar, where he spoke to the waiter. He spoke briefly to the girl, and then returned to the table. "Come on, let's get outta here."

Kiplock's suite was on the seventh floor. It had an uninterrupted view over the trees on the Embankment to the river. He walked Bill to a circular table by the window. Almost immediately there was a knock on the door. He walked across the room and opened it. "Come on in, Sam."

The waiter walked in with a bottle of champagne and two flutes on a tray. "Your sandwiches will take about half an hour, Mr Kiplock."

"That's fine, Sam."

The waiter extracted the cork and poured, then headed for the door. Kiplock followed him out into the corridor.

Bill heard murmured voices.

Kiplock came back into the room, closed the door and sat down opposite Bill. "Right," he said briskly. "You were about to tell me about moving to the States."

Bill sat forward in his chair and interlocked his fingers. "I was head-hunted by a mill in North Carolina, and I spent three years there."

"What was your territory?"

"Initially, New England, the upper mid-west, the deep south and two provinces of Canada. And then Western Europe and Scandinavia. I built a European agency network for them. I was away seventy percent of the time."

"Tough on the family."

"Very. My wife …"

"Angela, isn't it?"

Bill smiled. "You've been doing your homework. Yes, Angela. She handled it well. I couldn't have done what I've done without her support."

"Yeah, a wife who's prepared to support her husband when he's building a career is worth her weight in gold."

The phone on a walnut writing desk warbled. "One second, Bill." Kiplock crossed the room and picked it up. "Oh hi, doll. Everything okay? Good. Yeah, I'm fine. Busy, as usual. Kids OK? Good. Tomorrow? I'm in Paris tomorrow. Honey, can I call you back? I'm in a meeting right now. Sure, soon as I'm finished. No, strike that. I have another meeting after this one. I'll call you tomorrow. Love you, too. Give the kids a hug for me. Bye, hon."

He replaced the receiver and walked to the window. "What a view! People would give their right arm for a view like that. There's nowhere quite like London. It's much more civilised than New York." He sat down and took a swig of champagne. "So you developed a European network. And then what?"

"Then I got the chance to move to a bigger job in the upper Midwest."

"Dayton, Ohio. Correct me if I'm wrong."

Bill nodded. "Yes, Dayton, Ohio. But I had a problem with my boss, and left after two years."

"I know the guy, he's a mean son-of-a-bitch. So then you came back to the UK, right?"

"Right. I became managing director of the UK division of Trans Global Pulp and Paper Inc, operating from here, London. I was with them for five years."

"The president of the company's a member of my squash club in New York."

"Small world," Bill said. "Jim's a nice guy. At least I thought he was until he screwed me out of my profit sharing, accusing me of taking an agency off him."

Kiplock shrugged. "Shit happens."

"And that was when I started my own business."

"Which you've been running for how long?"

"Three years next month."

"Not easy starting a business from scratch, Bill, is it?"

"You can say that again," Bill said, with feeling.

Kiplock checked his watch. "Let me tell you why I wanted to meet with you. I'm looking for somebody to joint venture with in the UK. Somebody with your kind of experience, and your kind of presence in the market."

This was exactly what Bill wanted to hear. His pulse quickened.

"But I want you to know where I'm coming from," Kiplock continued. "Jacques Peterson does well in France because he does what we want him to do; I should say what I want him to do. He's doing well out of it, and so are we."

"So I understand."

Kiplock shifted in his chair, making himself more comfortable. "Bill, I've been asking you questions I already knew the answer to, and this was because firstly, I wanted to know if you would embellish the truth. And I'm pleased to see you haven't. And secondly, to see if there was chemistry between us, which, from my perspective, there is. I think we would get along just fine."

"I'm inclined to agree with you," Bill said. And he meant it. So far, he had seen nothing about the American that would have put him off going into business with him. But it was early days.

The phone rang and Kiplock walked across the room and picked it up. "Hello." He listened, and said, "Ten minutes, Sam." He replaced the receiver and walked back across the room.

After he had sat down, Bill asked him what he would bring to the table if they formed an association.

"More sources of material than you could shake a stick at," the American replied. "What I will bring to the table will make you a very rich man indeed."

Bill noted that he had said will bring to the table, rather than would bring to the table, and this augured well. He responded accordingly. "Sounds like I'm going to be busy."

"You will be busy. You'll need to take on another man. You have your existing sources to take care of, and there's no way you could handle it all by yourself."

"What about finance, Gerry? Without putting too fine a point on it, I'm not in a position to bring capital to the table."

"Let's not worry about that for the moment. So, my friend, are you interested?"

"I'm very interested, Gerry. I'd be a fool not to be."

"Great. I was hoping you would say that."

"So where do we go from here?" Bill asked.

"I want you and Angela to come to New York, to meet my executive group. Then, if my guys like you, and I know they will, we'll talk about putting a deal together." He checked his watch. "Sorry, Bill, but I'm going to have to wrap this up." He got to his feet and escorted Bill to the door. He put out his hand. "Great meeting you, pal, and I shall look forward to working with you. Expect to hear from me within the next few days."

As Bill headed for the lift, the girl in the red dress passed him. He pressed the button to summon the lift and then turned and watched her knock on the door of Kiplock's suite. The door opened and Kiplock's honeyed voice drifted down the corridor. "Well hello, my dear. Come in, come in."

"Said the spider to the fly," Bill muttered, as the door to Kiplock's suite closed behind her.

It was 8.10pm, and the smoked salmon sandwiches had never arrived. A morsel of food had not passed Bill's lips since lunchtime, and he was ravenous. On his walk back to King's Cross, he stopped at a McDonald's and ate a jumbo-sized hamburger and an extra helping of fries.

To Angela's surprise he was home by 9.30pm. And while she could tell he had had a drink, it was obvious he had had very little. "Is something wrong?" she asked anxiously. "Did it not go well?"

"It couldn't have gone better," he said. He grabbed her round the waist and spun her round, and then held her at arm's length and looked into her eyes. "How does a trip to New York grab you, you gorgeous creature?"

Chapter 6

"And how much of an extension to your overdraft facility will you need for this jaunt of yours?" Cummings asked.

Bill sighed and shook his head. Bankers! What did they know? "I'd hardly call a trip to New York to meet his management group a jaunt, Bob," he said into the phone.

"And why does Angela need to go?"

"Because Gerry said he wanted her there, and because that's how Americans do things. They interview the wife as well as the husband. If they don't like the wife, the husband doesn't get the job. And I'm sure you'll agree that with Angela's looks, and the way she handles herself, she should come with me. I have no better asset."

"I doubt anyone would disagree with that," the banker said. "You're a very lucky man in that regard."

"Not to mention she's a director of the company."

"In name, perhaps."

"I shouldn't let Angela hear you say that. She'd have your guts for garters. And if you took little more interest in my business, you would know that Angela does a lot more than just carry a title. I couldn't run the business without her. And while we're on the subject, when she and I came to your office the other day, I didn't appreciate your boss patronising her. A man in his position ought to know better."

"Yes, I'm sorry about that, Bill. She's such a beautiful woman that I think she intimidated him. I have to admit that I was intimidated until I got to know her better. So, how much do you need the overdraft extending by?"

"I should think £3,500 would cover it."

"That's a bit steep, Bill. Why will you need so much?"

"Return air fares for two; hotel accommodation for three or four days, and New York hotels are not cheap. And we have to eat."

"Could you not manage with less?"

"And there'll be incidentals."

"Such as?"

"Angela will need a new outfit. She hasn't had any new clothes for quite some time, and I need her looking her best."

"And how much are you budgeting for a new outfit?"

"Angela reckons £500."

"Good Lord! My wife could buy a whole new wardrobe for £500."

Bill thought, yes and I've seen your wife and she probably could.

"What are you planning to buy her?"

"She'll need a dress, shoes, a handbag, and a warm coat. New York will be a heck of a lot colder than Welwyn Garden City at this time of the year, and I don't want her catching a cold. And, considering the importance of the occasion, she won't be shopping at C&A."

"And what's wrong with C&A?" He sounded indignant. "My wife shops at C&A and I've never had reason to complain about what she wears. Does the £3,500 include flying economy?"

"Absolutely," Bill said. He had no intention of flying economy. He never flew economy. He always flew business class, and why should he start flying economy with the prospects he now had ahead of him? "I'll have my secretary shop around to see what she can find. She should be able to find us something on Air India, or Aeroflot."

"I think that would be prudent, Bill, all things considered. Well, you go ahead with your trip, Bill. And don't forget to tell Angela what I said about C&A."

"I certainly will, Bob. I'm sure she'll appreciate your advice."

He hung up and snorted, "As if."

Jason's bedroom was at the front of the house, which meant it overlooked the semi-circular drive. His father was cleaning his car immediately below. He opened his bedroom window and leaned out. "You're making a nice job of the car, Dad," he said.

Bill was bent over washing the Jaguar's nearside front wheel. He raised himself to an upright position and stretched his aching back. He glanced at his watch and looked up at his son. "Jason, it's eleven o-clock and it's a Saturday so you have no school, and you should be down here helping me, not standing up there in your bedroom telling me I'm making a good job of cleaning my car. Now you get dressed and get down here and help me. I'll give you five minutes, and if you're not down here by then, there'll be no TV for you for a week."

"But Dad," Jason wailed, "it's cold out there."

"So put your coat on. Jason, you're old enough to be pulling your weight around here now. My father never let me get away with half of what I let you get away with."

"But, Dad, it's Saturday morning."

"Yes, and it's Saturday morning for me too, Jason. And nobody ever gives me a Saturday morning off."

"But you've nearly finished the car."

"Then you can go shopping with your mother."

"But I hate shopping. Besides, I haven't had breakfast yet."

"Then I'll give you twenty minutes." Bill checked his watch again. "Nineteen-and-a-half, nineteen."

Jason vanished. He knew how far he could push his father.

Bill finished washing the wheel and threw half a bucket of clean water over it. He heard the phone ring in the house. He had just finished cleaning the fourth wheel when the door to the house opened and Angela appeared. She was crying.

"Hey," he said, "what's all this? What on earth's the matter?"

Angela sobbed, "It's my mother. She's had a heart attack."

Bill tossed the sponge into his bucket of soapy water and hurried over and threw his arms round her. "Darling, I'm so sorry. How bad is it?"

"I'm not sure, my father wasn't making any sense. He was crying. It sounds bad. She's in intensive care in Torquay General. Bill, I have to go down there. My father can't manage on his own."

"Yes, of course, sweetheart. Why don't you take my car? It's a long drive and it'll be more comfortable than yours."

"But you're going to Scotland next week. You'll need your car."

"I'll cancel my trip. The buyers will understand. I can reschedule it."

Angela wiped her eyes with the palms of her hands. "I'd rather take my own car. It will be easier to handle if I run into snow and ice. What about the children, Bill?"

"I can run them to school, and as you know, I can make a mean beans on toast. You go to Torquay and forget about us. We'll be fine."

A couple of hours later, Bill and the children waved her off.

"You two are going to have to help me around the house while your mother's away," he said, ushering the children back into the house. Neither of them said anything, but from the looks he got, he realised it was going to be an uphill struggle.

Later in the day, Angela phoned to say she had arrived safely and that her mother was holding her own. She asked how he was coping.

"I'm coping fine," Bill said. "Don't you go worrying about me. You look after things down there. I'll be fine."

Over the weekend, Bill's patience was sorely tested, especially by Jason, and on the Sunday evening, as he cleared the dishes away after a meal of sausage and beans, he put his foot down. "Jason, you are not watching TV until you've done your homework. And that's final."

"But, Dad ..."

"But Dad nothing!" his father retorted. "I'm not paying all that money in school fees just to have you fail your exams because you haven't been doing your homework."

"I like homework," Melanie said brightly. "And when I grow up, I'm going to marry a rich man like you, Daddy." She stuck her tongue out at her brother. "So there. You won't be able to do that, so you have to do your homework."

The next morning, Bill drove the children to school and then drove to the office.

"I thought you were supposed to be in Scotland this week," Maureen said, surprised to see him.

"I was," Bill said. He explained about Angela's mother having a heart attack. "So, I'm going to reschedule my appointments." He spent the morning phoning buyers he should have been meeting during the week.

The children came out of school at 3.30pm and, at 3.20pm Bill left the office to pick them up, telling Maureen he would be coming back in the evening to catch up with stuff he had not been able to finish.

That evening, Bill made beans on toast for their evening meals, despite Jason's protestations that they had already had beans three times since their mother left. They ate in the kitchen, at the breakfast bar, where they had been eating all their meals since their mother had left. As he loaded the dirty dishes in the dishwasher, he told the children he had to go back to the office because he had some work he hadn't been able to finish during the day. "And I expect you two to behave while I'm away," he said. "Can I rely on you to do that?"

"Yes, Daddy," Melanie said.

"Jason?"

"What time will you be back?" Jason asked, all innocence.

Bill looked at him suspiciously. "I'm not sure. Why do you ask?"

"No reason," Jason said. "I just wondered."

Whenever Jason looked like butter wouldn't melt in his mouth, Bill was suspicious. He found the TV guide and checked what was on that evening. "Jason, if it's this film on ITV at nine o'clock you had in mind, you can forget it. You're not old enough for that. And, anyway, I might be home by then."

There was a cinema in Welwyn Garden City, an old cinema with one screen. Standing in line waiting for its doors to open, was a tall shaven-headed youth wearing boots with a fleur-de-lys motif engraved on the toecaps.

Bill drove by, on dipped headlights.

The youth spotted him. He watched Bill turn off the road and head in the direction of the station, and then said something to the three male friends with whom he had come to see the film.

On both sides of the street outside the building in which Bill's office was located, were double yellow lines. The nearest official car park was a purpose built three-storey car park at the far end of the station, but there was what passed for a car park behind the supermarket just across the street from the office and whenever Bill worked late at the office, which was rarely, he used it.

It was a space of perhaps half an acre, and it was laid to cinder. It was bounded on one side by the rear wall of the supermarket, and on the other three sides by fences, behind one of which were the railway lines leading to and from the station. It was basically for the use of customers at the supermarket, and delivery vehicles. Access was available 24/7, and parking was free. The main disadvantage to using this car park on a dark night, which was why women rarely used it after dark, was that there was only one light. It was a sodium light, which was affixed to the wall of the supermarket. There were no other vehicles in the car park, and Bill parked immediately under the light. He climbed out of the car and pressed the remote to lock the car and alarm it. As he left the car park, an Intercity Express thundered by. It was travelling at such a speed that, in the darkness, the lights from the carriages looked like a continuous ribbon of light.

Maureen had left the heating on for him, and his office was pleasantly warm. He hung his coat on the hook on the back of the door, and then took off his jacket and hung it over the back of his chair. He had left everything he needed to work on in a file on his desk, and he opened the file and settled down to work.

About fifteen minutes later, he heard the door to the street below open and close. He looked up, curious. There was another tenant on his floor, a solicitor, but it was unusual for them to work in the evening. He heard the click-clack of a woman's heels on the tiled floor in the downstairs hallway, and then he heard creaks as someone climbed the stairs. He heard footsteps in the corridor, and then his office door opened and Maureen walked in.

She was dressed to kill.

He smiled at her. "I wondered who it was," he said. "You look nice. Are you going somewhere special?"

Maureen shook her head. "I'm not going anywhere, Bill. I came to see you."

Bill wondered what could be so important that it wouldn't wait until morning.

Maureen closed the door and snipped the Yale lock, meaning the door couldn't be opened from the corridor, even with a key.

Bill watched, fascinated. He wondered what on earth she was up to.

At right angles to the front of his desk, forming a T-shaped arrangement, was a table down each side of which were two seats with chromium-plated legs and brown cord cloth, allowing Bill to have meetings with four people at once, and after locking the door Maureen walked to the table and stood with her hands on the back of one of the chairs. "I came to take you up on your offer," she said, by way of explanation.

Bill had no idea what she was talking about. He put his pen down and sat back in his chair. "What offer?"

"Don't be coy, Bill," Maureen said. "You know what I'm talking about. You asked me how I was doing in the family department and I told you I thought Ted was firing blanks. You said to let you know if you could help, and that's why I'm here."

Bill had no recollection of any such conversation, but he had no doubt what she was getting at. "You surely don't mean ..."

She nodded. "Yes, I do."

Maureen opened her coat. She was wearing a see-through blouse and no bra, and her nipples were hard and erect. "Come on, Bill," she said, "I've seen the way you look at me. And don't try and deny it."

"Yes, but looking, and ... and ... what you have in mind are two very different things." He tried to drag his eyes away from her swollen nipples. He felt stirrings from below. His mouth had gone dry. He licked his lips. "But what about Ted?" he said. "How would he feel about another man fathering a child by his wife?"

"I won't tell him if you won't."

"What about Angela?"

"She'll never know from me."

"But I'll know," Bill said. "And I don't cheat on Angela. And how would you expect me to feel if, in years to come, I saw you walking round town with a child that looked exactly like me? I'm sorry, Maureen. It's out of the question. I think you'd better leave."

Maureen started to undo her blouse.

Bill felt himself hardening. "Maureen," he croaked. "Don't do this. Please."

The light switch was by the door and Maureen walked over and flicked it off, leaving the room bathed in a dull yellow glow from a sodium light across the street. She took the glass ashtray off the table and put it on Bill's credenza, and slid the papers he had been working on to one side. She took off her coat, rolled it up and placed it on the middle of the table.

Bill croaked, "Maureen, please. Please don't do this."

Maureen finished undoing her blouse, and tugged it out of her skirt. She hitched up her skirt and, in one fluid movement, removed her tights and panties. She shifted one of the chairs to one side and climbed on to the table. She lay on her back with her knees bent and her head resting on her coat. She put her feet on Bill's desk and spread her legs. "This is the only chance you'll ever get, Bill," she said, addressing her remarks to the ceiling. "So don't waste it."

His heart pounding, Bill got to his feet. He shoved his chair away, undid his belt and dropped his trousers.

There was no foreplay. It was a case of wham, bam, thank you, ma'am and it was over in seconds. He climaxed with a shudder and stood over Maureen, panting.

Maureen waited a moment or two, then pushed him away and sat up. She climbed off the table and started to dress.

Bill stared stupidly at her. He felt used and abused. Raped almost. How could things ever be the same between them again? How could he allow her to continue working for him, and how could he explain to Angela if he decided his only recourse was to fire her? But that wasn't the most pressing problem. The most pressing problem was whether or not she had conceived. He fervently hoped that she hadn't.

He bent down and pulled up his trousers. He zipped them up and fastened his belt. Then he sat down, breathing heavily.

Maureen finished dressing and put on her coat. She walked to the door, unlocked it and opened it. "Thank you, Bill. I'll see you in the morning."

Bill sat there in the dark listening to the stairs creaking, then her heels click-clacking on the tiled floor. He heard the street door open, and close. He sat there calling himself all the names under the sun. But it was too late for recriminations. The deed was done.

He had lost all interest in work. He straightened his desk and got to his feet. He put on his jacket, put back the chair Maureen had moved and put back the glass ashtray. He put on his coat, switched off the light, stepped out in the corridor, locked his office door and left the building.

When he got to the car park, he had so much on his mind that it didn't register that the light under which he had parked his car was no longer lit, and that the car park was in total darkness. He could make out the outline of his car and he walked towards it. As he walked round the back of the car, he felt glass crunch under his shoe.

A blow to his back knocked him to the ground and he felt his teeth break as his face hit a patch of concrete. He had the presence of mind to curl himself into a ball as kicks and blows began to rain down on him.

Finally, a voice he recognised, snarled, "And that, you piece of shit, is for fucking my sister."

A savage kick to the side of his head delivered him into oblivion.

Chapter 7

"I don't think anything's broken, but you've lost some teeth."

The words came through a fog of pain. Bill opened his eyes. His vision was blurred and his left eye hurt like hell. He shook his head to try and clear his vision and groaned as a bolt of pain shot through his temple. As his vision cleared, he could see he was in a private ward in a hospital.

A dark-haired man in a white coat was standing over him. "Welcome back to the land of the living," he said, introducing himself as Dr Zahedi. "How do you feel?"

"Like I've been hit by a train," Bill said.

"I'm not surprised. That was quite a beating you took." The doctor peered at the side of Bill's face. "How did you come by that mark? Unless I'm very much mistaken, it's a fleur-de-lys."

Bill knew exactly how he had come by the mark, but he pleaded ignorance.

He needed time to think. That the youth with whom he had had the run-in on the train, the youth who had attacked him, was Maureen's brother seemed a staggering coincidence, and because of this he was going to have to box clever. If he disclosed that he knew who had attacked him, Angela would almost certainly find out about his ... whatever you want to call it ... with Maureen, and with so many other aspects of his life appearing on the cusp of taking a turn for the better, that was the last thing he needed. But, on the other hand, there was no way he could let Maureen's brother get away with the beating he and his pals had given him.

He had a moment of panic when he remembered the children. They were home alone and they wouldn't know where he was. They would be worried sick. "Doctor, can you get someone to call my home. My children are …"

"Your children are fine," the doctor said. "They are here at the hospital. It seems your son called the police when you didn't come home. And they brought the children here."

"Thank God for that," Bill said. He looked at his watch. It was 10.22pm. At least Maureen's brother hadn't stolen his watch. He supposed he should be thankful for that. "How long have I been here?" he asked.

"You were brought in at a quarter to nine. The police found you and called an ambulance."

"Am I at the QE11?"

"Yes, you are. And there's a policeman waiting in the waiting room with your children. He asked to have a word with you when you recovered consciousness."

"I'd like to talk to my children first."

"Yes, of course. I'll have a nurse bring them in. I'll drop in on you later."

When Melanie saw her father, she burst into tears. "Oh, Daddy." She ran to the bed and hugged him.

"Oh, steady, sweetheart," he said, wincing. "My ribs are sore."

Jason stood by the side of the bed, inspecting the damage. "You've lost some teeth, Dad," he said.

"I know. By the way, Jason, you did exactly the right thing calling the police when I didn't come home, so well done you. I'm proud of you."

70

Unaccustomed to having compliments from his father, Jason said a sheepish thank you.

"I don't suppose you thought to bring the phone number of your grandparents' home in Torquay?"

Jason fished a piece of paper out of his pocket. "Yes, I did. I got it when the police came to collect us."

"Well done, Jason. You need to give your mother a call. Tell her what's happened and where I am. Tell her I'm all right, and not to think about driving straight home. The last thing we need is her driving home in the dark in a panic and having an accident. I'm sure the hospital will get through for you. And ask her to phone Auntie Betty, to see if you and Melanie can stay with them tonight. You can't stay in the house on your own."

"We can manage, Dad," Jason said. "We'll behave, I promise."

Bill was in no mood to argue. "Jason, I'm probably already in trouble with the police for leaving two under-age children in the house on their own, so please, for once in your life, do as you're told."

After the children had gone, Bill said he was ready to talk to the policeman, who introduced himself as Sergeant Bob Schembri of the Welwyn Garden City police. "Well," he said, inspecting the damage to Bill's face. "Whoever did this, certainly did a number on you."

Bill needed to get something off his chest. "Sergeant, I know I shouldn't have left the children on their own, but ..."

"Don't give it another thought, sir. Your children are fine, and we have more important things to think about. By the way, you have two fine children, and your son is very organised."

71

"Thank you, Sergeant. That's kind of you. For the record, I was only planning to be gone a couple of hours. My wife's mother …"

The sergeant held up his hand. "You needn't bother explaining, sir. Your son told us about your wife's mother. Do you feel up to telling me what happened? The sooner we start looking for him, the better."

"Not him," Bill said. "Them."

"So there were at least two of them." The sergeant took a pad and pencil from the breast pocket of his uniform

"It was dark and they came at me from behind, so I didn't see them, but I suspect there were three or four of them."

"Did they say anything? Could you pinpoint a voice, or an accent?"

"I don't recall any of them saying anything," Bill lied. "There just seemed to be a lot of grunting and heavy breathing."

The sergeant made a note. "Can you think of anyone you might have upset recently?"

Bill needed to put a stop to this. He needed time to think. "Sergeant, would you mind if we did this in the morning? I really don't feel well."

"That's perfectly all right, sir," the sergeant said. He got to his feet and put his pad and pencil back in the breast pocket of his uniform. "It's understandable after the beating you've taken. By the way, we found you by a Jaguar. Would that happen to be your car?"

"Yes, it would. Have they damaged it?"

"Not that we can see, but it is very dark there. If you'll let me have the keys, I'll have it picked up. It's much too valuable to be standing there unattended."

When Bill woke up the next morning, there was barely a square inch of him that didn't hurt, and when he dragged himself out of bed and saw his face in his bathroom mirror in daylight, he blanched. His bottom lip was twice its normal size, the left side of his face was a mass of bruises, and his left eye was surrounded by bruises and closed completely. He opened his mouth to inspect the huge gap left by his missing teeth, and then he looked for the fleur-de-lys on the side of his face. It was there, albeit barely noticeable.

So he could check out the damage to his body, he slipped off his hospital gown and stood there naked. He remembered lying on his right side and curling up into a ball when the attack began, and by using a hand mirror a nurse had provided, he could see that his right side was unscathed. His left side, however, was another matter. His left arm, his left leg, and much of the left side of his back, were covered in welts. Across his upper back was a welt about four inches wide, and he had a vague recollection of hearing the sound of wood splitting when he felt the blow that had knocked him to the ground.

He had another visit from the police sergeant soon after breakfast. He told him as much as he could about what had happened, without revealing the fact that he knew the identity of one of his attackers.

Bill had asked a nurse to contact Maureen and tell her what had happened, and where he was, and she dropped in to see him later in the morning. When she saw the extent of his injuries, she looked genuinely distressed. She gave no sign of having any knowledge that her brother had been involved in the attack. Neither did she mention what had happened between them the previous evening. She had brought some correspondence she thought he should see from the morning mail, and it was all strictly business as usual. She left after fifteen minutes or so, because with Angela away, there was no one to answer the phone.

Angela drove back from Torquay and drove straight to the hospital, arriving at around 2.30pm.

Bill was sleeping. He awoke when she kissed him. He yawned. "Hi, sweetheart. How's your mother?"

Angela sat in the chair beside the bed and took his hand. "She's holding her own. But what's more to the point, how are you? You look awful, Bill. What on earth happened?"

Although it pained him not to tell her the truth, he stuck to the story he had given the police sergeant.

"And you've no idea who did it, or why?"

He shook his head. "The police think it was probably a random attack."

"Does Maureen know what happened?"

He nodded. "Yes, she does. I had one of the nurses call her. She dropped in to see me this morning."

Angela stayed for a half hour or so and then left, saying she would drop in on him again in the evening.

She had brought him a Financial Times, and he was sitting up in bed reading it when one of the nurses walked in. "Present for you," she said, pouring four teeth into his hand. "The police found them in the car park and Dr Zahedi thought you might like to have them as souvenirs. Dr Zahedi is known for his sense of humour." She grinned.

"Tell him I'll have them strung and wear them round my neck, to remind me of him," Bill said dryly.

"We think you've lost six teeth, so you might have swallowed the other two. But I shouldn't worry about it, they'll find their own way out. Eventually."

"I see Dr Zahedi is not the only one with a sense of humour," Bill said, getting back to his newspaper.

Shortly after Bill had finished eating his evening meal, there was a knock on the door of his room and a familiar voice announced, "Well, you have been in the wars."

"Bas!" Bill exclaimed. "Well this is a nice surprise. Come on in." He pressed a button on the remote to switch off the TV.

Basil, husband to Betty, was Bill's friend. He walked across the room and handed Bill a bag of grapes. "Best I could do at short notice," he said apologetically.

"Thanks," Bill said, putting the grapes on the table at the side of the bed.

"How are you feeling, old man?"

"Probably how I look," Bill said. "I've felt better."

Basil sat in the chair by the side of the bed. "Betty sends her love, and best wishes for a full and speedy recovery."

"That's nice. Please thank her for me. How is she?"

"She seems a bit down in the dumps at the moment. I can't think why. I hear you've no idea who attacked you."

"The police say it was probably a random attack."

Basil shook his head. "Things didn't used to be like this. I hear you're off to New York, old man."

"Yes, in a couple of weeks. With me looking like this, it's just as well we're not going earlier. Speaking of New York, Bas, has Angie said anything to you about asking Betty if Anne could sit for us while we're away?"

"It's all arranged, old man. Anne will stay overnight at your house while you're away, and Betty will pick Jason and Melanie up in the mornings and take them to school, and pick them up again in the afternoons and take them home."

"Thank you, Bas. That's brilliant."

Basil shrugged. "That's what friends are for."

"Tell you what, Bas, in exchange for Betty and Anne looking after the kids, Angela and I will take you and Betty into town for a slap-up meal when we get back."

"You're on," Basil said. "You look tired, Bill, so I'll be off." He got to his feet. "I'll drop in again tomorrow evening, assuming you're still here in the hospital."

Shortly after Basil left, Angela arrived. She pecked Bill on the cheek, and sat down. She was wearing a perfume he didn't recognise.

"Did I buy you that perfume?" he said.

"You bought it me ages ago," Angela said, making light of it. "You've probably forgotten. I haven't worn it recently. How are you feeling?"

"The soreness is wearing off, although my ribs still hurt. How's your mother?"

"She's on the mend. Dad says she should be out of hospital soon."

"Good, I'm glad to hear it. You just missed Bas."

"How was he?"

"He seemed fine."

Angela seemed restless, and Bill asked her if she was all right.

"Actually I've got a terrible headache," she said. "Bill, do you mind if I leave?"

"But you've only just got here."

"I know, but I'll make it up to you by staying longer tomorrow."

"Well if you must."

She got up and headed for the door. "I'll see you tomorrow. Goodnight, Bill."

"Hey," he said. He tapped his cheek, the uninjured one. "Where's my kiss?"

"Oh, sorry." She walked back to the bed and planted a kiss on his cheek. "Goodnight, and sleep tight."

"Night, sweetheart. Give my love to the kids."

"I will."

Her perfume lingered after she had left, and try as he might, Bill could not for the life in him remember buying it for her. He usually bought her Chanel N°5, and what she was wearing was not Chanel N°5.

Chapter 8

When Bill reached up to get Angela's coat from the Boeing 747's overhead locker, he winced.

"Ribs still hurting?" Angela asked, before bending down to collect her handbag and the magazines she had brought to read on the flight.

"Not as much as they were." He helped Angela on with her coat, before getting his own coat, and briefcase, down.

"Your lip looks better," she said, peering at his mouth. "The swelling's almost gone now."

"How does my eye look?" He turned his head to give her a better look.

She touched his cheek as she inspected his eye. "It's still a bit yellow." She gently patted his cheek. "You'll live."

He ran his tongue over his teeth. The dentist had made him a partial denture and it felt like he had a mouthful of rocks. Fortunately, the six temporary teeth had not affected his speech.

Because they had travelled business-class, they, along with the first-class passengers, were allowed off the plane first. After the warmth of the plane, stepping into the jetway was like stepping into the Arctic.

Immigration was a nightmare. With wide-bodied aircraft arriving from all over the world, the immigration hall was packed.

Gerry Kiplock's secretary, Marcia, had told Bill in their telephone conversation the day before they left that she would have a car meet them at JFK, and after they had collected their luggage and passed through customs, Bill looked for a board with his name on it. Despite the crowd in the arrivals hall, he soon spotted it. It was held by a heavily built black man of indeterminate age. He was wearing a dark blue raincoat and a chauffeur's cap and he was standing with a group of other men who were similarly attired and holding boards.

Trundling their suitcases on a trolley before him, Bill made his way over to him. "Hi," he said. "I'm Bill Smith."

The driver welcomed them to New York, and touched his cap deferentially to Angela. "Ma'am."

The pavement outside the British Airways terminal was piled high with dirty snow, which was rapidly turning to slush on account of the fact that it was raining heavily. Their driver was carrying a furled umbrella and he opened it and handed it to Bill, before hurrying to a stretched Cadillac limousine with their luggage. He opened the boot and loaded the luggage, before opening the driver's door and switching on the vehicle's engine to get the heater going, and then opening the rear door.

Bill took Angela's hand as she picked her way through the slush in her new high-heeled boots.

As they pulled out into the traffic, Bill engaged the driver in conversation, learning that his name was George and that he worked for the Kiplock group. "I mostly drive Gerry and his father, because they don't own cars," he said. "And I pick up visitors from the airport."

Bill asked him how long he had worked for Gerry.

"Five years, give or take."

"Is he good to work for?"

"You do what you're paid to do, he's fine. You screw up ..." George eyeballed Angela in the rear view mirror. "Pardon my language, ma'am; he'll let you know about it. It's smart to keep on the right side of him. You been to New York before, Mr Smith?"

"Quite a few times," Bill said.

"You, ma'am?"

"Just once," Angela said.

It had been some time since Angela had been to New York, so Bill pointed out landmarks as they passed them; including Shea Stadium, which was the home of the New York Mets baseball team, and La Guardia airport. In a long line ahead of them they could see the lights of inbound aircraft.

Manhattan is bounded to the west by the Hudson River and to the east by the East River and, to cross the river, they had two options: The Queensboro Bridge, or the Holland Tunnel. As they approached the East River, George asked, "Bridge, or tunnel, Mr Smith?"

Since the Queensboro Bridge would give them a great view of Manhattan and the Holland Tunnel would be dark, dirty and congested, it was a no-brainer. "Bridge please, George."

When George drew up outside the Park Avenue entrance of the Waldorf Astoria, Angela looked at Bill with concern. Keeping her voice down so George wouldn't hear her, she said, "We're surely not staying here, Bill. Isn't this horribly expensive?"

"It is," Bill replied. "But Marcia booked us in here and, when I'm trying to give Gerry the impression I'm running a successful business, I could hardly tell her we can't afford to stay here. We'll just have to bite the bullet."

"The bank manager would have a fit if he knew."

"He doesn't see my expense statements, so don't worry about it."

Not only had Marcia booked them into one of the most expensive hotels in New York, she had also booked them a small suite. It was on the tenth floor and it had a sitting room with French Provincial furniture, a marble bathroom with gold fittings, and a bedroom with a bed big enough to comfortably accommodate four people.

What appeared to be at least a couple of dozen yellow roses stood in a crystal vase on an inlaid walnut table in the sitting room, and there was a card. Angela picked it up. "They're from Gerry." She read the card out loud: "Welcome to New York, and I look forward to seeing you tomorrow. Well, isn't that nice? I think I'm going to like Gerry."

The doorbell chimed and a voice called, "Room Service."

Bill walked to the door and squinted through the spyhole. It was a waiter, in tails. He opened the door.

"Good afternoon, sir. Welcome to the Waldorf." The waiter walked in with a silver tray, on which stood a silver ice bucket containing a bottle of champagne and two crystal flutes. "Compliments of Mr Kiplock," he said. "Good afternoon, ma'am." He put the tray on a table. "Shall I uncork it now, sir?"

Angela said, "Bill, why don't we leave it until we have something to celebrate?"

"Yes, let's do that," Bill said. "Just leave it there, waiter. Thank you."

"As you wish, sir," the waiter said. "Enjoy your stay." He bowed slightly to Angela. "Ma'am." He let himself out.

"Gerry's keen," Angela said. "Roses and champagne. He wouldn't be doing this if he wasn't seriously interested in us."

"I agree," Bill said. "I'd say we've got off to a very good start."

They would have liked to have taken a walk after unpacking their luggage, but by now it was dark outside and it was still raining heavily, so they scrapped the idea. Instead, they took a shower, put on their pyjamas and dressing gowns, and ordered a meal from room service. They were in bed and asleep by 10pm local time. Which, their weary bodies were telling them, was 3am English time.

The next morning, for the meeting with Gerry Kiplock and his management team, Bill wore a charcoal grey pinstripe suit, a white shirt with a button-down collar, and a red and blue striped tie.

Angela wore the knee length, slim-fitting, fine wool dress with long sleeves and turtleneck, which Bill had bought her from Harvey Nicholls in Knightsbridge. So much for the bank manager's suggestion of C&A. Her hair was swept back and tied at the back with a black velvet bow, the way Bill liked it. The only jewellery she wore, the only jewellery Angela ever wore, was the diamond stud earrings Bill had bought her for her thirtieth birthday, the watch he had bought her as a Christmas present, and her wedding and engagement rings. She looked sensational, and he told her so.

"As long as it helps get the job done," she said, shrugging off his compliment.

Angela always shrugged off the compliments he paid her, and he paid her many. She was the least vain person he knew.

When they stepped out of the hotel at 8.45am, the Cadillac was waiting for them with its engine running.

A cold front had moved in overnight and they were glad of their warm coats. What had been slush on the pavement when they had arrived the previous day, was now hard-packed and crisp. As much of the sky as they could see, which because of the high rise buildings by which they were surrounded, was not that much, was blue broken only by the vapour trails from arriving and departing commercial jets. The Park Avenue traffic was heavy, with yellow cabs in abundance.

The drive took less than ten minutes. They could easily have walked.

The offices of the Kiplock organisation were located in a high rise building on East 42nd Street, a couple of blocks up from Grand Central Station. George dropped them off in the street outside the building and told Bill to take the lift to the twenty-second floor. "I'll let them know you're on your way," he said.

They stepped out of the Cadillac to a cacophony of sound from traffic banging over potholes and honking their horns. Commuters streamed out of Grand Central Station like a river in flood, and there was the smell of roasting coffee beans from the cart of a nearby vendor. A United Airlines Boeing 737 flew low overhead, its landing wheels down, no doubt heading for La Guardia.

When their lift stopped at the twenty-second floor, an attractive woman in her mid to late fifties stood there waiting to greet them. With her steel-grey hair swept back off her face and her rimless glasses, she looked the epitome of efficiency. "Mr and Mrs Smith, I presume," she said, smiling.

"Bill and Angela," Bill said. "Good morning."

"I'm Marcia, Gerry's secretary."

"Nice to finally put a face to a voice," Bill said.

Marcia's handshake was firm, more like a man's than a woman's. She greeted Angela warmly, but didn't offer to shake hands with her. Angela knew it was unusual for American women to shake hands with other women, and she didn't take offence.

"Right, let me take your coats, and then I'll take you to the conference room. They're waiting for you." She hung their coats in a small cloakroom off the reception area.

As Marcia led them to the conference room, Angela asked her if she was responsible for the flowers in their suite.

"I organised them," Marcia said, "but yellow roses was Gerry's idea."

"I must remember to thank him."

"Do that. He'll be pleased. I take it you do know the significance of yellow roses here in America."

"You use them to welcome people home," Bill said. "As in the song, 'Tie a Yellow Ribbon', etc."

"Exactly. So I think you can be assured of a warm welcome."

When they got to the conference room, Marcia knocked on the door and opened it. "Your visitors are here, Gerry."

Sitting at the far end of a long conference table were six men, all of whom were in shirtsleeves. Gerry Kiplock sat at the head of the table. They all got to their feet.

Ever the gentleman, Bill stepped back to let Angela walk in first.

When Kiplock saw her, his eyes locked on to her in the way they had locked on to the girl in the American bar at the Savoy Hotel in London. "Well hello, my dear," he said, walking down the room with his hand out. "Come in, come in."

To Bill, Kiplock's words had a familiar ring. They were exactly the same words he had spoken to the girl, for whom Kiplock had cut short his meeting and turfed him out, when they had met in London.

Kiplock shook Angela's hand, and held on to it. Looking deep into her eyes, he said, "You didn't tell me you had such a beautiful wife, Bill." He finally let go of her hand.

"What happened to you?" he said, looking at the remnants of Bill's bruises. "You didn't look like that the last time we met."

"I've been trying to get away with telling people I walked into a door, but nobody's believing me."

"And the real version?"

"A gang of youths decided they didn't like the colour of my eyes."

"And here's me thinking England was a civilised country," Kiplock said. "Right, let me introduce you to my management group."

"Shall I organise coffee, Gerry?" Marcia said.

"Yeah, coffee would be good, Marcia."

The last man to whom they were introduced was a big man with piercing blue eyes and steel grey hair who looked to be in his mid-sixties. "And this old reprobate," Kiplock said, "is my in-house attorney, Oscar Blackman. He helped my father start the company."

"And he now spends most of his time trying to keep Gerry out of trouble," the lawyer said, a smile on his lips. "Good to meet you, Bill. Gerry's been telling me a lot about you. And before you ask, it was all good."

When the introductions were over with, Kiplock sat Angela to his right and Bill to his left.

Blackman sat at the far end of the table, facing his boss. He was there to listen, and observe.

The coffee arrived and they broke for a while, chatting and getting to know each other.

Angela took the opportunity to thank Kiplock for the flowers. "Marcia tells me that roses were your idea. I love roses; they remind me of my mother."

"I'm pleased to hear it, my dear. Roses for an English rose." He patted her hand.

Fifteen minutes later, with empty cups littering the table, Kiplock rapped on the table to get everybody's attention "Okay, you've all been circulated with what I know of Bill, and now you can get it from the horse's mouth. Bill, you have the floor."

Bill cleared his throat and sat forward in his chair. "Thank you, Gerry. Gentlemen, I've been in the paper business since I left school, and ..." He talked for almost an hour, and he spoke without notes. No one interrupted him.

For much of the time, Oscar Blackman sat back in his chair with his hands behind his head staring at the ceiling, as if his mind were elsewhere. Occasionally, he would nod in agreement at something Bill had said.

Gerry Kiplock alternated between sitting, and pacing the room. Occasionally he would stand at the window and look down on East 42nd Street.

Finally, when Bill had said everything he had wanted to say, he sat back in his chair. "Well, that's about it. There's not much more I can tell you."

Kiplock looked down the table at Oscar Blackman. "Well, was I right, or was I right?"

"You were right," Blackman said. "Great stuff, Bill. Very impressive."

"Okay, guys," Kiplock said, "Bill's done his stuff, and now it's time for us to tell him what we can bring to the table." He gestured to the man sitting next to Angela. Bernie Levy was vice president of Kiplock's kraft linerboard division. "Bernie, let's start with you. And then we'll go round the table anti-clockwise."

At noon, Kiplock called a break for lunch. By this time, Bill had filled several sheets of foolscap with notes.

Kiplock took Bill and Angela to a small French restaurant a couple of blocks from the office. He ordered champagne.

Angela asked him if he was ordering champagne because he had something to celebrate.

"No, my dear," he said. "I'm ordering champagne because that's all I ever drink."

They were back in the conference room by 1.30pm, and the afternoon meeting went on until almost 5pm.

When his executives had all left the room, Kiplock invited Bill and Angela to dinner. "And we can take in a Broadway show afterwards if you like. I can get tickets to all the shows at short notice."

Angela was exhausted. All she wanted to do was have a night in and put her feet up. "Would you mind if we didn't, Gerry," she said. "It's been a long day, and I'm still on English time."

Bill was tired, too. "I'm with you, Angie," he said. "We'll take a rain-check if you don't mind, Gerry."

"Okay, we'll do it some other time. I'll have George drive you back to your hotel. We have a lot to get through tomorrow, guys, so we'd better make an early start. Okay if I have George pick you up at eight forty-five?"

"No problem," Bill said.

Back in their room, Angela took off her coat, kicked off her shoes and threw herself into a chair. "I could sleep for a week," she said. "I'm pooped."

"G and T?" Bill said, heading for the mini-bar.

"Please."

They sipped their drinks and talked about the day. Angela asked him how he thought everything had gone.

"I would say it went very well," he said. "And if Gerry's guys can bring to the table half the sources they say they can bring, we'll do very well indeed out of it. Speaking of Gerry, Angie, what do you think of him?"

"You mean apart from him having an eye for the ladies? I quite like him. I'll tell you one person I did like, and that was Oscar. I really liked him."

"So did I. It's an odd thing to say about a corporate lawyer, but I had the feeling I could trust him."

"Me too," Angela said. "Could you trust Gerry, do you think?"

Bill paused before answering. "I'm not sure. Let's say the jury's still out on that one."

New York – Day Two

The meeting the next morning consisted of just four people: Gerry Kiplock, Oscar Blackman, Bill and Angela. It took place in Kiplock's office.

Kiplock got down to it without preamble. "You guys ready to cut a deal?"

His surprise at the speed at which things were moving registered on Bill's face, and Blackman laughed. "Bill, when you get to know Gerry better, you'll find out that once he's made his mind up he doesn't hang around."

"I can see that," Bill said. "Well, I'm ready. Darling?"

"It's your show, Bill," Angela said.

"Okay. What did you have in mind, Gerry?"

"A partnership."

"Fifty, fifty?"

"Fifty-one, forty-nine."

"In whose favour?"

"Mine. Fifty-one percent Kiplock, forty-nine percent Smith."

"But I'll be running the show, Gerry."

"And I'll be supplying the product."

"That's as maybe," Bill said. "But if you had controlling interest, I would feel I was reporting to you and that wouldn't work for me. I'm too used to being my own boss. If anything, I think I should have fifty-one percent."

"And that wouldn't work for me," Kiplock said. "Because I have controlling interest in all our offshore offices."

"Well, I'm sorry, Gerry, but having a minority interest won't work for me."

Oscar Blackman stepped in. "Gentlemen, if I can say something. It seems to me you both want this to work, and it would be a pity to blow it out of the water for a paltry one percent. The way I look at it is that you're both grown men, and you've both tongues in your heads if things go wrong at some point in the future. I think you should agree fifty-fifty."

Kiplock thought about it for a moment or two and then concurred. "You're right, Oscar. We are grown men, and we do have tongues in our heads. I'll agree fifty-fifty if you will, Bill."

It wasn't ideal, but rather than have the deal go sour at this stage, Bill agreed.

Kiplock ticked something off on a piece of paper on his desk. "Next point. Capital. We're both going to need to put money into this, because your expenses will be going up. You couldn't hope to sell everything we'll be bringing to the table on your own. You'll have to take on a new man, and he'll need an office, and a car, and a secretary, and travelling expenses. What do you say to us putting in a hundred grand each, to begin with?"

Bill almost choked.

"Are we talking dollars, or pounds, Gerry?" Blackman said.

"Dollars should do it. That okay with you, Bill?"

"Gerry, I told you in London I wasn't in a position to bring capital to the table. You told me not to worry about it, and I took that to mean I wouldn't have to find any money."

"Well, if you're expecting me to put up all the capital, it sure as hell ain't gonna be fifty-fifty."

"Could your bank help, Bill?" Blackman suggested.

Bill shook his head. "Not at the moment they wouldn't, Oscar."

"Not even if you call them from here, right now, and told them you've got the business if they loan you the money?" Blackman glanced at his watch. "It's 9.35am here, which means that in England it's 2.35pm, so you should be able to get hold of somebody."

"There's no point, Oscar," Bill said. "They won't play ball."

"He's right," Angela said. "They won't play ball."

"The only way we could raise that kind of money would be to sell our house," Bill said. "And we're not going to do that."

"No, you're not," Blackman said emphatically. "You're not selling your home just for the privilege of doing business with the Kiplock group. Are they, Gerry?"

"Hell no, we're not having you doing that. There is another option, Bill, and one that won't require capital on your part."

Bill knew what he was going to say.

"That is, you act as our agent."

"But that's not what you want, Gerry, is it?" Blackman said. "You've always said everybody and his brother has agents offshore, and you wanted to be different. You wanted to have your own offices."

"Yeah, you're right. So how do we make this work?"

"There is a way it might work," Blackman mused. "Bill, would you and Angela mind waiting in the conference room while I have a word with Gerry?"

"Not at all," Bill said. He was glad of the excuse to get out from under. With the cat out of the bag as to the state of his finances, his self-esteem was taking a pounding.

Blackman walked them to the conference room. "Back in five," he said. He walked out and closed the door.

Angela sat. Bill paced the floor.

"Bill, take it easy. You're going to give yourself a heart attack."

His forehead was creased in a frown. "I've never had an opportunity like this before, and I'm scared of losing it."

"You won't lose it, darling. Oscar will come up with something. I know he will."

Blackman came back smiling. "Come on, let's get on with it." He led them back to Kiplock's office. "Do you want to tell them, Gerry? Or shall I?"

"You tell 'em," Kiplock said. "It was your idea."

The lawyer perched on the corner of Kiplock's desk. "How would you feel about selling Gerry half your company? That way, you get cash in hand, you don't have to go cap-in-hand to the bank, and you don't have to sell your home. And you get Gerry's business."

"That sounds like a wonderful idea," Angela said.

"Does it?" Bill said.

The others looked at him in surprise.

"I'd like a word with Angela," he said.

"Use the conference room again," Blackman said.

In the privacy of the conference room, Angela asked Bill what his problem was. "As I see it, they've taken into account everything you've said, and they've come up with what seems to me like an ideal solution."

Before Bill could answer, there was a knock on the door and Blackman appeared. "Okay if I come in, guys?"

"Of course it is," Bill said. "Come on in."

Blackman walked in, closed the door and stood with his back against the window. "Bill, I don't understand your problem. Considering your circumstances, it seems to me like an ideal solution."

Angela was on the point of saying that was exactly what she had just said, but she thought better of it.

"You do want this deal, don't you?" Blackman asked.

"Of course, I do. There's nothing I want more."

"Then what's your problem? You'd probably make so much money out of the deal you'd be able to retire in ten years if you wanted to."

"And think about it, Bill," Angela said. "We'd probably never have to worry about money again. How nice would that be?"

"Worrying about money's for the birds," Blackman said. "You could make money and have yourselves and your children a wonderful lifestyle. That's what you want isn't it? It's what most of us work for."

"Of course it is, but …"

"But what, Bill?" Angela said.

"Okay," Bill said, "I didn't want to say this in front of Gerry but in a nutshell, if he owns a part of my company, and knowing now how he thinks he would probably want to own at least fifty percent. I would have no control of my own company."

Blackman threw up his hands in frustration. "But, Bill, with three thousand miles between you, how could Gerry have any control over your company? And he's travelling most of the time. He won't be breathing down your neck. He doesn't have the time."

"Oscar's right, Bill," Angela said. "And as you've both agreed, if you work together, everything should be fine."

"Oscar, what happens if it doesn't work out between us? What would happen to my existing business then?"

"Then you pay Gerry back what he paid you for your shares, and you get your business back - lock, stock and barrel."

"I would need that in writing."

"I'll be drawing up the agreement. I'll make sure you get it."

"There is one other thing, Oscar."

"What's that, Bill?"

"I've heard some things about Gerry, things of a personal nature, that are not exactly complimentary."

"Everybody's heard things about Gerry that are not complimentary, Bill, and some of them may be true. But we all have our foibles. Gerry's not a monster. Sure, he's not the easiest guy in the world to work with, but what successful person is. They have to be hard to get where they've got."

"How long have you worked for Gerry, Oscar?" Angela asked.

"Twenty-six years, give or take. His father took me on and I watched Gerry grow up and I watched his father bring him into the business. Gerry's a talented and astute businessman because his father taught him, and taught him the hard way. He'll make you more money than you can possibly imagine. And isn't that why you're here? When all is said and done, money is all business is about. Everything else is incidental."

"Oscar's right, Bill," Angela said. "And without putting too fine a point on it, you can be pretty difficult yourself. Gerry may end up being the one with the difficulty."

Bill knew she was right. He looked from one to the other, making up his mind, finally, he nodded. "All right, Oscar. Let's do it."

Back in Kiplock's office, Kiplock said, "Well, what's it to be? Are we doing the deal, or are we not?"

"If we can come to terms on the price of the shares in my company, we're doing the deal," Bill said.

"That's easy enough," Kiplock said. "There's a standard formula American companies use in situations like this. For half the shares in your company, I'll give you half the current net book value of the company."

Bill knew that the net book value of the company was currently a big fat zero, and half of a big fat zero, is a big fat zero. But he also knew that in order to make a contract legal, there had to be offer, acceptance, and consideration, the consideration being the price paid. So money had to change hands. Bill also knew that, despite his company being a closed company, meaning that the company's accounts were not open to the public, Kiplock would have done his homework and would know that the company was virtually worthless. "If getting half the company for a dollar is what you had in mind, Gerry," he said. "You can forget it."

"Gerry bought Jacques Peterson's company for a dollar," Blackman said. "Jacques had debts that kept him awake at night, and no assets. Now he has no debts, he sleeps at night, and he makes a shed load of money."

"Bill, considering how difficult …" Angela started to say.

"You'll need to stump up $250,000," Bill said.

95

"In your dreams," Kiplock said.

"Then make me an offer."

"A hundred grand."

"Pounds, or dollars?"

"Dollars. We're talking dollars."

"Way too low. Make it two-hundred thousand."

"Way too high. A hundred and a quarter."

"Way too low," Bill said. "Make it one and three quarters."

"I'll tell what I'll do, Bill. I'll offer you $150,000, and that's my final offer." Kiplock put out his hand. "Do we shake on it?"

Bill ignored the outstretched hand and shook his head. "No, I sleep on it."

New York – Day Three

The next morning, Oscar Blackman met them when they stepped out of the lift at the office. "You guys are going home tonight, right?"

"We're planning to," Bill said.

"Then we need to put this deal to bed. No offence Bill, but all things considered, that was a very fair offer Gerry made you yesterday."

"No offence taken," Bill said. "But what Gerry offered me yesterday was less than half what it would cost him to run his own office in the UK for just one year."

"You're kidding!" the lawyer said, astounded. "I'd no idea the UK was so expensive."

"It's a hell of a lot more expensive than the US, Oscar, and that was why I needed to sleep on it. Gerry would be getting a hell of a deal. But I'm going to accept his offer, anyway. I'm not turning an opportunity like this down."

Blackman slapped him on the back. "Bill, that's just great. Gerry's gonna be over the moon. Let's go and give him the good news." He walked them to Kiplock's office.

Kiplock was at his desk working on some papers. He sat back in his chair. "Morning. Well, are we going to shake on it?"

"Yes, we're going to shake on it."

Kiplock got to his feet and pumped Bill's hand. "You won't regret it." He gave Angela a hug. "Smart fella, this husband of yours," he said, after finally letting her go.

They settled down to talk about logistics: taking on more staff, office space, etc., and then got down to discussing how the joint venture should be structured. They settled on leaving Bill's company exactly as it was, at least as far as the outside world was concerned, and setting up a new company, a fifty-fifty joint venture to handle the Kiplock materials, with Bill as chairman and managing director, and Angela, Gerry, and Gerry's father, as directors.

Bill saved something that had been nagging at him until last. It was one thing the Kiplock group saying they had all these American sources of material to bring to the table, but he only had their word for it. He needed it in writing. The question was, how best to bring it up without causing offence. "Gerry," he said tentatively.

"Shoot, partner."

"Gerry, don't take this the wrong way, but ..." He paused.

"Spit it out, Bill," Blackman said. "You're among friends."

"Well, I'm not doubting anybody's word, but these sources your guys say they can bring to the table."

Kiplock looked at him suspiciously. "What about them?"

"I'd like to have them in writing."

Kiplock frowned. "Why, don't you trust me?"

"Sure he trusts you," Blackman said. "And if the boot were on the other foot, Gerry, you would want to have them in writing."

Kiplock nodded. "Yeah, I guess I would."

"I'll make sure it's covered, Bill," Blackman said. "Was there anything else?"

"I can't think of anything else. Can you, darling?"

"No, I can't think of anything else," Angela said.

"Well, I suppose there is one other thing," Bill said. "When are we likely to get the money? I'd like to get the bank off my back."

"How soon can you get a contract drawn up, Oscar?" Kiplock said.

"Well, I guess I can have a draft contract drawn up in about a week."

"Is that the best you can do?" Kiplock said. "I want to get this show on the road."

Gerry Blackman stared at his boss. "Do you want it drawn up quickly, or do you want it drawn up right? I mean, if you want it full of errors ..."

"All right, all right. Point taken."

"Bill, I'll fax you a draft within a week. And assuming you're happy with it, I'll get the contract drawn up formally and DHL you two originals. Sign both copies, and DHL one of them back to me. Once I get that, I'll have the guys in accounts wire the money into your bank account. It shouldn't take more than ten days, two weeks tops."

"From now?"

"From now."

"Any more questions?" Kiplock said.

"Not from me," Bill said. "Darling?"

Angela shook her head. "Not that I can think of."

"Good," Kiplock said. "Now, I don't know about you guys, but all this talk of money is making me thirsty. Who's for a glass of champagne, to celebrate?"

They celebrated their deal with a lunch of oysters on the half shell and quail in a white wine sauce washed down with vintage champagne at the Four Seasons Restaurant on East 52nd Street. Their celebration meal went on until late in the afternoon, by which time six empty champagne bottles had been carted away.

When Bill said they had to leave for the airport, Kiplock shook his hand warmly. "Don't worry about your bill at the Waldorf," he said. "It's been taken care of. And you look after this lovely wife of yours, you hear?"

"I will," Bill said. "And thanks, Gerry. You've just made our lives a whole lot easier. I'm really looking forward to working with you."

"Me too, pal." He gave Angela a hug. When he finally let go of her, he looked into her eyes. "You look after that husband of yours, okay? He's a valuable commodity, not to mention a hell of a nice guy."

"Don't worry, Gerry, I will."

Blackman shook Bill's hand. "You have any problems, you call me. You hear? I'll always be available."

"I will, Oscar, and thank you. Thank you for everything. I don't think it would have worked without your input."

"Sure it would. Don't sell yourself short. You're a very capable guy."

Bill and Angela walked out to the waiting stretch Cadillac leaving Gerry Kiplock and Oscar Blackman trying to reach agreement on whether they should go back to the office, or order another bottle of champagne.

Chapter 9

"Hello, sleepyhead."

"What?" Bill struggled to open his eyes. "Oh hi, sweetheart. God, I'm tired. What time is it?"

"It's three in the afternoon. You've been asleep for five hours."

"Good grief!"

"You didn't get much sleep on the plane, did you?"

"I didn't get any. Too much on my mind."

"I'm not surprised. I've brought you some coffee."

"Good, maybe it will help me wake up."

"I've unpacked your case and put your things in the wash."

"Thank you. Aren't you tired?"

"I slept on the plane. I feel fine."

Angela walked across the bedroom and drew back the curtains. The sky was dark and threatening and rain was beginning to spot the windows. She walked to her side of the built-in wardrobe that ran the length of the wall and opened the door. "I'm just off to pick the children up from school," she said. She rifled through the rail, looking for a warm coat.

Bill was in bed in his pyjamas. He sat up and reached for his coffee. "Great trip, eh?"

"It was amazing." Angela found herself a warm coat and slipped it on. She headed for the bedroom door. "By the way," she said, stopping by the door, "I called

Maureen to see if everything was all right at the office, and she asked that you call her."

"Did she say what about?"

Angela shook her head. "She said it was something only you could deal with. She sounded to be in one of her moods."

"I'll call her when I'm dressed."

"And Bas is asking when we are taking them out for the celebration dinner you promised him. He sends his congratulations, by the way."

"Oh, did he call? I didn't hear the phone."

Angela picked a piece of imaginary fluff off her coat. "I called Betty. He answered the phone."

"He must be taking the afternoon off."

"I suppose he must. Do you want to give me a date?"

"Let's leave it until after I've signed a contract with Gerry, just in case."

After Angela had gone, Bill finished his coffee and got out of bed. He showered, shaved, and dressed and then went downstairs and phoned Maureen.

Angela was right; Maureen was in a mood. She was using her *I'm-pissed-off-and-I'm-going-to-let-you-know-it* tone of voice.

"I know that tone of voice," he said. "What's up?"

"I started my period yesterday."

Which meant she wasn't pregnant. Bill was so elated he felt like punching the air. Now he needn't worry about bumping into her with a child that resembled him.

"Have you nothing to say?" she demanded.

"What do you want me to say?" he said

"You could at least say you're sorry."

This was ridiculous. She was his secretary, and she was talking to him as if they were lovers. But he knew Maureen's moods and he knew that in her present mood he needed to proceed with caution. "All right," he said. "I'm sorry."

Maureen pulled a face. "You could at least sound as if you mean it."

Bill was tired and jet-lagged from his trip and he was getting fed-up of this. He threw discretion to the winds. "Quite frankly, Maureen, whether or not you are pregnant is not the most important issue in my life right now. I have much more important issues to think of."

"I could change all that," Maureen said, bridling.

Bill frowned. "Are you threatening me?"

"I could tell the police you raped me."

"I raped you?" Bill snorted. "You come to the office all tarted up and with one thing on your mind, and you accuse me of raping you. If anyone raped anyone, you raped me."

"I could tell Angela."

Bill heard car doors slam and the children's voices in the driveway. "Maureen, I have to go. We'll talk about this in the morning."

The next morning, Bill was in early. He was reading through the masses of notes he had taken during the trip and trying to make sense of them and get them in order.

When Maureen came in, she banged around her office and then brought in a week's worth of mail and dumped it unceremoniously on his desk. If her face had been any longer, she could well have tripped over it.

Bill knew he needed to get this sorted, and fast. Fortunately, Angela had some shopping to do and wouldn't be in until later. He pointed to a chair; the chair Maureen had shifted so she could climb on to the table when he and she had … he winced at the thought. "Sit down, Maureen."

Maureen dragged out the chair and plonked herself down. Her expression was more that of a spoiled child than a well paid and highly qualified secretary.

"Maureen," he said sternly, "before you got me into this, you promised me you wouldn't tell Angela. So why the change of heart?"

"I would have thought that was obvious."

"Well it isn't to me, so why don't you enlighten me."

"I wanted you to get me pregnant, and you didn't." She made is sound so simple, and so logical.

"So I didn't get you pregnant. Is that a reason to blackmail me?"

Maureen just looked at him.

He felt his temper rising. He kept it in check. "Maureen, need I remind you that you are my secretary. Are you going to drop this nonsense, or am I going to have to consider my options?"

"Now who's threatening who?" Maureen said. "I'll drop it if you'll try again."

Bill couldn't believe what he was hearing. "I don't think so, Maureen," he said, trying to stay calm despite the turmoil going on inside him. "But if you persist in this nonsense, I'll tell you what I will do. I'll tell Angela what happened, and then I'll have a word with the police about your brother."

It was evident from the look on her face that Maureen had no idea what he was talking about. "What does my brother have to do with anything? How do you even know I have a brother?"

"Your brother's the one who beat me up. At least he was one of them."

"That's ridiculous," Maureen said. "My brother doesn't go round beating people up." She looked at him suspiciously. "Besides, how do you know it was my brother? You've never met my brother."

Bill smiled. "Ah, but that's where you're wrong, Maureen. I've met your brother on two separate occasions, and I have to say that on neither occasion was it a pleasure. The next time you talk to your brother, ask him about the run-in he had with a man on the train from Knebworth to Welwyn Garden City on the evening of my meeting in London with Gerry Kiplock. I was the man on the train. I reported him to the guard for his behaviour."

"And you assume it was my brother who beat you up because?"

"Because of what he yelled at me just before he kicked me in the head, and because I recognised his voice."

"How do I know you're not making it all up?" Maureen said. "And anyway, it wouldn't stand up in court."

"The imprint of the fleur-de-lys on the toes of his boots would."

Maureen was shaking her head, mystified. "What are you talking about?"

"When I was taken into the hospital, after your brother and his pals had beaten me up, I had the imprint of a fleur-de-lys on the side of my face. The hospital took a photograph of it."

Maureen leaned forward and took a look at his face. "I don't see anything other than a yellowish bruise. And anyway, if you knew who attacked you, why didn't you tell the police?"

"Isn't it obvious? If I'd told them it was your brother who had attacked me, you would have been brought into it, and what you and I did would almost certainly have got back to Angela. And I didn't want that to happen."

"My brother could get rid of his boots."

"Ah, so you admit it was your brother?"

"I'm not admitting anything."

"Getting rid of his boots wouldn't change anything. The guard on the train saw the boots, and the hospital will give the police the photograph of the fleur-de-lys impression on my face. So what do you say, Maureen? Are you still thinking of telling Angela?"

Maureen was beginning to look a lot less sure of herself. "Would you give me time to think about this, Bill?"

"What, and have this hanging over me?" Bill snorted. "I don't think so."

"If I promise not to tell Angela, will you promise not to talk to the police?"

"You promised not to tell Angela once before. Why should I believe you this time?"

"Bill, please. My brother's been arrested for grievous bodily harm before, but he got away with a suspended sentence. If he gets arrested again, he'll go to jail."

"Perhaps jail is where he should be," Bill said with a shrug.

"Please, Bill."

"If you promise not to talk to Angela, and to never bring up the subject again …"

"I promise. Anything. Just please don't …"

"All right, Maureen, but if you break your word." He left the sentence hanging. He got his paperknife out of a drawer in his desk and started to open the mail. "Now, if you don't mind, Maureen, I have things to do."

Bill had just finished reading the mail when Maureen buzzed him. "I have Mr Cummings on the line from the bank, Bill."

"Put him through."

"Good morning, Bill. So you're back from your trip, then."

"Yes, we got back yesterday. I was going to call you later today to tell you how we got on."

"I look forward to hearing about it. Meantime, there are some papers I need you to sign. Could you and Angela drop in this afternoon?"

Bill was not aware of any papers that needed to be signed. "What papers would those be, Bob?"

"The papers covering the extension to your overdraft facility."

Bill frowned. "You're surely not talking about the money you advanced us for our trip."

"One and the same. And since the mortgage on your home is in joint names, Angela will need to sign, too."

"You mean you want to secure the costs of our trip, a paltry £3,500, on our home. And after we've made the trip. Are you serious?"

"It might seem a little extreme, but ...

"A little extreme? That's putting it mildly. I would say it's just plain bonkers. You don't even know how we got on."

"What time would work for you, Bill? I can be flexible this afternoon."

"I'm not sure any time would work for us, Bob, because frankly I'm appalled that after all that's been said and everything we've been through together, you feel it necessary to secure the costs of our trip on our home. That shows no confidence in us whatsoever. And now, Bob, I don't want to say any more. I need to talk to

Angela about whether we continue to bank with you. I'll
get back to you."

He hung up.

Chapter 10

It took only one reading of the draft contract Oscar Blackman had prepared for one thing to become clear; it was heavily slanted in Gerry Kiplock's favour. So much for believing Blackman was on my side, Bill thought.

It was a complex document running to several pages and covering every conceivable eventuality. So he had something on plain paper to work with, Bill had Maureen photocopy the fax. Then he read it again, and again. Then, using felt-tip pens, he highlighted in yellow, the clauses he wanted amending, and in red, the clauses he wanted deleting. And he made pencil notes in the margin of items he wanted to add. He worked on the contract for most of the day, before finally dictating a reply to Maureen.

He signed the letter and then had Maureen fax it all back to New York.

A couple of hours later, Blackman phoned. "Got a pencil?"

"Hang on a sec." Bill grabbed his copy of the paperwork, and a pencil. "Okay, shoot."

"Let's start with the requested amendments that Gerry accepts."

As Blackman reeled them off, Bill ticked them off his list.

"Right," the lawyer said finally, "that's it for that list."

Bill gulped a mouthful of coffee while he had the chance. It was cold.

"Now, let's take a look at what Gerry doesn't necessarily agree with, but is prepared to compromise on."

Ten minutes later, they had reached agreement on that list.

"Make sure you're happy with what we're doing, Bill, because we can't come back to this once the contract's been signed."

"Don't worry," Bill said. "I'll make sure I'm happy."

"Right, then let's move on to the list of items you want deleted."

The next few minutes went by smoothly enough, until Blackman said, "Page four, clause eight. He won't agree to deleting this clause."

The clause in question stated that Bill was not to take on any other source of product without written permission from Gerry Kiplock personally.

"Oscar, that clause effectively relegates my position to that of underdog. I would be happy to agree to talk to Gerry before taking on another source, but to have to get his written permission beforehand, I don't think so."

"Bill, Gerry has that clause in his agreement with all his offices."

"And are all his offices partnerships?"

"Paris is. He owns the others outright."

"Well I'm sorry, Oscar, but I'm a partner, and I want that clause deleted."

"Bill, Gerry's point is that you might take on sources that compete with ours."

"I do understand this business, Oscar. You're forgetting I already have sources of my own. I want this clause deleted."

Blackman gave an audible sigh. "All right, Bill. But he's not going to like it. Now, on the subject of you repaying the $150,000 in the event of the partnership going belly up."

"Oscar, there's no way on God's earth I'm agreeing to repaying the $150,000 in the event the partnership goes belly up."

"All right, Bill, I'll tell him. But you're going to have a problem with him on that one. Now, as to the sole and exclusivity clause, there isn't one."

"I know there isn't one, and I want one included. We talked about this in New York."

"Yes, we did, and if I remember rightly, the idea was thrown out."

"Oscar, without a sole and exclusivity clause, Gerry could sell his material in the UK through anyone he liked, leaving me high and dry. And that's not acceptable. I need that covering in the contract."

"Bill, you keep your nose clean and work hard, and you'll have nothing to worry about. Trust me, I know Gerry."

"What about the list of suppliers and products Gerry's guys said they could bring to the table?"

In the silence that ensued, Bill heard Maureen moving around in the next room and traffic in the street below.

"Oscar, I need that list."

"All right, Bill. I'll ask him again. Is that it?"

"Subject to a lawyer taking a look at it."

"Jesus, Bill! You're having a lawyer look at it at this stage? Gerry will go ballistic."

"Oscar, if your draft had not been so heavily slanted in Gerry's favour, I wouldn't have needed a lawyer."

Bill's friend Basil ran his own business and he had often talked about how good his lawyer was. He had offices in London. Basil gave Bill the number and Bill called him.

"Andrew Buckley."

"Andrew, it's Bill McLaren. Basil Sutherland suggested I contact you."

"Yes, Bill, I've been expecting your call. What can I do for you?"

"I've got a contract I'd like you to give me your thoughts on."

"I'll be happy to."

"If you let me have your fax number I'll fax it to you. Meantime, let me give you the background."

Buckley listened quietly while Bill explained. "I think I get the picture."

"The thing is, Andrew, that time is of the essence. How long will you need?"

"Well, I'm pretty busy right now. I could probably let you have an opinion in say a couple of weeks' time."

"That gives me a problem, because New York are all over me. I was hoping for something yesterday."

"Since you're a friend of Basel's, I'll slot you in. Fax me the draft and I'll see what I can do."

A week later, Oscar Blackman called. He sounded harassed. "Any news, Bill?"

"I'm still waiting for my lawyer."

"Gerry thinks you're stalling and he's threatening to pull out. So I would suggest that if you're seriously interested in putting this deal together, you get on the phone to your lawyer and tell him to pull his finger out."

Bill hung up and called the lawyer.

"I was just about to send you a fax," Buckley said. "I'll have it on your machine within the next two minutes."

Bill stood by the fax machine until the fax arrived. When he read it, he realised he had wasted his money. The lawyer was telling him nothing he didn't know already. He dictated a fax to Oscar Blackman.

Blackman phoned within the hour. "Got your fax, Bill. Not good news, I'm afraid. Gerry won't budge."

"On what?"

"On the clauses you want deleted. Especially the one concerning paying back the $150,000 in the event the partnership fails."

"So I'm just supposed to knuckle under, am I?"

"You have to admit that Gerry's given way on a number of major issues."

"Let me ask you a question, Oscar: who decides that the deal hasn't worked out, and at what point is it decided?"

"I'm not sure I understand you."

"Well let's take the scenario that the money has come through and we've hired a new guy, and we've got him a car, and we've got him an office and we've hired him a secretary, and then Gerry has a fit of pique about something and tells me what to do with myself. What happens then?"

"I don't think you need to worry about that, Bill. You'll have made loads of money by then."

"Not if it happens in the first year I won't. You don't just walk into a UK buyer's office and expect him to start taking product from a source he isn't familiar with, just because you're on each other's Christmas card list. It takes time. It can take years."

"I take your point. Same here in the US."

"I can live with not deleting the other clauses Gerry has a problem with, but I can't live with this one. To Gerry, $150,000 is a mere bagatelle. To me, it's the difference between keeping my head above water and sinking without trace. Is he there, Oscar? I'd like a word with him."

"He's on his way to Peru. I'm joining him down there. We'll be gone for two weeks. We're talking to some potential new sources, some of which could come your way. Be careful, Bill. You don't want to blow what could be the opportunity of a lifetime for you."

"I'm not planning to blow it. I'm just making the point that Gerry could blow me out of the water any time he liked."

"Then that's probably something you're just going to have to live with, Bill. He is what he is. I can't change him."

"This is not a good start to a new relationship, Oscar."

"You're over-reacting, Bill."

"Would you ask him again? Please. It's very important to me."

"All right, Bill. I'll ask him again. But don't hold your breath."

A couple of days later, Bill got a call from the bank. "When do you expect to get the money from New York, Bill?" Cummings asked. "Head office is asking."

"Soon, Bob."

"I expected to hear something by now."

"I know. You'll get it soon, I promise."

Expecting Oscar Blackman to call him back, Bill made no attempt to contact him. But after a week had gone by and nothing had happened, he phoned New York.

"I'm sorry, Bill," the girl on the switchboard said, "Oscar's in Peru with Gerry and we're having difficulty contacting them. The phone systems are not great down there."

"I understand. But would you try to get a message to Oscar and ask him to phone me, please. It's extremely urgent."

"Sure, Bill. I'll see what I can do."

Two days later, Blackman phoned. There was the hum of machinery in the background. "I hear you've been trying to get hold of me."

"You said you'd have another word with Gerry, about the repayment clause. I thought you'd be getting back to me."

"We've been busy. He won't budge, Bill. He says that if you don't agree to leave the clause in, the deal's off."

"And if I agree to leaving the clause in?"

"We go ahead."

Bill knew he had no choice. It was either moving forward under terms that were well short of satisfactory, or selling the house and virtual oblivion.

"All right, Oscar. I agree. Leave the clause in."

"Fine, I'll tell him. Bill, a word to the wise: you're going to have to mend some fences with Gerry, because right now he's wondering if he made the right decision in approaching you."

Two days later, Bill got a call from the bank. "The money's in the account, Bill," Cummings said. "I'm glad you decided to continue banking with us."

Chapter 11

For their celebration dinner with Basil and Betty, Bill had booked a table at a London restaurant at which he had entertained on a number of occasions prior to starting his own company. It was an expensive restaurant in Park Lane. Bill had never felt he could justify the expense of eating there under his own steam, but with Gerry Kiplock's $150,000 converted to sterling and tucked safely away in the bank, and the promise of much more where that came from when the Kiplock business started to flow, he had felt like pushing the boat out.

The arrangement was that he and Angela would pick Basil and Betty up from their house and drive them into London, but it was clear from the moment Basil and Betty climbed into the back of the Jaguar, that something was wrong. They didn't seem to be speaking to each other, and Betty looked as if she had been crying.

The fifty-minute drive into London was taken up by a three-way conversation between Bill, Angela and Basil, mostly about how the trip to New York had gone, with Betty staring through the window and only speaking when she was spoken to.

The maître d' at the restaurant recognised Bill. He beamed and said, "Very nice to see you again, sir. It's been a while."

"Indeed it has," Bill said, "it's been over three years. But with a bit of luck and a following wind, you might be seeing more of me in the future."

The maître d' suggested an apéritif before sitting down at the table, and when Bill said that sounded like an excellent idea, he collected menus and a wine list and led the way into the bar area, which was busy. He sat them down at one of two available tables and handed Bill the wine list and each of them a menu, and raised a hand to summon a member of the bar staff, before returning to his post.

"It makes a difference when you're spending your own money, doesn't it, old man?" Basil said, opening his green leather covered menu.

"Doesn't it just," Bill said. "I must say it's nice to be back." He looked around the room to see if there was anyone he recognised.

"The last couple of years have been difficult for you, haven't they?" Basil said. "You never complained, but I could tell."

"It has been difficult, Bas, but hopefully it's behind me, now."

They ordered drinks, toasted happy days, and studied their menus.

When the waiter came to take their order, Bill asked him if he was recommending anything in particular.

"The chateaubriand is always good," the waiter said.

"Ah, yes," Bill said. "I remember the chateaubriand. It was always excellent."

"Chateaubriand's fine with me," Basil said.

"And with me," Angela said.

Bill looked at Betty.

She didn't respond. She looked preoccupied.

"Betty?"

"What?"

"Would you like chateaubriand?"

"Oh, I'm sorry, Bill. I was miles away. Yes, chateaubriand is fine."

Bill hated any sign of blood in his beef. "Pink in the middle, everyone?" he said.

"Fine with me," Basil said.

"And with me," Angela said.

"It's fine with me too, Bill." Betty said.

"Pink in the middle it is," the waiter said, making a note.

For starters, they agreed on prawns rolled in smoked salmon.

Bill wanted everything to be just-so, and he took his time choosing the wine. He finally settled on Chablis to go with their starters, and a Chateau-bottled claret to go with the beef.

Twenty minutes later, the maître d' told them their table was ready and led them into the restaurant.

When Bill had made the booking, he had asked for the table in the alcove at the far end of the restaurant, because he knew this to be the only table in the restaurant with a view of Hyde Park.

As they waited to be served, Basil, who was sitting across the table next to Angela, told Bill that his face was looking better.

"It's fine now," Bill said. "And I'm seeing my dentist next week. That should be the end of it."

The wine waiter arrived with two bottles of wine.

Bill tasted the Chablis and nodded to the waiter. He asked him to uncork the claret to let it breathe.

"Again, old man," Basil said, raising his glass to Bill, "well done in New York. I knew you could do it."

"Do the police have any idea who attacked you, Bill?" Betty asked, speaking for the first time since she had agreed to chateaubriand in the bar.

"Not as far as I'm aware, Betty. At least no one's said anything to me."

Betty was clearly not herself. Something was bothering her. A vivacious person by nature, she was almost always bright and enthusiastic, but not tonight. Bill recalled Basil saying something about her not being herself when he had visited him in the hospital. To try and draw her out and get her to engage in the conversation, he asked her how her wine was.

She gave him a little smile. "It's lovely, Bill. Thank you."

"What kind of a man is this Gerry Kiplock?" Basil said.

Bill took a sip of his wine before answering. "He's very successful, and he knows his business. But I would say he's not a man to be trifled with. What do you think, Angie? How would you describe Gerry?"

"I agree that he's not a man to be trifled with, but on the flip side, he's very good looking." She winked at Betty.

Betty looked away.

"You kid about that," Bill said, "but you watch yourself. I know more about that side of him than you do."

Angela looked at him curiously. "Why haven't you mentioned that before?"

"Because I didn't think it was important before. But just have a care, that's all I'm saying."

Angela was wearing the dress Bill had bought her for the trip, the grey wool one with the turtle neck, and Basil remarked on what a beautiful dress it was. "It's lovely, isn't it, Betty?" he said.

To Bill's certain knowledge, this was the first time Basil had spoken directly to his wife since he had picked them up in the car.

Betty glanced at Angela's dress and nodded. "Yes, it's very nice." She got back to her meal.

"How are things going at the bank now, old man?" Basil asked.

"Things are fine now Gerry's money has come through," Bill replied.

Throughout the meal there were lengthy silences, and what little conversation there was, was stilted. To Bill it all seemed to revolve around Betty. Finally, he came right out with it and told her she was very quiet tonight. He asked if she was all right.

Basil answered for her. "She's not been feeling herself recently, have you, old girl?"

Betty glared at him. "I can speak for myself," she snapped. "And I do wish you'd stop calling me old girl."

"Hey, come on, old girl. This is supposed to be a celebration. I know you're a bit off colour, but that's no reason to spoil everybody's evening."

"Me spoil the evening?" Betty said angrily. "That's rich, coming from you."

"Come on, Betty," Angela said. "As Bas said, this is supposed to be a celebration."

Betty glared at her. "Well just maybe I don't feel like celebrating." She threw her napkin on the table, pushed her chair back and got to her feet. "I need some air." She headed for the exit, her shoulders set.

"I'm sorry," Basil said, making to get to his feet. "Really not herself. I'd better go after her."

Bill beat him to it. "I'll go, Bas," he said, getting to his feet. "You get on with your meal."

The restaurant was on the first floor of a five-star hotel and was accessed via a sweeping staircase from the hotel lobby. To catch up with her, Bill almost had to run down the stairs. He caught her as she reached the bottom of the staircase. He caught her arm. "What is it, Betty?"

There were tears in her eyes. She shook her head. "Not here. Let's go to your car."

Bill had parked his car in the hotel's basement garage, which meant walking out into the street and down a ramp at the side of the building.

It was a cold night and Betty's shoulders were bare. She was shivering. Bill took off his jacket and draped it over her shoulders. When they got to the car, he started the engine and turned up the heater.

Betty stared through the windscreen, a picture of abject misery.

"What is it, Betty?"

Tears were now running freely down her cheeks.

He handed her his handkerchief.

"It's those two."

"Which two? Are you talking about Bas and Angie?"

"Yes, those two."

"What about them?"

"They're having an affair."

"Nonsense."

Betty turned to face him. "I knew you wouldn't believe me. It's true, Bill. They're having an affair."

"I don't believe it, Betty. I would have known."

"How could you know, when you're never here? You're always away on business. At first I thought it was his secretary, but I've watched them together, and it's not her. Then I noticed his behaviour when Angela was around."

"I haven't noticed anything."

"I mean when you're not around. He moons around her like a lovesick puppy. And it's the same when he's talking to her on the phone. I'm not making it up, Bill, they're having an affair."

"But if they were having an affair, there would be absences. How does he explain his absences?"

"I think they meet mostly during the day. With you away, and the children at school, it wouldn't be that difficult. And he's been coming up with cock-and-bull stories about having to go back to the office in the evenings. He never used to go back to the office in the evenings, but he's been doing it a lot over the last few months."

"The last few months? Are you saying it's been going on for months?"

Her tears were drying up. She dabbed at a loose one with his handkerchief. "When I think back, it could have been going on for a year."

"But how could I not have noticed, for a year?"

She patted his hand. "Don't reproach yourself, Bill. You weren't here. You weren't to know."

"But when he said he was going to the office, did you call his office to check if he was actually there?"

"I did, on several occasions. And I always got the answering machine. And when I asked him why he didn't answer the phone, he told me he let the machine take it so he wouldn't be disturbed while he's working."

"Did you ever go to the office, to see that he was actually there?"

"I did once, and he wasn't there. When I asked him where he'd been, he made an excuse that seemed entirely plausible."

A thought occurred. "Betty, do you happen to remember if Basil went out on the evening I was in hospital? I mean after he had been to the hospital to see me."

Betty thought for a moment or two, and then said, "Yes, I believe he did go out that evening. If I recall, he went out around nine.

"And Angela left the hospital about then. And she was wearing a perfume I hadn't bought her, although she told me that evening that I had. As a matter of fact, she's wearing it again tonight."

"I know she is," Betty said. "I noticed it as soon as I got into your car when you picked us up. That's one reason why I'm upset tonight. I helped him choose that perfume. He told me he wanted something for his secretary, for Christmas."

"And after all the time he and I have been friends. How can you be so wrong about someone?"

"My sentiments exactly," Betty said miserably.

Bill turned to face her. "What will you do, Betty? Will you leave him?"

"I don't think so, Bill. The reason I haven't precipitated anything is that I have no money of my own, and at my time of life I don't want to have to start again. I'd rather have him than be on my own."

"Has he had affairs with other women? To the best of your knowledge, I mean."

"None that I'm aware of. What will you do, Bill?"

"Right now, Betty. I haven't a clue. I need time to think." And speaking of time, he realised they had been away from the table for quite some time. He checked his watch. They had been gone for almost twenty-five minutes. "If you're all right now, Betty, we should be getting back. They'll be wondering what we're doing. Not that I give much of a damn about what they're thinking."

Neither of them wanted to go back to the table and pretend everything was hunky-dory, and as they walked up the staircase they agreed that Betty would say she wasn't feeling well and would like to go home.

Neither Angela nor Basil appeared surprised by what Betty had to say, and Bill asked the waiter for the bill.

That night, Bill lay awake until the early hours.

Angela lay sleeping beside him. At least he thought she was sleeping.

Finally, he slipped quietly out of bed, put on his dressing gown and went downstairs and made himself some tea. He carried it through into the sitting room and sat in the dark, his mind in turmoil.

A sound behind him startled him.

It was Angela.

He got a whiff of her perfume, the one his so-called friend had bought her. He wondered how many times she had worn it in bed with him.

"Can't you sleep?" she said.

He didn't answer. He was afraid of where this might lead, and his heart was pounding and he was finding it hard to breathe.

She knelt on the floor beside him and put her hand on his knee and her chin on her hand. "Problem, Bill?"

"You could say that."

"Do you want to talk about it?"

"I'm not sure."

"A problem shared, and all that."

"Okay," Bill said. "You want to know what's wrong, you are what's wrong. You and that bastard I thought was my friend."

"I thought so. You know, don't you?"

"About you and him?"

"Yes."

"Yes, I know. Betty told me while we were sitting in the car."

"I thought she had. You were gone from the table for so long."

"How do you think she feels?"

"Wretched, I should imagine. I know I would in her position."

"Why, Angela?"

"You only call me Angela when you're upset with me."

"Wouldn't you be upset if the boot was on the other foot?"

"I think that would be putting it mildly. You're taking it much better than I thought you would." She got to her feet and sat in a chair facing him.

It was dark, but he could see her outline. She was sitting forward with her elbows on her knees. Even from a distance of five or six feet he could smell the perfume. He wanted to tell her to go and wash it off. Scrub it off, even.

"I'm sorry, Bill."

"Sorry for what, Angela? Sorry you've been caught, or sorry for what you've done to Betty and me?"

"I'm sorry it ever happened, and I'm dreadfully sorry for what I've done to you and Betty."

"But why was it necessary? Was it something I said? Something I did, or didn't do? Or do you not love me anymore?"

"I think it started with a need to feel desired."

"Don't I make you feel desired?"

"You're never here. And when you are here, you're tired because you've just got back from a trip, or you've been drinking."

"But why with my so-called best friend?"

"Because you weren't here, and he was, I suppose."

"How long has it been going on?"

"Almost a year."

"Christ almighty! A year? How can I have missed the signs for a year?"

"I don't know, Bill. It's actually not very flattering that you have missed them. It shows how little attention you pay to me. That's another of the problems. You're so wrapped up in your business. Sometimes I feel like an appendage, like something to parade around to impress people, like the bank, or Gerry Kiplock. I sometimes feel more like a trophy, than your wife."

"But why have you never talked to me about this? How am I supposed to know if you don't tell me?"

"I'm telling you now."

There followed a lengthy silence, a silence lasting several minutes.

It was Bill who finally broke it. "So what are we going to do about it?"

"I don't know, Bill. I suppose that's really up to you. Since you're the injured party."

In the dark Hertfordshire countryside, a fox barked. Its bark sounded like some unfortunate creature dying in agony.

"I don't want us to split up," Bill said. "We've gone through too much to throw it all away now, even considering the seriousness of what's happened. And there's too much to lose, especially now with Gerry Kiplock on the scene. Do you love him? I can't even bring myself to mention his name."

He could see the silhouette of her head shaking, no. "It was never love. In fact, at times I actually find him quite boring. It's you I love. The question is, Bill, do you love me? Because I can't honestly remember the last time you told me you loved me."

"Then that's remiss of me, and I apologise. I do love you, Angie. I've always loved you, and I probably always will. And perhaps if you'd told me I wasn't telling you I loved you, you wouldn't have had to turn to him for comfort."

"You called me Angie again. Does that mean you're not angry with me anymore?"

"I'm not sure what I am at the moment. Beyond confused, and hurt."

"Can you find it in your heart to forgive me, Bill?"

"If we're going to stay together, I'm going to have to, although it might take some time. But you're going to have to break it off with him."

"It's done. We ended it tonight, while you and Betty were away from the table. You were gone from the table so long, we suspected what was going on."

"There's one other thing I need you to do for me."

"Of course, Bill, anything."

"Throw that bloody perfume away."

Chapter 12

"I have Marcia on the line for you," Maureen said.

"Put her through."

"Good morning, Bill."

"Good morning, Marcia. Or good afternoon, as it is in my neck of the woods."

"Bill, Gerry's planning to come over to England the week after next. He's arriving on the Tuesday evening, May 10th, and he's leaving for Rome on the evening of Thursday, May 12th. He wants you to set up interviews for the sales manager's job on the Wednesday, and he said you should have a board meeting to elect the officers for the joint venture at your offices on the Thursday morning."

Bill took a quick look at his desk diary. He was planning to be in Scotland that week. He would have to reschedule. "Okay, Marcia. I'll set it up."

"Would it be out of your way to collect Gerry at Heathrow and drive him to the Savoy Hotel?"

This was music to Bill's ears. An hour alone in the car with him would give him the chance to start mending some of the fences Oscar Blackman had been talking about. "Not at all," he said. "I'd be happy to pick him up."

"I'll fax you his itinerary. Say hi to the lovely Angela for me."

"I will."

Marcia hung up.

Bill hung up and put a note in his desk diary. Then he sat back and started to think about how he was going to set up interviews for a senior sales executive at less than two weeks' notice. Hiring a secretary could be done locally, but finding someone with the knowledge and experience to be able to walk straight in and build volumes of product from American mills, was going to be a whole other ball game.

His thoughts went back to when he had been working in London for an American forest products company, prior to starting his own company, and he had needed a sales executive. He had used a head-hunter who hired exclusively for the pulp and paper industry. He remembered that the guy operated from offices in the financial district of London, the square mile as it was known, but he couldn't for the life of him remember his name. He found it by searching through his extensive collection of business cards.

His name was Ian Penhaligen. Bill got his phone number from his card and picked up the phone and called him. They chewed the fat for a few moments, getting reacquainted, and then Bill told him what he was looking for.

"It's going to have to be somebody I already have on my books, Bill, because it takes time to advertise a new position. But off the top of my head, there are three guys who might fit the bill." He gave Bill a quick rundown on the individuals in question, and Bill asked him to fax him their CVs.

Next, Bill had to think about office accommodation for the new man. There were a couple of vacant rooms down the corridor from his suite of offices and he phoned the landlord, Welwyn Garden City council, who sent a man round with a set of keys.

The rooms turned out to be a suite of two inter-connecting rooms, each room the same size as Bill's room. And like Bill's room, one of them had French windows. They had been empty for as long as Bill had been a tenant in the building and they were in dire need of decorating, which Bill lost no time in pointing out to the man from the council.

"A lick of paint and some new wallpaper and they'll be as right as rain," the man from the council said airily.

"And new carpet," Bill pointed out. Where people had sat at their desks and shuffled their feet, the carpets were threadbare. "And by the way, when you say they will be as right as rain, I don't need them both. I only need one room."

"I'm sorry," the man from the council said firmly, "but we can't break up a suite. Council policy."

"Then perhaps I should look for offices elsewhere. Come to think of it, I would quite like to have a change."

That brought an immediate and hasty response. "I don't think there's any need for you to look elsewhere, Mr Smith. I'm sure we can work something out."

Bill walked through the inter-connecting door into the room with the French windows. "So," he said, standing by the grime-encrusted windows and looking down on the street, "the council will redecorate and put down new carpets in both rooms. Right?"

"Correct," the man from the council said, making a note on his clipboard. "Do I take it you're interested?"

"I could be if you give me both rooms for the price of one. As I said, I'm only looking for one room."

"You're a hard man, Mr. Smith," the man from the council said. "But I think we can accommodate you."

Gerry Kiplock's Visit – His Arrival

When Gerry Kiplock walked into the arrivals hall at Heathrow, Bill had to restrain himself from laughing out loud. If he had turned up at his golf club wearing the loud check jacket and bright red trousers his partner was wearing, he would have been asked to resign his membership. He greeted him cheerfully. "Hi there, partner. Good flight?"

The American's response was a less-than-enthusiastic. "Okay, I guess."

Kiplock was carrying a suitcase in one hand and a briefcase in the other, and Bill reached forward to take the suitcase. "Let me take that, Gerry. It looks heavy."

Kiplock sidestepped him. "I'm good."

It was clear from his body language and the expression on his face that he was in a foul mood and they walked to the multi-storey car park in silence.

When he saw that Bill was driving a Jaguar, he exclaimed, "Jesus Christ! A Jaguar?" He pronounced it *Jagwar*, in the way Americans do. "And here's me thinking you had no money."

Bill opened the boot. "Gerry, I've been driving this car for five years. I bought it from my previous employer for a lot less than it was worth, and it has well over a hundred thousand miles on the clock."

Kiplock tossed his luggage in the boot. "It's still a Jaguar. In the States, if I turned up for a meeting in a

Jaguar, I wouldn't get the business. The guy would think I was making too much money."

Bill slammed the boot lid, annoyed at being lectured at. "You turn up for meetings in a much more upmarket vehicle than I do. You turn up in a chauffeur-driven stretch Cadillac."

"I'm talking about when I fly and drive."

"I don't rent Jaguars when I fly and drive"

"Well I think you should think about changing it."

"Gerry, I'm not changing my car just because you think I should. And perhaps you should remember than I'm your partner, and not the hired help."

Neither of them spoke again until they were approaching the slip road to the M4 motorway. As he accelerated up the slip road, Bill glanced at his partner. "Gerry, have I done something wrong?"

"Since you ask, yes you have. You've cost me an agency."

Bill checked his side and rear-view mirrors. There was a gap in the traffic on the motorway and he accelerated first into the slow lane, then into the middle lane, and then into the fast lane. "Would you care to explain?" he said, adjusting his speed to that of the rest of the traffic.

"I had a board mill in Alabama wanting us to act as their agent in the UK, but the guy changed his mind because you were stalling and went with another agent."

Bill checked his rear-view mirror. A pair of flashing headlights was bearing down on him. He indicated left and pulled into the middle lane. A black Ferrari thundered past.

"You can hardly blame me for that, Gerry. If the initial draft had not been so heavily slanted in your favour, we could probably have reached agreement in half the time. You surely didn't expect me to agree with everything you wanted."

"You didn't agree with anything," Kiplock said. "But that's not what I'm talking about. I'm talking about you only sending the contract to a lawyer at the last minute. That's what caused us to lose the agency."

"Well this might seem like a silly question, Gerry, but how was I supposed to know if you didn't tell me?"

"Jesus, you can be so irritating at times," Kiplock said.

They rode for the next few miles in silence. As they drove round the Chiswick flyover roundabout, Bill said, "Gerry, can I say something?"

"Sure, go ahead. Get it off your chest."

"With the contract as it stands, you can pull the plug on me any time you like, and I would have to pay you back the $150,000. I hardly think that's fair."

"So make sure we never get to the stage where I want to pull the plug on you."

They drove on, in silence.

Bill waited until they had to stop at the traffic light at Earls Court before he raised his next point. "Gerry, why have you not sent me a list of the suppliers you are bringing to the table. Oscar promised me that list, in your office, in front of you."

"Maybe I was just pissed off with you."

"That's no reason not to send me that list, Gerry. That list is fundamental to the agreement. Without it, I could be hiring a new guy and taking on a lot of additional cost, and there could, and I say could and not would, be nothing for him to sell. Where would that leave me?"

Kiplock looked across the car at him. "Why the hell would I pay you $150,000 for fifty percent of a company that isn't worth a plugged nickel, if I didn't plan to bring sources to the table?"

The light changed and Bill pulled away.

They drove in silence until they were passing the Victoria and Albert Museum, when Bill turned to his partner and said, "Gerry, while we're getting things off our chests, is there anything else you want to say? And then we can move on."

"Since you mention it, yeah, there is something else. You refusing to accept my collect call from Mexico City really pissed me off."

As they drove through Knightsbridge, Bill pulled out to overtake a taxi that was stopping to pick up a well-dressed woman with her hands full of designer label shopping bags. "But if you look at it from my point of view, Gerry, you can afford international phone calls a heck of a lot better than I can."

Kiplock said, "Let me explain, and then perhaps you'll understand. Marcia called me and told me you wanted to speak to me urgently. I was in a meeting with the owner of a linerboard mill in Mexico City, and when I got Marcia's message I interrupted my meeting to call you. The guy offered me the use of the phone on his desk, but I didn't want him to have to pay for the call so I asked the overseas operator to call you collect. When you refused to pay for the call, it was embarrassing for me. And if there's one thing I hate in life, it's being embarrassed. I was so pissed off about it that I told Oscar I was pulling out of the deal. Fortunately, for you that is, he talked me out of it."

"Gerry, I'm sorry. If I'd known …"

"Bill, one of your problems is you don't think before you act. When I do something there's usually a reason for it, and you would be well advised to remember that."

"All right, Gerry. Point taken."

As they drove up the Strand, Bill asked his partner if he was free for dinner the following evening. "Angela and I would like to take you out for dinner to celebrate our new partnership."

"Sorry, I already have a dinner appointment tomorrow evening."

Bill was taken aback. Since his new partner was in London for such a short time, he had thought he would have been spending most of his time with him. To cover his surprise, he said, "Anyone I know?"

"Bill, if I had wanted you to know who I was having dinner with, I would have told you."

Bill pulled into Savoy Street and stopped the car outside the Savoy Hotel. He got out of the car and opened the boot.

The uniformed commissionaire recognised the American. "Good afternoon, sir. And welcome back. Let me help you with your luggage."

Kiplock asked Bill what time the first appointment was in the morning.

"It's at ten o'clock, Gerry. We can take a taxi from here. I'll meet you here at 9.15."

"Right, see you in the morning." The American turned on his heel and followed the commissionaire into the hotel. No thank you for the lift, or offer to shake his hand.

When Bill got home, Angela asked him how he had got on.

"I'm not sure," he said, "I'm a bit shell shocked." Over a large gin and tonic he told her what had happened.

"He might have some problems you're not aware of," Angela said. "I'm sure he'll be fine in the morning."

Gerry Kiplock's Visit - Day One

Ian Penhaligen's offices were on the first floor of a four-storey building in the heart of the City of London, the square mile as it was known. He ushered them into a small conference room with a table with seating for six.

The first applicant, Jeremy Wood, was forty-three. He was married, but without children. His CV indicated that he was a three-handicap golfer.

When Penhaligen wheeled him in, there was a bead of sweat on the applicant's top lip, and he looked mildly terrified.

Bill recognised immediately that he was nervous. In fact, from the look in Wood's eyes, he was close to having a panic attack. To put him at his ease, Bill, a golfer himself, immediately went to common ground. "I see you're a golfer, Jeremy."

A brief look of gratitude appeared. "Yes, I am," he said. "But I haven't played for a year." The look of gratitude vanished as quickly as it had appeared.

"Are you a member of a club?" Bill asked.

Wood shook his head. "Not at the moment."

Kiplock flicked through his three-page CV. "You gave the reason for leaving a previous employer as incompatibility with your boss. What does that mean?"

Wood coughed. It was a dry, nervous cough, almost a choke. "He didn't appreciate what I was doing for the company, and I thought he made irrational decisions."

"I see. And what was your boss's name?"

"Phil Thomas."

"Is he English?"

"Yes, he's English. He's from Yorkshire. Which is in the north-east of England."

"I know where Yorkshire is," Kiplock said. "There's an Englishman by the name of Phil Thomas running Atlantic Paperboard out of Framington, New Jersey. Could he be the same Phil Thomas?"

"He could be, I suppose. I understand he did go to America."

Kiplock tossed the CV on the table. "Good judge of character, are you? Because for someone who makes irrational decisions, that Phil Thomas turned Atlantic Paperboard from a rundown company with one board mill into a highly profitable business with seven board mills along the US Eastern Seaboard. As a matter of fact, we act as his agent in Japan, and the Philippines."

"I didn't know that," Wood said, wishing the earth would open and swallow him up.

"No reason why you should," Kiplock said agreeably. "Is there anything else you'd like to say about him?"

"Not really. Except that I've always thought he drank too much."

Kiplock nodded. "Yeah, he does. But then anyone who is anyone in this industry drinks too much. Isn't that right, Bill?"

"It certainly is," Bill said.

"Your résumé ended a year ago," Kiplock continued. "What have you been doing for the last twelve months?"

"Could I have a glass of water, please?"

"Sorry about that," Penhaligen said, after showing the applicant out. "I don't know what came over him. I was impressed with him the first time I met him."

"He was nervous," Bill said.

"He was an asshole," Kiplock said.

"Who's next, Ian?" Bill asked.

Penhaligen checked his notes. "A Scot. Angus McPherson."

"I hope he isn't a golfer," Kiplock said.

"No, he's a course fisherman."

Kiplock shook his head. "Why does everyone in this country insist on putting what they do in their spare time on their résumé? Who gives a shit what they do in their spare time? It's what they do during business hours that matters. Who's the third guy?"

"Patrick Flood."

"Is he any good?"

"I would say he's the best of the three," Penhaligen said. He was about to add that there would have been more, but he hadn't been given enough time to advertise the position.

"Then why don't we skip number two and go straight to number three?"

"I'd rather not do that, Gerry, if you don't mind," Penhaligen said, "because he's flying down from the north of Scotland specially to see you."

"In which case, Gerry," Bill said, "we should give him a chance."

"Then you give him a chance, Bill. You interview him. I have some phone calls to make. Have you got an office I can use, Ian?"

"Yes, of course, Gerry. Use my office."

After showing Kiplock to his office, Penhaligen came back and said, "Boy, you've got your hands full with that one."

"Tell me about it."

"Angus is here. Shall I wheel him in?"

"Might as well."

Kiplock walked back into the conference room an hour later. Bill and Ian Penhaligen were sitting at the table having coffee. "Has the course fisherman gone?" he said, sitting down.

"He left a few minutes ago," Bill said.

"Was he any good?"

"I wasn't overly impressed," Bill said. "But it wouldn't work anyway, because he didn't want to leave Scotland."

"So? I have people all over the US working for me. If that can work for me, why can't it work for you?"

"Gerry, that might work for you, but it wouldn't work for me."

Kiplock shrugged. "Whatever." He picked up his copy of the third applicant's CV. "What time's this Patrick coming?"

"He's here now," Penhaligen said. "We've been waiting for you to finish your phone calls. He's in our reception area."

"Then wheel him in."

When Patrick Flood walked in, Kiplock said immediately, "Don't I know you?"

"Yes, you do, Gerry," Patrick said. "We've met before."

"Refresh my memory."

"We met at the DRUPA exhibition in Düsseldorf in 1996, and we met again at the official opening of Enso's big new board mill in 1999. You might remember that we ended up in the sauna that night, with a bunch of drunken Finns."

"Yeah, I remember. We were beating the hell out of each other with birch twigs, and chucking beer all over the place. That was one hell of a party."

"It certainly was," Patrick said. "And I'm still doing business with some of those guys today."

"So am I."

"I'm Bill Smith," Bill said, offering his hand.

Patrick's hand was soft and fleshy, but his handshake was firm. "It's good to meet you finally, Bill," he said. "I've been hearing your name for a long, long time."

Bill had never heard of Patrick, but then the pulp and paper industry was a big industry.

Patrick was a big man, in all respects. Standing around six feet tall, he had a girth to match. The buttons on his shirt were threatening to pop off and fly across the room. He had fair hair and pale blue eyes and an almost boyish face. He had a warm and ready smile. He was the sort of man to whom few would take offence. Bill liked him instinctively. He was a man he felt he could trust.

Kiplock pointed to the chair across the table from him. "Sit down, Patrick."

Bill sat down and picked up Patrick's CV. "Your CV doesn't say if you're married, Patrick."

A shadow crossed Patrick's face. "I'm widowed, Bill. My wife died six months ago. She had cancer of the liver."

Everyone expressed condolences.

"You didn't mention it when we met, Patrick," Penhaligen said.

"I don't wear my problem on my sleeve, Ian. I'm trying to put it behind me and move on."

"How are you managing?" Bill asked.

"Not terribly well." Patrick patted his more than ample stomach. "I'm eating a lot of junk food. I can't be bothered cooking properly for myself, which is probably why I've been putting on so much weight."

"Tough break," Kiplock said. "How old was your wife, Patrick?"

"She was thirty-two, Gerry. And it's because she died that I want to change my job. We worked for the same company. It's the memories, you see." He looked close to tears. "I need to get away, have a fresh start."

"I can understand that," Kiplock said. He re-read an item on Patrick's CV. "Who, or what, is this Finnglomerate, Patrick? I've never heard of them."

To give Patrick time to recover his composure, Bill answered the question himself. "It's a conglomerate of Finnish companies operating out of offices in Mayfair, here in London, Gerry. They have agencies for several Finnish paper and board mills, including some of the grades you're bringing to the table. Patrick's experience could be very useful to us."

"Then let's continue this discussion over lunch," Kiplock said. "Because I want to hear more."

Chapter 13

Bill was standing on the platform at Welwyn Garden City station when the Edinburgh-bound 9.05am train from Kings Cross rumbled in.

Most of the passengers had disembarked and were heading up the stairs towards the exit when Gerry Kiplock emerged from a first-class compartment at the front of the train. He was wearing his loud check sports jacket and red trousers, and he was visibly unsteady on his feet.

He spotted Bill and staggered towards him. He looked like he had just stepped out of a nightclub. He reeked of alcohol and his clothes stank of cigarette smoke. "Jesus," he croaked, "what a night."

Bill took his arm. "Come on, let's get you to the office and see if we can't find something to help you."

As Bill helped him up the stairs, Kiplock stumbled, almost tripping up a man who was charging down the stairs with his briefcase in his hand and his coat tails flying to try and catch the train before it left the station.

On the way to the office, Bill had to stop and let his partner sit down twice, once on a bench and once on a low wall, because he said he thought he was going to throw up.

When he finally got him to the office, Bill sat him down in his room and opened the interconnecting door into Maureen's office. He almost had a fit at what he saw.

Maureen was wearing the blouse she had worn the night she seduced him. At least she was wearing a bra this time. But this, if anything, actually made it worse, because it was an uplifting bra resulting in her already significant cleavage being drastically enhanced.

Bill quickly shut the door. "Maureen, for God's sake."

"What?" Maureen said, a picture of innocence.

"You know perfectly well what. What the hell are you doing wearing that blouse today, of all days?"

"I didn't hear you complaining the last time I wore it," Maureen said, smirking.

A jacket was hanging over the back of her chair.

"Is that your jacket?"

"Since it's hanging on the back of my chair, it would hardly be anyone else's, would it?"

"Then put it on. And leave it on until my new partner's gone."

Maureen got to her feet and put on her jacket. "That better?"

She looked marginally more business-like, but putting on her jacket had done little to conceal her cleavage.

"Can't you button it?"

"What, with my breasts?"

Bill took his wallet from the inside pocket of his suit jacket. He took out a £20 note and handed it to her. "Go down to Threshers and get me a bottle of Fernet Branca."

"Ferny what?"

"Fernet Branca." He wrote it down for her. "And if Threshers don't have it, try the off-licence at the other end of the station."

Maureen looked at what he had written down. "And what, when it's at home, is Fernet Branca? I've never heard of it."

"It's alcohol. In this case, it's the hair of the dog. My partner's got a hangover."

Angela arrived while Maureen was away. She was wearing the suit Bill had bought her to commemorate his new partner's first visit to the office, and the inaugural board meeting of the joint venture, and it emphasised her height and her long slim legs. She looked sensational.

Kiplock tried, unsuccessfully, to get to his feet.

Bill mouthed. "He's drunk."

"Don't get up, Gerry," Angela said. She bent over and gave Kiplock a peck on the cheek. "It's lovely to see you again."

"I'm shorry," Kiplock slurred. "I mushed have had too much to drink lash night."

"Is Maureen in, Bill?"

"She's in, but I've just sent her to the off-licence to get something for Gerry."

When Maureen came back, she knocked and walked in with a bottle of Fernet Branca and a glass on a tray. "Good morning, Angela," she said. "Good morning, Mr Kiplock."

Bill said, "Gerry, this is my secretary, Maureen."

Angela took one look at Maureen's chest and gave her a look that would have frozen mercury.

When Kiplock saw the bottle, his face lit up. "Ah, Fernet Branca. That little baby's saved my life more times than I care to remember."

Maureen put the tray on the table. "Shall I pour, Bill?"

Kiplock was staring at Maureen's chest with his mouth open, and Bill just wanted her to leave. "Thank you, Maureen. I'll pour."

Bill unscrewed the cap on the bottle and poured a large shot of the dark-coloured liquid into the glass. He handed it to his partner. "There," he said, "that should make you feel better."

Kiplock swallowed half the contents of the glass and breathed a sigh of relief. "Ah, that's better." Looking at Angela and then Maureen, he asked, "Bill, how the hell do you get any work done when you're surrounded by beautiful women?" Then he casually asked Maureen if she was married.

"Yes, she is," Angela said. "And that will be all, Maureen, thank you." She followed Maureen into her office. Although she had closed the door, her words, "I want a word with you," could clearly be heard in Bill's office.

"As you can see," Bill said, "Angela doesn't like Maureen."

"Looking like that, my wife wouldn't like her either," Kiplock responded.

Angela finished telling Maureen what she thought of her and the way she was dressed, and walked back in leaving Maureen banging about in her office.

With two large glasses of Fernet Branca under his belt, Kiplock was soon functioning normally again. "So what do we do about Patrick, Bill?"

"I think we should make him an offer."

"So do I. You know compensation packages in this country better than I do; what did you have in mind?"

"A basic salary he can live on comfortably, and a level of commission that will allow him to make virtually as much as he likes."

"I like it. Anything that makes a guy work for his money, works for me."

"So, do we go for it?"

"Yeah, go for it."

"I'll give Ian a call when we've had our board meeting."

"Why not call him now? No time like the present."

Bill picked up the phone.

"What did you think of Patrick?" Penhaligen said.

"We liked him, and we'd like to make him an offer."

"I'm sure he'll be pleased to hear it, and so am I. What did you have in mind?"

Bill spelled out what he and Gerry had discussed.

"I think that's a very generous offer, and I like the way you've structured it," Penhaligen said. "I'll put it to Patrick and let you know what he says."

Bill ended the call and hung up.

"Well?" Kiplock said.

"He thinks it's a generous offer and he likes the way we've structured it. He's calling Patrick and getting back to me."

"Let's hope we get him. I like Patrick, I like him a lot."

Angela was company secretary of Bill's company, and she had agreed to be company secretary of the joint venture. She knew what she had to do, and she handled matters with dignity and aplomb. She and Bill were appointed directors of the joint-venture, which was to go by the name of Smith-Kiplock Ltd, with Bill as chairman. Gerry Kiplock and his father were appointed directors.

When everything was done and dusted, Bill declared the meeting closed.

At noon, Bill asked his partner if he was ready for lunch.

"Sure am," Kiplock said. "Is Maureen joining us?"

"Not if I have anything to do with it, she isn't," Angela said.

"Why not?" Kiplock said, grinning. "It might be fun."

"Not for me, it wouldn't," Angela said.

"Indulge me, Angela. I'm only here for a day. By the way, Bill, where's your rest room?"

"Turn right down the corridor, and it's the first door on the left."

When Kiplock had left the room, Angela hissed, "Bill, do something."

"Like what?" Bill said. "Come on, sweetheart, it's only for lunch."

"But she looks like a tart. People will think we picked her up on the street."

"Darling, if Gerry wants her to go, we should take her. I want him to leave here feeling good about his visit."

With British Aerospace, De La Roche Pharmaceuticals, Nagasaki Sumo Bank and several other large employers within five miles of Welwyn Garden City, the town boasted several good restaurants, and one of the best of them – The French Connection – was within a short walk of the office. Maureen had reserved a table for three, and she gleefully telephoned the restaurant to say it would now be for four.

As they were shown to their table, Angela heard a business-suited individual say, as Maureen walked past him, 'Christ, will you look at that. I wouldn't mind getting my hands on her', and she arrived at the table stony-faced. She caught Bill's arm before he started seating them. "Bill, don't put me opposite Maureen. I'm not sitting there looking at her boobs for the next two hours."

Bill had no choice but to sit Angela and Maureen side-by-side on one side of the square table, and his partner and himself side-by-side on the other side. This left Kiplock with an unrestricted view of Maureen's chest, with which he seemed inordinately happy.

Even though Bill was picking up the tab, Kiplock insisted on champagne.

"Not for me, Bill," Angela said. "I have to pick the children up at three-thirty. I'll just have a glass of white wine."

But Kiplock was having none of it. "Hey, come on Angela, we're celebrating. At least have one glass of champagne."

"Up to you, sweetheart," Bill said.

"All right. But only one."

Before the champagne arrived, a waiter put a basket of crusty bread rolls on the table.

Before Bill had a chance to pick up the basket and offer the bread to the others, Maureen reached over and grabbed a roll and bit into it. A piece of crust dropped down the front of her blouse. Seemingly unconcerned, she stuck her hand between her breasts, fished out the piece of crust, put it in her mouth and ate it.

"Oh, please," Angela muttered. "Excuse me," she said, getting to her feet. She marched off to the ladies' room. She waited until she had regained her composure, and then returned to the table.

During the meal, Kiplock spent most of his time talking to Maureen. Business hardly got a mention. At one stage, he asked Maureen if she had any children.

"Not yet," Maureen replied. "But I'm trying for one. Aren't I Bill?" she said, glancing slyly in Bill's direction.

"Yes, you are," Bill said, turning it into a joke. "You're very trying." He shot her a warning look.

On the way back to the office, Maureen walked ahead with Kiplock. They were chatting away as if they had known each other all their lives.

Angela said, "Bill, what did she mean by saying 'aren't I, Bill?' when she said she was trying for a child?"

"I've no idea, sweetheart. She was probably just making conversation."

Back at the office, Maureen went into her room while Bill, Angela and Gerry Kiplock went into Bill's office

"Bill, are we done here?" Kiplock asked.

"We are unless you'd like me to show you the rooms we'll be taking on down the corridor, Gerry."

"Nah, I don't need to see 'em. You know what you're doing. Will you be needing Maureen this afternoon?"

"I won't be needing her, but she might have other things to do. We have a couple of vessels arriving soon and she'll have shipping documents to send out. Why do you ask?"

"I thought she might come back to London with me. You know how much I like London and I thought she might show me some of the sights."

"It's not the sights of London you have in mind," Angela muttered under her breath.

Maureen confirmed that she did indeed have some shipping documents to send out, but she pointed out that the two vessels were not due for another ten days and she could send them out first thing in the morning. "They'll get to the buyers in plenty of time."

"Then I see no reason why she can't go with you, Gerry."

"Thanks, pal," Kiplock said, pumping Bill's hand. "It's been a great visit. Keep me posted about Patrick, and get him on board as soon as you can."

"Will do."

Kiplock gave Angela a hug. "You did a great job today. I'm proud of you. And look after this husband of yours. We need him."

"No need to worry on that score," Angela said. "I need him too." She patted Bill's cheek affectionately.

"Ready, Maureen?"

"I'm ready, Gerry."

Bill and Angela stood at the French windows and watched Gerry and Maureen walk down the street towards the station. They were giggling like teenagers.

"What are we running here?" Angela said. "A brothel?

"Sweetheart, as long as Gerry's happy, who cares?"

After Angela had left to pick up the children from school, Bill got a call from the head-hunter. "Bill, I'm afraid I have got some bad news for you."

"You're not going to tell me he's turned our offer down."

"No, he hasn't turned it down. He's had a better offer."

"Do you believe him?"

"I do, actually. I don't think he's the kind of man who would lie about that sort of thing."

"Any idea who the other party is, Ian?"

"I asked him that, but he said it wouldn't be fair to the other party if he told me. What do you want me to do, Bill?"

"I need to try and get hold of Gerry. He left here an hour ago, and he's flying to Rome tonight."

"Don't take too long getting back to me, Bill. Patrick said he has to give the other party a decision by close of play tomorrow."

"Ian, would you mind if I had a word with Patrick myself? Maybe I can get some more information out of him."

"I wouldn't mind at all, Bill. Let me give you his number?"

"I already have it, Ian. It's on his business card."

Bill ended the call and got Patrick's card from his wallet.

"I thought I might hear from you," Patrick said.

"Patrick, are you serious about having another offer? I'd be disappointed if this was just a way of getting us to increase our offer."

"I wouldn't do that to you, Bill. I genuinely do have another offer."

"I'm not getting into a Dutch auction, Patrick."

"It won't come to that, Bill, I promise."

"Are you going to tell me who the other party is?"

"I'd rather not. I haven't told them who you are, so it's only fair that I don't tell you who they are."

"Would you at least tell me if it's a UK company?"

"It's an American company."

"Eastern Seaboard? West Coast?"

"Eastern Seaboard. But beyond that, I'd rather not say."

"By how much do we need to increase our offer?"

"With respect, Bill, I rather think that's up to you."

151

"It sounds awfully like a Dutch auction to me, Patrick."

"Bill, make me one more offer and then I'll make my decision. That's a promise."

"All right, Patrick. I'll go along with that. I'm going to have to try and get hold of Gerry. He was here in my office this morning, but he's gone now and he's supposed to be heading off to Italy tonight. I'll get back to you as soon as I can."

"I need to know by close of play tomorrow, Bill. That's the deadline with the other party."

"Our time, or Eastern Seaboard US time?"

"Our time."

"Right, I'll get back to you."

Bill ended the call and hung up.

He had no idea how he could get hold of his partner. Kiplock was supposed to be on his way to Rome that evening, but with Maureen in the frame Bill suspected his partner would not be taking the flight. The only thing he could think to do was call the Savoy. He explained who he was and why he was calling, and they told him that Mr Kiplock had phoned and said he would be staying another night. Bill said he needed to speak to him urgently and asked that they please leave a message for him to call him as soon as possible.

By eight that evening he had still not heard, so he called the Savoy from home. He was informed that Mr Kiplock was in his suite, but he had left instructions he was not to be disturbed.

Chapter 14

The next morning, Bill had already opened the mail when Maureen wandered in. There were dark shadows under her eyes and she was wearing the same clothes she had worn the previous day.

He looked at his watch. It was 10.06am. "What time do you call this?"

Maureen shrugged. "Gerry asked me to stay."

"As a matter of interest, Maureen, where did Ted think you were?"

"I told him I was staying with a friend."

"And did he believe you?"

"He believes everything I tell him. He loves me."

"Good thing he does. You do know Gerry's married, Maureen. Oh, I forgot; it's married men you go for, isn't it? Does this mean you're letting me off the hook?"

"Hopefully."

"Hopefully nothing!" Bill snapped. "We're not going there again. I take it he knows you're trying for a child."

"I mentioned it over lunch yesterday, in case you've forgotten."

"So you did," Bill said sarcastically. "That wasn't very clever of you, Maureen."

"Did Angela notice?"

"That's none of your business. Where's Gerry now? I need to speak to him."

"He left the Savoy at seven this morning. He said he was going to return your call when he got to Heathrow."

"If he left the Savoy at seven, why didn't you leave when he did? You could have gone home and changed and been here at the time you're supposed to be here."

"Because Gerry suggested I stay and have breakfast in the room."

"And he's your employer, is he?"

"Well no, but ..."

"Maureen, go home and change. And don't ever come to the office in that blouse again."

While Maureen was away, Bill got a call from the Welwyn Garden City police. "So you're back from your trip then, sir."

Bill frowned. He hadn't been anywhere since he came back from New York. "Which trip are you referring to, officer?" he said.

"New York, I believe it was. When you didn't return our call, we thought you must have extended your trip. We left a message with your secretary."

"I didn't get the message. She must have forgotten to tell me. What can I do for you?"

"We think we've found the youth who attacked you, or one of them, and we want to set up an identity parade. We had in mind the day after tomorrow, say two thirty in the afternoon. Would that be convenient for you?"

"Hang on, let me check my diary." Bill covered the mouthpiece with his hand and got his brain in gear. Maureen must have suspected that the call from the police had something to do with her brother attacking him, which begged the question when, if ever, she was going to tell him they had called. It was decision time. Maureen's brother had to be stopped. Next time he could kill someone. But if he identified him, it would get in the papers and Angela would certainly find out. Still, considering the fact that she had had an affair with his

154

best friend, ex-best friend, lasting a year, his one-night stand with Maureen would surely result in nothing more serious than a blazing row.

"Two thirty tomorrow afternoon will be fine, officer," he said.

When Maureen came back, she was dressed in a plain white blouse that was buttoned almost up to her throat and a straight black skirt. Bill asked her why she hadn't told him the police had called.

"Isn't it obvious?"

"He's not getting away with it, Maureen. I'm attending a line-up tomorrow, and if he's in the line, I'll point him out. He's got to be stopped. He could have killed me, kicking me in the head like that."

"And how's Angela going to react when I tell her about you and me?"

Bill no longer cared. "Do whatever you have to do, Maureen."

Later that afternoon, Kiplock phoned. "Hey, partner."

"Hi, Gerry. How's Rome?"

"Noisy and congested, but that's nothing new. It's always noisy and congested. I've just cut a deal with Patrick."

"You've what!"

"I've just cut a deal with Patrick."

"Do you mean you've talked to him direct?"

"Yeah, his number was on his business card."

"Do you mean you've cut Ian and me out of the loop?"

"Hey, come on partner, don't get all shit-faced on me. Penhaligen won't mind, as long as he gets his money. I had some time to kill between meetings, so I thought I'd give Patrick a call. He told me he'd had another offer, and I told him we'd match it."

"And how much was the other offer?"

"A salary of a hundred thousand dollars, whatever that is in sterling, and a dollar a ton commission."

Bill was appalled. "But that's twice what you and I agreed yesterday. For what he'll be doing, he's not worth that much. Nobody's worth that much."

"Bill, the other guys have been looking for somebody for over a year, and they were about to start advertising for an American. They figured that's what they would have to pay an American, so that's what they offered Patrick. They set the price, not me."

"And what if I don't agree to pay Patrick twice what the job's worth?"

"It's too late, pal, it's a done deal. Gotta go, buddy. I have another meeting. Ciao."

Bill hung up fuming. He waited until he had calmed down, and then called Patrick. "I understand we've just hired you."

"Yes you have, and I'm over the moon."

"As a matter of interest, Patrick, why did you tell Gerry who the other party was, when you wouldn't tell me?"

"Because he mentioned a name, and it happened to be the right one. I thought it was churlish not to confirm he was right, and he would have found out at some point, anyway."

"I see. And am I to be privy to when you're making a start?"

"Four weeks from today. I'm handing in my notice tomorrow. You don't sound too happy, Bill. Is something wrong?"

Bill sighed. "It's nothing you need concern yourself about."

Chapter 15

At the identity parade, Bill spotted Maureen's brother immediately. He ignored the other five youths in the line and walked straight to him. "So we meet again," he said grimly. "And this time, on my terms."

The youth eyed him contemptuously.

"This is the one who attacked me," Bill said to the police officer accompanying him.

"You're sure about that, sir?"

"I'm absolutely certain. I didn't actually see him attack me, because as I reported at the time it was dark and he and his pals came at me from behind. But I'll know for certain if I hear him speak."

"What do you want him to say?"

"How about, 'And that, you piece of shit, is for what you did to my sister.'"

"You heard the man."

Maureen's brother shrugged. "And that, you piece of shit, is for what you did to my sister." He said it in a bored, dull monotone, nothing like his normal voice.

Bill smiled. "I didn't expect you to cooperate. This is definitely the man who attacked me, officer."

"You're sure, sir?"

"Officer, I am a thousand percent certain."

Maureen's brother smiled mockingly. "Prove it."

It was a Thursday morning and Bill was away for the week. He was travelling in the north of England. Angela was sitting at his desk working on some figures for New York. It was detailed work, and she was giving it her full attention.

Maureen knocked and walked in. "Do you have a minute, Angela?"

Angela frowned at the interruption. "What is it, Maureen? I'm busy."

"There's something I think you should know."

Angela put her pen down and sat back. "All right, Maureen. But make it quick. I've got to get these figures off to New York today."

Maureen pulled a chair out from under the table and sat down. "You're not going to like it."

"Maureen, for goodness sake …"

"While you were away in Torquay, when your mother was ill …" Maureen hesitated.

"What about it?"

"You're not going to like it."

"Maureen, you either tell me what it is you have to tell me, or you let me get on with my work. I don't have time for games."

"The night you went to Torquay, Bill came back to the office and he … how can I put it … he had his wicked way with me." Maureen patted the table. "Right here, on the table."

"Don't be ridiculous."

"I'm not being ridiculous. It's true."

"Maureen, I don't know what you hope to gain by telling me this, but you've told me downright lies before, and this sounds like another of them. I don't believe a word of it."

"Then ask him!"

"I don't think I'll bother. Now, if there's nothing else, Maureen, I have work to do."

"That afternoon he had to leave early to pick the children up from school, and he came back in the evening because he hadn't got through his work."

"Maureen, why are you telling me this?"

"Because I thought you should know."

"No, there's more to it than that."

"He has a mole under his shoulder blade. The left one, I think. And it's very prominent. I remember thinking he should see a doctor about it."

The colour drained from Angela's face.

"And one of his testicles is bigger than the other."

Angela made it to the ladies' toilet just in time to throw up.

Bill was stopped at a red traffic light at a busy junction in the heart of Leeds city centre. He was late for a meeting with the managing director of a paper mill in Otley, six miles away. He had a telephone built into the armrest of his car and it rang as he waited for the light to change. The illuminated screen revealed his home phone number. He plucked the phone from its cradle and put it to his ear. "Darling, it's not convenient at the moment. Can I call you back?"

"Don't you 'darling' me," Angela snapped. "You make me feel as guilty as hell about my affair with Bas, and all the time you were hiding your grubby little secret with Maureen."

Oh, shit! "Darling, I can explain. It's not what you might think it is."

"So you're not denying it then."

"Well no, but you need to let me explain." The traffic light changed to green. "Damn! Darling, I'm stopped at a traffic light and it's just changed to green, and there's a police car right behind me. I'll have to call you back."

Angela hung up on him.

Bill put the phone back in its cradle and clicked it firmly in place. He shifted the gear selector into drive, and pulled away. He drove a couple of miles out of Leeds and found a convenient place to stop. He parked and switched the engine off. He called the mill to inform them he was going to be late for his appointment, and then phoned home. There was no reply.

He drove to the mill, which was situated right next to a river, parked in the visitor's car park, which overlooked a weir, and phoned home again. There was still no reply. After his meeting, he phoned again.

Angela phoned him as he was driving to his next appointment.

He grabbed the phone. "I'm driving, Angela," he said hastily. "Give me a minute. Let me find somewhere to park." He found a lay-by half a mile ahead and pulled in. He stopped the car and switched the engine off. "Right, I can talk now."

"Why on the table?"

"Does it matter?"

"It matters to me. Why on the table?"

"It was her idea."

"She said it was your idea."

"Angela, she's lying. She set the whole thing up. I was working late at the office and she came to the office, and …"

"Is making love to your secretary on the table in your office some kind of fetish of yours?"

"Darling, it wasn't like that. It was her idea."

"So you say."

"And I certainly wasn't making love to her."

"So what were you doing, reading her a bedtime story?"

"Well, no, but … what I mean is … oh, hell. Darling you're getting me all confused. All I know is that she came to the office wearing the blouse she was wearing when Gerry came, except that that night she wasn't wearing a bra."

"Too much information."

"Sorry. And she told me Ted was firing blanks and she wanted me to give her a child."

"And you were only too happy to oblige, because I was away and you thought I would never know."

"Darling, it wasn't like that. Well, I suppose … oh, shoot. I don't know what it was. Anyway, you'll be happy to know she started her period."

"That's way too much information."

"All I meant by that was that she's not pregnant." He checked his watch. He had to go. His next buyer was a stickler for visitors arriving on time. "Sweetheart, I'm sorry but I've got another appointment. Can I call you later?"

Angela hung up on him.

Fifteen minutes later, she called him again.

"Hang on, let me find somewhere to park." He was driving through a small Yorkshire town and he parked outside a branch of Barclays Bank. He was on double yellow lines and he left his engine running in case the police or a traffic warden turned up and he had to make a quick getaway. "Okay, darling, go ahead."

"Wasn't that the night you were beaten up?"

"Yes, it was."

"Was there some link between you being beaten up and being with her?"

Bill didn't want to go there, but he knew he had no choice. Better to get it all out in the open, once and for all. "Yes, there was. It was her brother who beat me up. Well, he and some other young thugs."

"The plot thickens. Do tell."

"Darling, I can't now, because I have to be on my way."

"You told me you had no idea who attacked you, and you told me you told the police that. You said they thought it was probably a random attack, a case of you being in the wrong place at the wrong time."

"But don't you see, darling, if I had told you and the police that I knew who had attacked me, the story would have come out about Maureen and me. And that was the last thing I wanted."

"So, you lied to me, and you lied to the police."

"Yes, I did, and I'm very sorry, especially for lying to you. I lied to you because I didn't want you to be hurt by what I'd done."

"Pull the other one, Bill. You lied to me because you didn't want me to find out. Do the police know you lied to them?"

"No, they don't."

"Is that the full story, or is there some other sordid little detail you haven't told me?"

"That's the full story, I promise. Darling, can we discuss this later? I really do have to go."

"No, we can discuss it now."

"But I have a meeting in forty minutes, and I have thirty miles to go. I'll never get there on time."

"Then you'll just have to be late for your meeting, won't you? Are you going to fire Maureen now?"

"Darling, be reasonable. With Patrick just about to start, I can't fire her. Well not at the moment." He was talking to any empty phone.

Angela had hung up on him.

He phoned back, but she didn't pick up. He tried again, and again, and then headed off to his next appointment.

When he got to the next mill, he spent an hour extolling the virtues of Heikki Pentilla's material to the mill manager and left with an order for a trial 100 tons for immediate shipment. After his meeting, he sat in his car in the mill yard and dialled home again. He got no reply, so he called the office.

He gave Maureen the details of the order he had just picked up so she could relay it to Heikki Pentilla, and then said coldly, "So you did it. You told Angela."

"I told you I would if you talked to the police. My brother's in custody."

"Which is where he should be. The bloody hooligan could have killed me. Telling Angela make you feel better, did it?"

"Not specially. Just so you know, she told me to find myself another job. But Gerry doesn't want me to leave."

"What the hell does this have to do with Gerry?"

"I thought he should know, so I told him what happened."

"You did what! Need I remind you, Maureen, that ..."

"He wants you to call him."

She hung up on him.

That night, Bill was staying overnight at the County Hotel in Durham, a delightful four-star hostelry with an excellent restaurant in the shadow of the Cathedral. He stayed there whenever he was in the area. It was late evening and he was on the A1(M) motorway approaching the Durham turnoff. That day, he had visited four mills and driven over two hundred and fifty miles, and he was tired.

The phone rang. The number on the screen showed a 001 prefix, which meant the call was coming from the States. He had no doubt it was his partner calling, and he had no doubt why he was calling. He was still two or three miles from the Durham exit, so he indicated left and pulled over on to the hard shoulder and stopped. Lorry after lorry hurtled past. He checked his mirrors. There was no sign of a police car, but he put his hazard lights on and left his engine running, anyway.

"Who's been a naughty boy, then?" Kiplock said. He sounded amused.

"It's not funny, Gerry."

"That's what comes of dipping your pen in company ink. I don't want you to fire her."

"Gerry, she's my secretary, not yours. I don't tell you what to do with your secretary."

"You don't own half my company, Bill."

"Ah, so that's it. Is this how it's going to be from now on, Gerry?"

"Bill, for the sake of the business, at least do nothing until Patrick's on board and has things under control. That's as much in your best interests as it is in mine."

Bill couldn't fault his logic. "All right, Gerry. But then she has to go."

The next day, Friday, Bill visited a mill in Sunderland, where he picked up another trial order for Heikki's material, and then headed south. He made visits to two mills in east Lancashire, and finally got home just after 9.30pm He was exhausted and not best pleased to see Basil's car in the drive.

The house had a sweeping semi-circular drive and he had plenty of room to pass Basil's car and park in front of it. He switched off the engine and climbed out of the car. He got his briefcase from the back seat and his suitcase from the boot, slamming the doors and the boot lid unnecessarily loudly at his annoyance at Basil being there.

Angela heard the commotion and came to the door. "You look tired," she said.

"I am, I'm exhausted." He nodded at Basil's car. "What's he doing here?"

"Betty's left him."

Bill stepped into the house, dropped his suitcase and briefcase on the floor in the hall, closed the front door and followed Angela into the kitchen. "Where is he?"

"In the living room."

"How long has he been here?"

"Three or four hours. I fed him. He hadn't eaten since breakfast."

"Where are the children?"

"They're upstairs. I sent them to their rooms when I heard you arrive."

"Probably just as well. Well, let's see what he has to say for himself."

"Don't be too hard on him, Bill. He's very upset."

Bill raised an eyebrow. "He's upset? How do you think I feel, knowing you and he were banging each other's brains out while I was away? And for a year?"

Angela winced.

Bill marched down the hall.

Basil was sitting on the sofa with a two-thirds empty bottle of Glenmorangie single malt scotch on the coffee table in front of him, and a half empty glass in his hand. Bill had no doubt it was the bottle he had bought a couple of days before he had headed north, and had not opened.

"Hello, old man," Basil said. "Betty's left me." His speech was slurred.

Bill loosened his tie and threw himself into an armchair, from where he regarded the man who had once been his best friend.

"Have you eaten, Bill?" Angela said.

"I ate on the motorway. Are you surprised she's left you?"

"I am, actually. We talked it through and I thought she'd forgiven me. Then, out of the blue, she upped and left me. She's gone to stay with her mother."

Bill got to his feet and walked across the room to the cocktail cabinet. He got himself a glass, picked up the bottle from the coffee table and poured himself a triple. He took a swallow and blinked as the amber nectar seared his throat. "So what are you doing here?" he asked Basil.

Angela said, "Bill, he didn't know where else to go. So he came here."

"For what it's worth, old man, I'm very sorry for what happened. We never meant it to happen, did we Angela?"

"Of course you didn't," Bill said. "It was all my fault for going away and working my arse off to give my family a lifestyle and put my children through school. Who started it, by the way? Who made the first move?"

"Does it matter?" Angela said. "Can I make you a coffee, Bill?"

"I'd like a coffee," Basil said.

"You won't be staying long enough for coffee," Bill said.

"Bill, please," Angela said.

"Please what, Angela? Please be nice to him? After what he's done, why should I?"

"I think I'd better go," Basil said, struggling to his feet.

"Yes, I think you'd better," Bill said.

"Let me call you a taxi, Bas?" Angela said. "You can't drive in that condition. You can pick your car up in the morning."

"I'll be all right," Basil said.

"Sure he will," Bill said. "He's driven in that condition more times than I care to remember."

As Basil made his way unsteadily towards the hall, he grabbed Angela's wrists and pulled her towards him. "Angela, come with me," he pleaded. "You know you love me. I can give you everything Bill can give you, and I'm never away."

Angela gently disengaged herself. "It's over, Bas. You might as well accept it."

"Please, Angela," Basil pleaded. "I'll never stop loving you. Please come with me." There were tears in his eyes.

Bill almost had to physically restrain himself from punching Basil's lights out. "Bas," he said through gritted teeth, "if you want to leave here with your teeth intact, I suggest you don't say another word." He led the way down the hall, and opened the front door.

As Basil staggered towards his car, Angela said, "He shouldn't be driving in that condition, Bill."

"Sure he should," Bill said. "Maybe he'll do us all a favour and drive himself into a tree." He left Angela at the door and walked back into the sitting room. He

poured the balance of the contents of his glass down his throat, and filled it up again.

With the sound of Basil's car receding down the lane, Angela closed the door and walked back into the sitting room. She looked weary.

For a while they sat in silence.

Bill could hear a television set upstairs. The children each had one in their room. He spoke first. "So where do we go from here, Angela?"

Angela sighed and shook her head. "I really don't know, Bill. I'm stumped."

"Can I make a suggestion?"

"I wish you would."

"Why don't we call it quits? Even Stevens. You've had your affair with Bas, and I've had my whatever-you-want-to-call-it with Maureen."

Angela let out a sigh of relief. "I was hoping you'd say that. I'd like that, Bill. I'd like that very much."

Chapter 16

"Do you plan to open the mail today?" Angela said.

Maureen blew on her wet nail varnish. "What's the hurry?"

Angela picked up the mail and walked into Bill's office, slamming the door behind her.

The phone ringing on the nightstand beside him woke him with a start. He was in Scotland on business and he was staying the night at the George Hotel in Edinburgh. He had just got off to sleep. He glanced at the combined radio/alarm clock on the nightstand. It was 11.16pm. It had to be Angela. Apart from Maureen, who had typed up his itinerary, only Angela knew he was staying there. And she wouldn't be calling at this time of night unless something was wrong. He rolled over and picked up the phone.

Angela heard the sleep in his voice. "I'm sorry, darling. Did I wake you?"

"It doesn't matter. What is it, sweetheart?"

"Bill, there's a car in the lane, and it's been there for over an hour. I'm scared."

There was a tremor in her voice and Bill realised she was genuinely frightened.

"What kind of car is it?"

"I don't know, it's too dark to tell, and you know I can't tell one car from another. It's a big car, like yours. But it's not a Jaguar, I do know that."

"Where in the lane is it?"

"It's in the passing place. And the driver's smoking; I can see the glow as he draws on his cigarette."

"So it's a man, rather than a woman."

"I think so. The shape looks too big to be a woman."

"Is there anyone in the car with him?"

"I'm not sure. There may be someone next to him, a small person. Or it might just be a headrest."

"Do you think he might just have stopped to enjoy a cigarette and the peace of the countryside?"

"For an hour? And at this time of night?"

"Do you think he's watching the house?"

"I can't say. But he does seem to be looking this way."

Bill's mind was racing through the cars of people they knew. "Can you tell what colour the car is?"

"No, it's too dark."

"Can you at least tell if it's a light-colour, or a dark colour?"

"It's a dark colour."

There was absolutely nothing Bill could do from four hundred miles away and he was at a loss as to what to suggest. "Sweetheart, if you're really worried, you should call the police."

"I didn't want to bother them. He's not actually doing anything wrong."

"Where are you? In the house, I mean."

"At the landing window."

"Do you think he can see you?"

"I doubt it. I don't have any lights on. The reason I'm calling is that he was here last night too."

"For goodness sake, why didn't you tell me?"

"I didn't want to bother you. You have enough on your plate when you're travelling. Wait a minute, Bill; I think he's leaving. He's just flicked his cigarette over the hedge, and I can hear that he's just started his engine. Yes, he's leaving."

"See if you can catch his face as he drives past the house."

"Hang on. No, I couldn't see his face. The willow tree was in the way."

"What about his registration plate number? Could you see that?"

"No, I couldn't. The tree was in the way. He's gone now, anyway."

There was nothing more Bill could do, beyond try to reassure her. "Sweetheart, I'm sure he won't bother you again tonight, but check the doors and windows and then try and get some sleep."

"All right, Bill. I'm sorry I disturbed you."

"Hey, no need to apologise. I'm just sorry I wasn't there. You can call me at any time, day or night. Okay?"

"Okay. Thank you, Bill. I feel better for talking to you. Goodnight, and sleep tight. Don't let the bed bugs bite."

"Goodnight sweetheart. I'll call you in the morning."

The next morning, Bill called Angela before he went down to breakfast. "Are you all right this morning?"

"I'm fine."

"Did you manage to get some sleep?"

"Some. It unsettled me a bit because it was the second time."

"I've been racking my brains to think who it might have been."

"So have I. It could all be perfectly innocent. Someone who lives in the village, or nearby, who ..."

"Who'd been out with his girlfriend and stopped for a smoke and to think what he was going to tell his wife when he got home," Bill joked.

Angela laughed.

Bill checked his watch. He had a meeting at ten, and it was at least a half hour drive away. And he hadn't had breakfast yet. But he had taken to heart what Angela had said about him seeming not to care about her, and he was determined to try and put that right. So he asked her how she was getting on with Maureen.

"The woman's a menace," Angela replied. "She's behaving as if she owns the company. I'm starting to feel like an intruder. And by the way, Bill, I've caught her on the phone to Gerry a number of times. She's been whispering and giggling like a love-struck schoolgirl. I think that from now on you should be very careful about what you say in front of her, because it's likely to get back to him."

Bill called Angela twice that day, and he called her again before he went to bed in Aberdeen. There was no sign of the car in the lane.

Bill had converted their fourth bedroom into a study, from which he worked from time to time in the evenings and at weekends, and he had had a telephone extension installed. On the Sunday evening, he was working in his study when the phone rang. Angela was downstairs watching TV with the children in the living room, and so she wouldn't have to get up and answer it, he picked up.

"Bill, it's Betty."

He sat back in his chair and made himself comfortable. "Well, this is a nice surprise. How are you, Betty?"

"I'm fine. Is Angela there?"

"She's downstairs watching TV with the children. Just a second, I'll get her for you."

"Hold on, Bill," Betty said hastily. "It's you I want to speak to. I don't want Angela to know I'm calling."

"Oh, okay. How are you, Betty? You say you're fine, but how are you really?"

"I'm hurt, angry, and confused, Bill."

"I can imagine. Are you calling from your mother's?"

"No, I'm at the Roebuck, in Knebworth. The children and I are staying here."

The Roebuck Inn was a hostelry with a halfway decent restaurant some three miles from where Bill was sitting. He and Angela had stayed there when they were looking for a house in the area.

"I thought you were going to your mother's."

"Which is what I told Basil because I don't want him to know where I am and I knew he wouldn't call her. They haven't spoken in years. They can't stand the sight of each other."

"How long have you been at the Roebuck?"

"Since I left him. And a hotel room can get very boring."

"Tell me about it," Bill said. "I spend half my life in hotel rooms. How are the children holding up?"

"As well as can be expected. They're fed up of being cooped up in one room."

"I can imagine. What are your plans, Betty?"

"The house is on the market and I thought I'd hang around until it's been sold. It will give me time to think."

"No chance of a reconciliation then?"

"Not a hope. After what he's done, I could never trust him again. There have been too many lies."

"I know what you mean. Are you still on speaking terms?"

"For the sake of the children, yes, we are. I call him once a week so the children can speak to him. I've sworn them to secrecy as to where we are, and so far they haven't let me down."

"Did he tell you he came here?"

"Yes, he did."

"He got quite emotional. Not to mention very drunk."

"It's hardly surprising. After having Angela, and me, he's lost us both."

"He never had Angela. Well, what I mean by that is that she never loved him."

"He's besotted with her."

"I can see that. He tried to persuade her to go away with him, in front of my very eyes."

"And he's been sitting outside your house late evenings, hoping to get a glimpse of Angela."

Bill slapped his forehead with the palm of his hand. He couldn't believe he hadn't thought of it being Basil. But he was relieved in a way that it had been Basil, because with him, Angela would not have been in danger. "So it was him!" he exclaimed. "Angela's seen him sitting out there, Betty, and he's been scaring the life out of her. She had no idea it was Basil. You'd better tell him to stop doing that, because the next time he does it, Angela will be calling the police."

"I'll tell him. How do you feel about Angela now, Bill? Knowing how long she was cheating on you."

"I won't say it hasn't put a dent in our relationship, Betty, but we've talked it through and we've decided to stay together."

"For the sake of the children?"

"Not just for the sake of the children. I still have feelings for her, and perhaps I'll come to love her again in the fullness of time. She assures me she still loves me."

"Do you believe her?"

"I do, actually. What will you do once the house is sold?"

"Probably leave the area. Make a fresh start elsewhere."

"What about the children?"

"Anne will move in with Basil. She and he are very close, even though he isn't her biological father. Claude and Giles will come with me. Basil's agreed to it, and the children seem all right with it."

"We had some great times together, Betty, didn't we? The four of us."

"Yes, we did. I have a lot of happy memories."

Bill needed to get on. He had work to do. "Well, it's lovely to hear from you, Betty, and I …"

"Bill, before you go … I wanted to ask …I don't know quite how to put this …I thought … I wondered if … oh, God, I didn't think it would be this difficult."

"Spit it out, Betty."

"I wondered if you and I could meet."

"With what in mind?"

"Don't make me spell it out for you, Bill. You know I've always been attracted to you."

"I don't think that's a good idea, Betty. And, anyway, it wouldn't be fair on you. You would …"

Angela walked in. "Coffee, darling? Oh, I'm sorry, I didn't realise you were still on the phone."

Bill smiled at her and mouthed a silent, no thank you.

"Was that Angela?"

"Yes, it was. And I should go, Betty. But before I do, let me give you a piece of advice. Find yourself a man, a single one. A married man will only cause you grief."

"Easier said than done, Bill. Well, it was lovely talking with you. Goodbye, Bill. And good luck."

"Goodbye, Betty. And good luck to you, too."

Bill hung up and went downstairs. He walked into the kitchen and wrapped his arms round Angela and gave her a hug.

"What brought that on?" she said, when he finally let her go.

"I just felt like it," he said.

"I'm glad you did," Angela said, getting some cups from a cupboard. "And I'm glad we decided to stay together."

"So am I," Bill said.

Chapter 17

Patrick had put on a significant amount of weight. His face had taken on an almost cherubic appearance, and the buttons on his shirt, which at interview had looked in danger of popping off, now looked in even more danger of doing so. He had put on so much weight that Bill wondered if he would be able to get behind the wheel of the car he had leased for him.

"Very nice to meet you, Patrick," Angela said, shaking hands with him.

"You too, Mrs Smith."

"It's Angela."

Patrick smiled. "Angela it is."

Maureen asked him how he liked his coffee.

"Milk and four sugars, please," Patrick replied. He giggled self-consciously. "I really must cut down on sugar." He grabbed a handful of flesh from his middle. It wobbled, like jelly on a plate.

Bill pointed to a seat at the table. "Sit down, Patrick. And you might want to sit in on this too, Angela. Then you know what's going on."

Angela sat down opposite Patrick, and said, "I understand you live south of the river, Patrick."

"Yes, I do, Angela. I live in Godalming, in Surrey."

"You have a long commute."

"I do. It took me two hours by train this morning. I'll probably move up here in due course."

Bill asked him what he had been up to since they last met.

"I've been informing the industry I'm changing jobs and telling people what the joint venture has to offer. I'm very excited about this, Bill. I don't know of any other company that has come into this market with the range of products we are going to have. I can see us cleaning up here."

"Good," Bill said. "It can't happen soon enough for me. How did Seppo feel about you leaving?"

"He wasn't best pleased about it."

"I didn't think he would be, but that's how the cookie crumbles, as our cousins across the pond would say. What I thought we'd do, Patrick, is have coffee and a chat and then Angela can show you your office. She organised the furniture and the decorating and I think you'll like it. And then I thought we'd spend the rest of the day getting to know each other and talking about how we're going to get this thing up and running. And later this afternoon, we'll collect your company car. I've leased you an Audi A6."

"Thank you, Bill. I shall enjoy that."

Patrick liked his office.

"As you can see," Angela said, "the furniture's not new, and it doesn't quite match, but we can do something about it when you're making money."

"It's absolutely fine," Patrick assured her. "I'll manage perfectly well with this."

Angela had had the walls and ceilings of both rooms painted in magnolia emulsion, and the doors, window frames and skirting boards painted in a bright white gloss. The new carpet was rust coloured. There was still a smell of paint and carpet adhesive, but it was beginning to fade.

Angela opened the French windows to let in some air. It also let in the sounds of traffic and voices, from the street below, and the high-pitched whine on an Intercity Express as it sped through the station en-route to Scotland.

To give the room a more homely feel, she had placed potted plants here and there, and she had added a couple of artificial trees in nice ceramic pots. "I'll water the plants," she said. "No need for you to bother."

Rather than hanging pictures on the walls, Bill had suggested a map of American pulp and paper mills, so Patrick could identify where the mills that produced the materials he would be selling were coming from. A glossary with the names of the mills, who owned them, and what they produced in terms of product and annual volume, lay on the top of the filing cabinet. On another wall was a colour photograph of a kraft linerboard mill in Texas. It was not a mill the Kiplock group was currently doing business with, but it helped fill a void.

The door into the adjoining room was open and Patrick wandered through.

Angela followed him. She went to the sash window and slid it open.

"Planning ahead?" Patrick said. "Space for more people?"

"We'll see how it goes," Angela said.

"What do I do about secretarial services, Angela? Typing, etc."

"Use Maureen for the moment, Patrick. We'll hire you a secretary when you need one."

Early that afternoon, Maureen buzzed Bill to tell him Gerry Kiplock was on the line and asking to speak to Patrick. "Put him through to Patrick's office," Bill said. "And then come in, Maureen. Because I want a word with you." He put the phone down. "Gerry wants a word, Patrick. Take it in your office. Come back when you've finished talking to him."

When Maureen came in, Bill did not invite her to sit. "I've been hearing things I don't much like while I've been away," he said, looking at her sternly.

"Such as?"

"Such as you behaving as if you own the place."

"I've been doing nothing of the kind," Maureen said indignantly.

"And making Angela feel like an intruder."

"I don't know what you're talking about, I'm sure."

"And the phone conversations you've been having with Gerry. Do you think that because you spent the night with him it somehow raises your status here? Because I can assure you it doesn't. You're still my secretary, nothing more, and nothing less."

"I know that, Bill."

"Then you'd better start behaving as if you do, because otherwise you will be looking for another job, whatever Gerry thinks. And while we're on the subject, I don't much care for the way you've been talking to me recently. Does this have anything to do with me identifying your brother at the identity parade?"

"Did you expect me to be happy about it?"

"Maureen, in the interests of getting things back on track, I'm going to tell you something I probably shouldn't be telling you. And that is that the police have not been able to find your brother's boots. And without the boots, they won't be able to secure a conviction."

A ghost of a smile appeared on Maureen's lips.

"I thought that would please you," Bill said. "Just as a matter of interest, Maureen, did you tell him to dispose of his boots? I wouldn't blame you if you had, because I

181

would have if I were in your position. And there's nothing the police can do about it now."

"Of course I told him to get rid of them. Anybody would have, to protect their brother."

"Not quite anybody," Bill said, taking a small recording device from the inside pocket of his jacket and switching it off. "Just the dishonest ones. Thank you, Maureen. That's all I wanted to know." He smiled at the look of horror on Maureen's face. "Let's call it my insurance policy. Now, any more nastiness towards Angela, or attitude towards me, and I hand the tape over to the police. And if you think I won't, Maureen, try me. Do I make myself clear?"

Maureen nodded, her head down. "As crystal," she murmured.

When Patrick had finished talking to Gerry Kiplock, he bounded into Bill's room barely able to contain his excitement. "Wow! I didn't expect anything to be happening so quickly."

"Like what?" Bill said.

"He wants me in New York next week."

Bill frowned. He knew nothing about this. "To do what?"

"To meet his management team. And Trevor Kingsley is flying over as well. Gerry wants him to meet them, too."

Bill was confused. "He's a competitor, for heaven's sake. Why does Gerry want him to meet his management team?"

Patrick looked dismayed. "Oh dear. I assumed you knew."

"Knew what? What's going on, Patrick? Do you know something I don't know?"

Patrick was clearly embarrassed. "Bill, I'm sorry, but I don't think I should say any more."

Bill needed to get to the bottom of this, and fast. "I'll call you when I'm done, Patrick," he said, and picked up the phone.

Patrick got the message and left.

Kiplock greeted him cheerfully. "Hey, buddy. How the hell are you?"

"I was fine until Patrick told me you want him in New York next week. What's all that about?"

"I want to introduce him to my guys. Like I did with you."

"Yes, but you don't just go telling him to make a trip to New York without me knowing a thing about it, Gerry. He reports to me, not to you."

"Yeah, I guess I overstepped the mark. Sorry, buddy."

"And what's this about you wanting Trevor Kingsley over there, too? He's a competitor of ours."

"Not any more, he isn't."

"What do you mean?"

"I've hired him."

"To do what, for Christ's sake?"

"Keep your hair on, Bill. I've hired him to work with Patrick. He's moving into your spare office."

"Like hell he is. I don't want him within a mile of my office. I can't stand the guy."

"I admit he's not everybody's cup of tea, as you Brits would say, but he's a great salesman. And I've taken him on as an independent contractor, so he won't cost you a bean."

"He won't cost me a bean? I hope you're not telling me you've hired Trevor Kingsley to work for the joint venture."

"Well, sure I have. Who else would I have hired him to work for? He'll pick up his own costs and expenses, and he'll provide his own car. And since you're getting your spare room for free, that won't cost you anything either. He'll be working on commission only."

"Gerry, Trevor Kingsley's a charlatan. I can't think of anybody with any degree of common sense who would buy a used car from Trevor Kingsley."

"Have a care, Bill. Remember I've just hired him."

"Then you'd better un-hire him, Gerry, hadn't you? And when you want Patrick to come to New York, you clear it with me first. Okay? It's about time you started treating me like an equal partner." Without waiting for his partner to respond, Bill hung up.

He walked down the corridor to Patrick's office, where Patrick was sitting at his empty desk twiddling his thumbs and looking glum.

"You won't be going to New York next week, Patrick."

Patrick looked visibly relieved. "That's fine, Bill, whatever you say. What can I do to get some business moving?"

"Give Bernie Levy a call. He's head of Gerry's packaging division. Ask him to send you a list of what he has available. Nice guy. You'll like him. Tell him hi from me."

Ten minutes later, Patrick walked into Bill's office and told him Bernie had told him he had nothing available.

"Nonsense!" Bill exclaimed. "He's got more tonnage than you can shake a stick at. He told me that himself. I'll have a word with Gerry. Sit down, Patrick." He picked up the phone, dialled the number, identified

going to be expensive, making international calls from a hotel phone was always expensive, but he frankly didn't care. Right now, the cost of an international phone call was the least of his problems.

"Kiplock Inc. How may I direct your call?"

He forced himself to sound as cheerful as possible. Whenever you feel afraid, whistle a happy tune, and all that. "Hi, it's Bill Smith. How are you today?"

"I'm good, Bill. How are you?"

"I'm fine, thank you. Is Gerry there?"

There was a pause. "I'm sorry, Bill. Gerry's not here today. He's travelling."

"Do you have a number I can call him on? It's important I speak to him."

There was another pause, during which Bill heard muffled voices. "I'm sorry, Bill, I don't."

"Is Oscar there?"

"I'll put you through.

"Hey, buddy," Blackman said. "How's it going?"

"It isn't, Oscar. Your boss has just well and truly screwed me."

There was an audible sigh. "What's he done now?"

Bill explained what Kiplock had done.

"I don't believe this," Blackman said. "Have you spoken to him about it, Bill?"

"That was the reason for my call, but I understand he's travelling."

"I haven't said this, Bill, but he's not travelling, he's here in the office. Well, this is as bad as it gets. What do you plan to do about it, Bill? The ball seems to be in your court."

"What I'd really like to do, Oscar, is turn the clock back. Because right now I wish I'd never set eyes on the son-of-a-bitch. What I'm saying is that I'd like to get out

195

of the partnership. But I can't do that, because I used two thirds of the money he paid me for the shares in my company to pay off the mortgage on the house, and if I have to pay him back, which according to the contract I would have to, Angela and I would have to sell the house."

"Jesus, Bill, I'm real sorry. I don't know what to say. I knew he was devious, but this goes way beyond devious. This is downright immoral."

"And that's not the end of it, Oscar. You're probably not aware of it, but when he came to my office for our first board meeting, he spent the night with my secretary."

"I wasn't. But it doesn't surprise me."

"And in the office now, I'm afraid of opening my mouth in case something I say gets back to Gerry. Angela has told me that, when I'm travelling, Maureen's on the phone to Gerry on a regular basis."

There was the sound of the lawyer exhaling breath. A lot of it.

Bill said, "Oscar, I hope all of this will stay between you and me."

"It had damn well better, Bill, because I've been telling you stuff that could have got me fired. When you've decided what you're going to do, let me know what you need me to do, okay? And keep your chin up in the meantime, buddy. Okay?"

"I'll try, Oscar. But that's going to be easier said than done."

The next morning, Bill had breakfast in his room and then phoned Heikki. "Heikki, would you be interested in starting your own business?"

"Are you serious?"

"Yes, I'm serious. I've been awake half the night and I've come up with an idea."

"Then I'd be a fool not to be interested. People are not exactly queuing up to offer me a job."

"Right, then here's what I suggest we do."

Chapter 19

Bill was approaching the Maidstone exit on the M20 motorway when he spotted flashing blue lights in his rear-view mirror. He was talking to a customer on his car phone. "I'll have to call you back, John," he said. He hurriedly switched the phone off and put it back in its cradle.

He checked his speed. He was doing eighty-five. He took his foot off the accelerator pedal and let the car slow down to seventy. The police car, a white Volvo, came up behind him and sat three or four car lengths away. The flashing blue lights were now almost blinding.

Bill's destination was Dover, some ten to fifteen miles ahead, where he had an appointment with a mill, but he indicated left and pulled on to the Maidstone exit ramp, believing it would be safer than stopping on the hard shoulder of the motorway. The Volvo followed. He stopped near the roundabout at the top of the slope, and put the handbrake on. He left the engine running. The Volvo stopped behind him.

There were two uniformed officers in the Volvo. The one in the passenger seat got out, put on his cap and walked towards the Jaguar. The driver remained in the car, speaking on the phone.

Bill pressed the button to let the window down. "Morning, officer. Lovely morning." Which was not an exaggeration. It was a lovely morning.

For reasons best known to himself, the officer didn't seem interested in talking about the weather. "Would you switch off the engine and step out of the car, please, sir?"

Bill switched off the engine and climbed out of the car. Trucks were thundering past a few feet away, and he hurriedly closed the door in case one of them clipped it.

To get away from the traffic, the officer walked to the nearside of the Jaguar, and indicated to Bill that he should do the same. Then he asked Bill if it was his car.

"Mine and the bank's," Bill said, trying to make light of the situation.

The policeman evidently wasn't interested in jokes that morning, either. "Do you happen to have your registration document with you, sir?"

To cover eventualities of this nature, Bill carried photocopies of the registration document and the insurance policy. He kept them in the car's glove box. He opened the Jaguar door, leaned in and opened the glove box. He kept the photocopies inside the front cover of the owner's manual, which he lifted out. He took out the photocopy of the registration certificate, and handed it to the officer.

The driver of the police car climbed out of the vehicle and joined his colleague. They went into a huddle and exchanged words that Bill was unable to hear.

"You are Mr William A. Smith?" the officer with the copy of the registration certificate asked.

"I was the last time I looked at my passport," Bill replied.

Unamused, the officer said, "If you'll just answer the question, sir."

Bill decided he had better take them seriously. "Yes, officer. I'm William A. Smith. What's this all about, gentlemen?"

"This car has been reported stolen," the police driver said.

"That's ridiculous!" Bill exclaimed. "I've been driving this car since it was new five, years ago. I think somebody's having you on."

"May I see your licence, sir?"

The other officer started to walk round the car, inspecting its condition and checking the tyres.

Bill wasn't worried about the condition of the car, or the tyres. He had the car serviced every three months and he had had a set of new tyres fitted a couple of months ago. With the punishing schedule he set himself, there was no time for breakdowns on motorways. He fished his wallet out of the inside pocket of his jacket, took out his paper driving licence and handed it over.

The policeman unfolded it, opened it up and studied it. "Getting a little close to losing our licence, aren't we, sir?" he said, looking up. "Two convictions for speeding, and one for a drink-related offence, all within the last twelve months."

Feeling like a hardened criminal, Bill said dryly, "And if you drove fifty-five thousand miles a year, you'd get done for speeding occasionally, too."

"We actually drive a lot more than that, sir."

"Do you have any other form of identification, Mr Smith?"

Bill was still holding his wallet in his hand. He opened it up again. "American Express? Visa? MasterCard? Take your pick."

The officer glanced at the cards without asking for them to be taken out of the wallet. "That won't be necessary, sir. You obviously are who you say you are. And we know the car is registered to you." He handed Bill back his licence, and the copy of the registration certificate.

"So where do we go from here?" Bill said, checking his watch. He had to be in Dover in fifteen minutes. He wasn't going to make it.

"Can you think of anyone who might want to inconvenience you? Perhaps as a prank?"

Bill's brain had been engaged on that possibility for the last two or three minutes. He knew of no one sufficiently small-minded to pull a stunt like this, but someone had. He shook his head. "Not off-hand."

"Well, if you think of someone, you might want to give us a call. We take wasting police time very seriously."

The officer who had just made this comment walked to the Volvo and came back with a Maidstone police compliments slip "Call this number at any time of the day, or night."

"I'll do that," Bill said, folding the compliments slip and putting it in his wallet.

"Well, on you go then, sir. And remember that the speed limit is seventy, not eighty-five. And the next time we catch you talking on the phone while you're driving, we'll do you."

That night, Bill was sitting in his hotel room in Lincoln watching the ten o'clock news on TV when the phone by the side of his bed rang.

It was Angela. "Bill, there's a car in the lane again." She sounded perfectly calm, as if seeing the car no longer registered as a threat.

Bill reacted immediately. "Is Alec home?" Alec was their next-door neighbour. He was a scientist involved in the development of nuclear reactors.

"I think so. His car is in his drive."

"Stay put, sweetheart. I'll call you back."

Bill had Alec's phone number in his Filofax. He dialled the number. "Alec, it's Bill."

"Hello, Bill. Away on another trip?"

Bill laughed. "I'm afraid so. No rest for the wicked. Alec, have you noticed a car in the lane?"

"The Mercedes? Yes, I'm looking at it as we speak."

A Mercedes. That let Basil off the hook. He had a Jaguar similar to his, but a different colour. "Any idea who it might be?"

"No, but he looks harmless enough. He just seems to be sitting there smoking a cigarette."

"Obviously not a burglar then," Bill said. "No burglar with even half a brain would sit there casing the joint in full view of two houses."

"No, and I can't imagine a burglar driving the latest E-class either," Alec said. "Is he bothering Angela?"

"Not so you'd notice. But the fact that she called me and told me about it, means she's not comfortable with it. Especially since we had something similar recently, twice as a matter of fact. Alec, would you mind nipping out and having a word with him. If he's not up to any mischief, I'm sure he won't mind."

"Be happy to, Bill. Give me a number and I'll call you back."

Bill gave him his hotel's number. "I'm in room 26."

Five minutes later, Alec called back. "That's the damndest thing. When he saw me walking down my drive, he took off like a scalded cat."

"Did you get a look at him?"

"No, and I didn't get a look at his licence plate either. He drove away with his lights off. He obviously doesn't want to be identified. I think we should call the police if he turns up again."

"So do I. Well thanks, Alec. I really appreciate it."

"No problem. I'll pop round and have a word with Angela. Put her mind at rest."

As Bill sat stewing over who the driver of the Mercedes might be, a thought struck him. He dialled directory enquiries and asked for the number of the Roebuck Hotel. When the hotel answered, he asked to be put through to Betty's room.

"Bill," Betty exclaimed. "How lovely to hear from you." She dropped her voice. "Are you calling to tell me you've changed your mind about meeting me?"

Bill could hear a television in the background. She was watching the same news programme he had been watching. He visualised her cooped up in the one room with the children, and his heart went out to her.

"I'm afraid not, Betty," he said. "I've actually called to ask if Basil has changed his car recently?"

"Well, yes he has," Betty said. "He's bought himself a Mercedes."

"Do you happen to know if it's a new one?"

"Yes, I understand it is new. It's an E-class something or other."

"You wouldn't happen to know if he's started smoking, would he?"

"Well, yes, he has. He said it was because of the stress of our break-up. Why all the questions, Bill?"

"Because he's started parking outside the house again."

"Oh, dear. I'm sorry to hear that Bill."

"Betty, would you pass on a message for me? Would you tell him that if I catch him sitting in the lane in front of our house in the dead of night, I will not be responsible for my actions."

Chapter 20

"Good morning, Bill. If I may call you Bill?"

The warmth in the Finn's tone surprised him. It was a stark contrast to the tone he had used the last time they had spoken. He was also surprised at the Finn's use of his Christian name.

"Yes, of course you may. Good morning, Mr Papilla."

"It's Erkki. I'm calling to let you know that your commission has been wired."

"Good. Thank you for that."

"And let me apologise for my behaviour the last time we spoke. I believe I was quite rude to you. At the time, I had no knowledge of your association with the Kiplock organisation. I only knew that you were associated with Heikki Pentilla, with whom I have, shall we say, certain issues."

Bill felt like pointing out that civility costs nothing, whatever the circumstances. "That's perfectly all right, Erkki," he said.

"Another reason for calling is that I wanted to check that you knew we wired the funds to the Kiplock account in New York, not to the UK account you specified."

To Bill, his words came like a blow to the gut. Only his partner could have orchestrated this, and this was commission on business transacted before he came on the scene. Now he had got his hands on Bill's money. Was there no end to the man's treachery?

"May I ask why you did that, Erkki?" Bill asked quietly.

"Because the day after I received your fax, Gerry called from New York and said that due to restructuring within the group, the funds should be wired to New York. He said he would clear it with you. I hope we did the right thing. You don't sound too sure about it."

There was only one way Kiplock could have got wind of his fax to Finland, and that was through Maureen. She must have told him about it. Perhaps she even faxed him a copy. There was nothing he could do other than reassure the Finn that he had done absolutely the right thing and that he would work it out in-house with Gerry. He ended the call and sat back in his chair in absolute despair.

The world was closing in on him and he needed space, fresh air, and time to think. He put on his jacket and told Maureen he would be out for a while, and he walked down the stairs and into the street.

Round the corner from the office were well-tended gardens with benches for people to sit and smell the roses, or watch the world go by, and he found an empty bench and sat down. Council employees were cutting the grass and hoeing the flowerbeds and they were laughing and joking as if they hadn't a care in the world. At that particular moment in time, he would give his eyeteeth to trade places with one of them.

Try as he might, he could not understand why his partner was treating him like this. It wasn't as if he had done anything wrong, well nothing he could think of. On the contrary, as far as he was concerned he had done everything right. He had done everything he thought his partner would have expected him to do, and he had done it to the best of his ability. And Patrick was doing a wonderful job. He had got trials of newsprint into two Fleet Street tabloids, and trial orders of packaging grades into three corrugated box producers. What was not to like? And why would Kiplock not take, or return, his calls? If he couldn't speak to the man, how could he hope to find out what he had done wrong?

He decided to have another word with Oscar Blackman. At least he got replies and something got done when he spoke to him. He sat there for a while, enjoying the warmth of the sun and watching ordinary people going about their everyday lives. He then went back to the office and called Maureen in.

His French windows were open and the sounds from the street reassured him that, despite the treachery going on around him, life in the outside world was going on exactly as it should.

When Maureen walked in, he had to admit that, physically at any rate, she was quite a woman. She could turn a man's head without a backward glance, and he was reminded how little effort it had taken on her part to persuade him to seduce her. He couldn't blame Angela for saying no after Maureen's interview, nor could he blame his partner for accepting the favours Maureen was bestowing on him.

Bill actually felt sorry for Maureen; because he knew that his partner was merely enjoying her favours in the way he would enjoy another meal. He was using her purely for his own personal gratification, and Bill knew that when he finally dumped her, and he would, she would be devastated.

"Pull up a chair," he said.

Maureen pulled a chair out from under the table and sat down. She crossed her legs, causing her tight skirt to ride up over her knees. She tugged it down again.

Bill swivelled his chair round and gazed through his French windows. The smell of cigarette smoke drifted up from the street, and he thought it was amazing how far the smell of a lit cigarette could carry, especially to a non-smoker like himself. He turned back to face her.

"Maureen, does the word 'conscience' mean anything to you?"

Maureen seemed puzzled by the question. "Yes, of course it does," she said finally. "Why do you ask?"

"What about the word 'loyalty'? Does that figure in your personal vocabulary?"

"Of course it does."

"That fax you sent to Helsinki the other day."

"The one about the overdue commissions?"

"That's the one. How did Gerry come to hear about it?"

Maureen shrugged. "I sent him a copy."

"Why did you do that?"

"Because he asked me to keep him informed."

"Did it not occur to you, Maureen, that sending Gerry a copy of that fax might cause me a problem?"

"No, why should it? I was just doing what I was told."

She was either very dim, or she was playing a game with him. He suspected the latter. Either way, this wasn't getting him anywhere.

"Yes, of course you were," he said. "All right, Maureen, we'll leave it there for the moment."

The fresh air from his walk had helped clear his head, and it had also made him realise the impossibility of his situation. If he let his relationship with Gerry Kiplock continue, he would end up being at the beck and call of a man he had lost all respect for, and if he ended the relationship, he and Angela would be worse off than they were before, and would certainly lose the house.

So there was no chance of Maureen hearing what he had to say, he phoned Oscar Blackman from home.

"Hey, buddy. It's a beautiful day here in the Big Apple. The sun's shining and the birds are singing. What's it doing in jolly old England?"

"I wish I felt as cheerful as you sound."

"Uh oh, what is it this time?"

"I don't know where to start."

"Then start at the beginning. I have the time."

"Good, because you'll need it."

For the next fifteen minutes, Bill bent the lawyer's ear. He left nothing out.

When he had finished talking, the lawyer said, 'Hmm, I see what you mean."

"Oscar, the last straw was Gerry diverting the funds from Finland. That was business I did before you guys came on the scene. He's not entitled to a penny of that money. I feel so angry about it that I've actually been thinking of calling the police. To me, it's outright theft."

"Don't do that, Bill. We don't want the police involved."

"I mean, it's not as if he needs the money, is it?"

"No, it isn't. That's small change to Gerry."

"I want that money, Oscar. It's mine, and I want it."

"Okay, Bill. I'll have a word with him and see what I can do. As to whether you continue with the relationship, I do sympathise with your position, but you must do whatever works best for you and Angela."

Bill was heading west on a dual carriageway between Basingstoke and Winchester, when he spotted the marked police car. It was in a lay-by screened by trees. He was doing seventy-three miles an hour against a speed limit of seventy, so he didn't panic.

Just then, a Vauxhall Vectra passed him going like a bat out of hell. In the absence of brake lights, it was clear that the driver had obviously not seen the police car. It must have been doing close to a hundred, and the blue lights went on immediately.

Bill watched the Vectra disappear into the distance and mentally calculated how long it would take the police car to catch it. But the police car showed no sign of following the Vectra. Instead, it tucked in behind him. When he realised it was him they were after, there was something horribly familiar about it.

There was a lay-by about a mile ahead and he pulled into it. The police car pulled in behind him.

As the officer approached, Bill got his wallet out of his jacket pocket and withdrew the Maidstone police compliments slip. He let the window down.

"Would you step out of the car, please?"

Bill said, "Officer, if you've stopped me to tell me my car has been reported stolen, you'd better take a look at this." He handed him the compliments slip. "The Maidstone police stopped me earlier this week and told me my car had been reported stolen. If you give them a call, I'm sure they'll corroborate that."

"Bear with me, sir." The officer walked back to the police car.

In his rear-view mirror, Bill watched the policeman speak to his colleague and hand him the slip. And he watched the driver put a phone to his ear.

The officer came back and handed Bill the compliments slip. "You're right, sir. And by the way, the Maidstone boys cancelled the stolen car report when they realised it had been a hoax call, so it must have been reported stolen again since then. Have you any idea who might be behind this?"

"Not off-hand I haven't. I can't see what anyone could hope to gain by it."

"Someone with a grievance against you perhaps."

"That's what the Maidstone police suggested." An idea occurred to Bill. "Officer, if somebody phones in to report a stolen car, would the phone number of whoever made the call be on record?"

"Yes sir, it would."

"And if both calls came from the same number? Bill looked up into the officer's eyes.

The officer nodded. "I get your drift, sir. You be on your way, and we'll look into it. And again, I'm sorry you've been troubled."

Later in the day, Bill got a call on his car phone from Oscar Blackman.

"Hang on, Oscar. I'm driving. Let me find somewhere to stop. Okay, now I can talk."

"Gerry diverted the funds to show you he could."

"And how am I supposed to explain that to the bank?"

"I'm sure you'll think of something."

"Isn't he being a bit childish, Oscar?"

"It's his way of teaching you a lesson, Bill."

"For what? For not letting him crawl all over me?"

"He thinks you should do as you're told. Like everyone else around here does."

"If he wanted a yes-man, he picked the wrong person. Is he going to wire me the funds?"

"He says not. He says he's going to hang on to them until you start behaving. Bill, all I can suggest is that you decide whether or not you want to stay in the relationship, and keep your nose clean in the meantime."

Chapter 21

When Maureen brought in the mail and his first coffee of the morning, Bill grinned.

"What are you grinning about?" she said, putting the mug on his Mickey Mouse coaster, a souvenir from a family visit to Walt Disney World.

"If I told you that, I'd have to kill you," Bill said, still grinning.

Maureen was wearing a dress he had never seen before, and Bill knew enough about women's dresses to know that it had undoubtedly cost a small fortune. "Ted been putting in a lot of overtime, has he?" he asked.

The sarcasm went straight over Maureen's head. She looked at him, puzzled. "Sorry?"

"The dress." Bill knew with absolute certainty that his partner had bought her the dress.

Maureen scoffed, "Ted couldn't afford a dress like this if he worked overtime every day for a year. This dress cost more than he paid for our car." She gave him a twirl. "Do you like it?"

Bill had to admit that it was a stunning dress, and he told her so.

Angela walked in from dropping off the children at school. "Have they been?" she asked.

"Not yet," Bill said. "I'm expecting them between nine-thirty and ten."

Maureen said, "Oh, are we having visitors this morning?"

Angela noticed her dress. "My goodness, Maureen, where did you get that dress? It's absolutely gorgeous."

"It came from Harrods," Maureen said proudly. "Gerry bought it for me."

"And did he buy you the watch as well?" Angela said, eyeing the slim gold watch on Maureen's wrist.

"Yes, he bought it for me in New York." Maureen's face was now flushed with pride. "It came from Bombit Tweller."

Bill corrected her. "Bonwit Teller."

"What?"

"It's Bonwit Teller, not Bombit Tweller," Bill said. "It's a department store in New York."

Maureen shrugged. "Whatever."

"How do you explain these things to Ted?" Angela asked.

"I haven't been home for the last two nights, so he doesn't know about them yet. But it doesn't matter what he thinks now, because I'm leaving him. Gerry is getting me a flat in London."

"Well we are going up in the world," Bill said. "Will it be a penthouse in Mayfair, or something overlooking Hampstead Heath? Or perhaps a garden flat in Kensington?"

"Well, he's not actually buying me a flat, he's renting me one. We've been looking in the Finsbury Park area. And before you say anything about Finsbury Park, it's a lot nicer than where I live now."

"I never said a word," Bill said. "You said you've been looking, Maureen. Does that mean Gerry's been over here?"

"He was here at the weekend. He's gone back to New York now."

"Nice of him to let me know he was coming. When did he get here?"

"He arrived late Friday evening."

"From where? New York?"

"From Finland. We spent Saturday looking at flats, and visiting Harrods. And he had a business meeting on Sunday afternoon."

"With whom?" Bill asked.

"I don't know. He sent me out. He told me to go and see a movie."

"Is he still in London?"

"No, he left yesterday morning."

"To go where?"

"To Paris."

"Is he coming back here from Paris?"

"No, he's going back to New York from Paris."

Angela was sitting there admiring Maureen's dress. "If I might make an observation, Maureen," she said, "that's more of an evening dress than a day dress. And it's much too nice to wear for work."

"I don't care," Maureen said. "I've never had a dress like this before. I don't ever want to take it off."

Angela knew that Gerry Kiplock would dump Maureen when he got tired of her, and she actually felt quite sorry for her. "Well, it's a lovely dress," she said, "and you enjoy it while you can."

Maureen beamed. "Can I make you a coffee, Angela?"

"Is there time, Bill?" Angela said.

Bill looked at his watch and nodded. "I think so."

"Then thank you, Maureen. I'd love a coffee."

Maureen left the room and closed the door behind her.

Bill shook his head. "Talk about a lamb to the slaughter." He needed a word with Patrick, who was travelling, and he put a quick call through to the phone in his car. "Patrick, did you know Gerry was in London over the weekend?"

"No, I didn't, Bill. Is he coming to the office?"

"Apparently not. When did you last hear from him?"

"I haven't actually heard from Gerry in some time, Bill."

"Right. How's it going out there? Still making progress?"

"I certainly am. I've got another buyer interested in a trial container of Canadian newsprint. That's two new trials this week, and it's only Tuesday morning."

"Brilliant. Well drive safely, Patrick, and keep me posted." Bill put the phone down.

Maureen came in with Angela's coffee and Bill told her to pull out a chair and sit down. He wanted to make her aware of something. As Angela sipped her coffee he said, "Maureen, have you given any thought as to what might happen if Gerry's wife finds out about you and Gerry? If he's renting a flat for you, he would have to sign a contract and that would leave a trail."

Maureen seemed unconcerned. "How can she find out? She's three thousand miles away."

Bill said, "Are you aware that she's a top-notch divorce lawyer?"

"He doesn't talk about his wife, so no I wasn't."

"Well I should just point out, Maureen, that she could freeze all Gerry's assets, including his bank accounts, credit cards, etc. She could stitch him up so tightly he wouldn't be able to move a muscle. And don't say it won't happen, Maureen, because I've seen it happen. It happened to a friend of mine in a previous job. His wife was a divorce lawyer and she hung him out to dry."

Maureen looked at them both, first at Bill, and then at Angela. "And who's going to tell her? I know neither of you will, and Ted would have a heart attack at the very thought of placing a phone call to New York. He's afraid of his own shadow."

"How do you know we won't?" Bill said.

"I just do. You're not those kind of people."

"I suppose we should take that as a compliment," Bill said. "But how do you know we won't tell her just to get our own back for the way you've been treating us?"

"Because if you did, Gerry would terminate his partnership with you."

"How could you possibly know that," Bill said. "Unless of course …"

There was the sound of heavy footsteps on the stairs from the street, followed a moment or two later by a loud knock on the door.

"Come in," Bill called.

The door opened and a policeman in uniform put his head round the door. "Mr Smith? You said the second door down the corridor, on the right."

Bill got to his feet. "Yes, come on in, gentlemen."

There were two of them and they were both in uniform. The one who had popped his head round the door had three chevrons on his sleeves. He introduced himself as Sergeant Mullens and his colleague as Constable Crofton.

Bill got to his feet and walked the length of his office to shake hands with them. "This is my wife, Angela."

The two policemen nodded politely to Angela, who remained in her seat. "Good morning, madam."

"Good morning, gentlemen."

With a sweep of his hand, Bill indicated Maureen, who was sitting there watching the proceedings with an increasing sense of nervous anticipation. "And this, gentlemen, is Mrs Maureen Pomfret."

"Ah, the lady we've driven up from Maidstone to have a word with," Mullens said.

"Have a seat, gentlemen," Bill said. "May I offer you coffee?"

"No, thank you, sir," Mullens said, pulling out a seat and sitting down. "We'll just get on with what we've come for, if that's all the same to you. His colleague remained on his feet, as if standing guard in case Maureen decided to make a dash for it.

At that particular moment in time, Maureen looked more likely to throw up than make a dash for it.

Mullens opened the manila file he was carrying and took out a sheet of paper. He put it on the table and slid it across to Maureen. "Do you recognise this?"

It was one of Bill's most recent itineraries and, since Maureen had arranged the appointments and typed up the itinerary, she could hardly deny recognising it. "It's one of Bill's … Mr Smith's itineraries," she stammered. She knew what was coming and her stomach began to churn.

"And do you recognise this?" Mullens slid a page from a BT telephone bill in front of her.

Maureen's face was now beginning to lose its colour. "It's a page from a telephone bill," she said in a low voice.

"Indeed it is," Mullens said. "It's a page from a telephone bill. And if you take a look at the name at the top of the page, you'll see who the bill is addressed to."

Maureen didn't need to look, she knew to whom the bill was addressed. "It's addressed to the company," she said. She looked at Bill, her eyes pleading with him.

Bill looked away.

"That's correct. Now would you take a look at the two phone numbers highlighted in yellow, and tell me if you recognise them."

Maureen looked at the highlighted numbers. She didn't recognise the numbers; after dialling each of them only once, who would? She shook her head. "They don't mean anything to me."

"Which is hardly surprising, since you probably only dialled the numbers once," Mullens said. "So let me help you out. One of the numbers is the number of the police station in Maidstone, and the other one is the number of the police station in Winchester."

Maureen looked at Bill, her eyes pleading with him. "I'm sorry, Bill" she said in a voice that was little more than a whisper. "It was only meant as a joke."

"So you admit to making the calls?" Mullens said.

"Yes, but …"

Bill snapped, "So you think it's funny being stopped by the police, with their sirens blaring and their blue lights blinding you, do you? Being pulled over and made to feel like a criminal? And twice in a week, for God's sake! Is that your idea of a joke?"

"Bill, I'm sorry. I swear I didn't mean to …"

"Yes, you did, Maureen," Bill said, lowering his voice to a near conversational tone. "It's just another example of your contempt for me since Gerry Kiplock came on the scene. Well as far as I'm concerned, Maureen, you can stew in it. You brought this on yourself and you deserve whatever you get." Bill got to his feet. "Gentlemen, if you don't need us, my wife and I will leave you to it. Come on, Angela. I need some air."

When Bill and Angela got back to the office forty-five minutes later, the two policemen had gone; the coffee cups had been removed, and the chairs had been put back under the table.

Maureen heard them come in, so she knocked and entered the room. Her face was ashen. "I'm sorry, Bill."

"And so you damn well should be," Bill retorted.

"It was only meant as a joke."

"What on earth did you hope to gain by it?" Angela asked.

Maureen spread her hands in a gesture of helplessness. "I didn't expect to gain anything by it. I've no idea why I did it. It wasn't even my idea."

"Let me guess," Bill said. "It was your brother's idea."

"It was," Maureen said miserably. "And I shouldn't have listened to him. It was a stupid idea."

Angela pulled out a chair and sat down. "What did the police say?"

"That they're going to prosecute me for wasting police time."

Bill sat down behind his desk. "What's the maximum you can get for wasting police time, Angela? Two years?"

Angela wasn't playing ball. She looked away.

Maureen pleaded, "Bill, can you do something? Please. I swear I'll never do anything like this again. Cross my heart and hope to die." She made the sign of the cross over her heart.

Bill ignored her.

Maureen looked close to tears. She turned to Angela. "Angela, please."

"There's nothing Angela can do, Maureen. You've made your bed and now you must lie in it."

"Please, Bill. If you'll get me off the hook, I'll do anything you ask."

A germ of an idea started to form in Bill's mind. "If you mean that, Maureen, and you promise never to do anything like that again, I'm prepared to do what I can to get you off the hook. But there's a condition, and that is that you confirm, in writing, that it was your brother who beat me up."

Maureen looked confused. "But how will that help?" she said. "The police have let him go. He can't be arrested twice for the same offence."

Bill realised she was thinking of double jeopardy. What she didn't know was that you can actually be arrested several times for the same offence; you just can't be tried twice for the same offence. "Then by confirming it in writing, you would have nothing to worry about, would you?" he said.

Maureen suspected he was up to something, but in her confused and upset state she couldn't think what. She needed to speak to someone. Someone she could trust. Someone she knew was be on her side. The obvious candidate was her brother. "I'll need to speak to my brother first," she said.

"Be my guest," Bill said. "Use the phone on your desk."

Maureen turned to leave.

"Before you go, Maureen, what's your brother's full name?"

Maureen looked at him suspiciously. "Why do you need that?"

"Because I want to put something in writing that I want you to read to him." When Maureen baulked at giving him her brother's full name, Bill said, "Fine, I'll get it from the Welwyn Garden City police."

"Please, Bill, don't involve the police again. My brother's in enough trouble as it is. His full name is Gary Charles Harrington."

Bill wrote the name down. "Will you be able to get hold of him now?"

"I should be able to."

"Right, then go and call him. And when you've spoken to him, come back in and tell me what he said."

While Maureen was away, Angela left saying she had some shopping to do and would be back in about an hour.

Maureen came back and told Bill her brother wanted to know what it was he wanted her to sign.

"Is he still on the line?" Bill said.

"Yes, he's holding."

Bill tore the message off the pad and handed it to her. "Read this to him. And read it to him from my phone, then I'll know he's got the message." He picked up the phone on his desk, pushed the button to connect with the line on which Maureen had called her brother, and handed the phone to her.

Maureen glanced at the message and took the phone.

"Are you there, Gary? It's only three lines. I'll read it to you."

Bill opened a drawer in his desk and switched on his portable dictating machine.

Maureen began to read. "I, Maureen Victoria Pomfret, do hereby declare today, July 23, 1982, that my brother Gary Charles Harrison, admitted to me that he lied to the police, and that he did indeed assault Bill Smith, occasioning him actual bodily harm on the night of February 21, 1982."

Bill switched the dictating machine off.

"That's it, Gary," Maureen said. Her brother said something to her. "Wait a minute," she said. She put her hand over the mouthpiece. "He said to ask you if you think he's stupid? He won't agree to me signing that." She handed the statement back.

"Not to worry," Bill said. "It was worth a try."

"Is that it?" Maureen said, looking mystified.

"That's it. You can hang up now."

"All right, Gary," Maureen said into the phone. "That's it. I'll see you at Mum's on Sunday."

Before he went home that evening, Bill paid a visit to the police station. He told the desk sergeant that Sergeant Schembri was expecting him.

"Right, sir. If you'd like to take a seat."

Schembri came out grinning like the proverbial Cheshire cat. "I'm not sure it's going to work, but I certainly admire your initiative."

Bill handed him the tape and followed him to the interview room.

Schembri slotted the tape into a tape player on a table by a wall and pressed play. He turned up the volume.

Maureen's voice came over loud and clear. "I, Maureen Victoria Pomfret, do hereby declare …"

After the tape had ended, Bill asked him what he thought.

"We can certainly bring him in again on the strength of the tape," the policeman said. "But considering how you came by the tape, whether we would get a successful prosecution is another matter entirely."

"What's likely to happen to my secretary over the issue of wasting police time."

"Probably nothing more than a stern warning."

When Maureen brought in the mail and Bill's first coffee of the day the following morning, she banged the mug down on its coaster so hard that the contents came perilously close to sloshing all over his desk.

"You tricked me," she said, furiously.

"Did I?" he said, a picture of innocence.

"Yes, you did. My brother's been arrested again. You won't get away with this, because I'm going to tell Gerry. He'll sort you out. You just see if he won't."

"I wouldn't recommend it, Maureen. You seem to think that all you have to do is pick up the phone and Gerry will drop whatever he's doing and come running. Well it isn't like that, and the sooner you realise it, the better. For you, that is."

"I don't agree," Maureen said. "Gerry loves me and he'll do whatever I say."

"Maureen, it's not you he loves, it's your body. He's using you. He probably has women at his beck and call all over the world. And if he hasn't, all he has to do is snap his fingers. Don't you see that?"

"No, I don't," Maureen said. "He told me he loved me, and I believe him."

"Well, if you want my advice ..."

"I don't. I work for Gerry, not for you."

Bill was rapidly losing interest in the conversation. "Whatever," he said. "But I suggest you don't put it to the test. Because if you do, you might find out just how tenuous a link you have with Gerry."

Chapter 22

It was 6.45am on the morning of Gerry Kiplock's visit to the office and Bill was already showered, shaved and dressed. He woke Angela with a cup of tea.

"You're early," she said, sitting up and glancing at the alarm clock. "What time's he coming?" She reached for her tea.

Bill sat on the edge of the bed and smoothed the duvet with the palm of his hand. "Marcia didn't say. She just said to make myself available."

"Did you ask Maureen if she knows what time he's coming?"

"Yes, I did. And she didn't know, either."

"What would happen if Gerry found out what you were doing with Heikki?"

"I don't know, sweetheart. The you-know-what would probably hit the fan. I'll just have to hope he doesn't find out until such time as Heikki and I are making enough money to be able to walk away from Gerry. It can't happen soon enough for me. I didn't sign up for what he's been putting me through."

"How's it going with Heikki?" She took another sip of tea.

There were the sounds of the children rising from their beds.

"It's early days, but I would say it's going as well as can be expected. I've got trials into the UK from both of the Finnish mills we're working with, and from the

Swedish mill. Now we have to hope that the trials work out and the customers like the quality."

"Are you going to ask Gerry when he plans to pay you the overdue commission?"

"I certainly am. And I'm going to be talking to him about a lot of other things as well."

"He's probably not looking forward to his visit any more than you are."

"Well tough! He's brought it all on himself."

"You know why he's doing what he's doing, don't you, Bill? He's doing it because he's a bully and he's used to getting his own way."

"And what am I supposed to about that, Ange? Grovel and kow-tow to him? I don't think so. That's not my style."

"And I admire you for sticking to your principles. How do you see our capital holding up if he doesn't pay the commission?"

"We're all right for the moment. But with money going out like it's going out of style, and nothing coming in, it won't be long before we're in trouble again."

"Does Patrick know about what you're doing with Heikki?"

"No, he doesn't. I thought about telling him, but I decided against it. The fewer people who know what I'm doing, the better."

"Who does know, Bill?"

"Well, obviously the mills we're doing business with know, and you, Heikki and I know. Apart from that, nobody knows. At least I hope they don't."

"Do you really need me in today, Bill? After the way Gerry's been treating you, I really don't want to see him. I might say something I live to regret."

"I can understand that, Ange, but I really think you should be there. If only to give me moral support."

"All right, if I must. What would you like me to wear?"

"How about the dress you wore in New York?"

"That was wintertime, Bill. Wool is a bit warm for July."

"I was thinking more of the effect that you wearing that dress will have on Gerry. In New York, he couldn't keep his eyes off you, and I think we need all the help we can get."

Bill got to his office at around 9am. There was no sign of Maureen. She was still not in at 10am and Bill was standing at the French windows of his office wondering when she was going to put in an appearance when he saw her walking arm-in-arm with his partner from the station.

He was wearing his loud check jacket and red trousers and she was wearing the dress he had bought her at Harrods. They looked the unlikeliest of couples and people were turning and looking at them as they walked past.

Bill sat at his desk and waited for them to arrive.

He heard Maureen unlock the door from the corridor to her office and he heard her offer him coffee, and him say, "That would be great, babe." Then the inter-connecting door to his office opened and his partner walked in.

Bill got to his feet. He didn't feel like getting to his feet, but the way he had been brought up prevented him doing otherwise.

"Morning, Gerry."

"Morning."

They briefly shook hands.

"Pull up a chair," Bill said.

Kiplock pulled a chair out and sat down.

Bill sat back down behind his desk. "It's been a while."

"Yeah, well you know how it is."

Bill had no idea how it was, but it would have been pointless to say so.

Through the open door, Maureen called, "Coffee, Bill?"

"Please."

There followed an awkward silence during which neither of them seemed to know what to say.

Bill broke it. "Patrick's doing well. He's bringing in a lot of business."

"Yeah, he's doing a great job."

There was another silence.

This time, Kiplock broke it. "Angela coming in today?"

"She'll be joining us later. What's on the agenda for today, Gerry?"

"Nothing you need worry yourself about."

Bill felt his hackles rising. "Gerry, this won't do."

"There you go again."

"What do you mean, there you go again?"

"I mean that nobody else talks to me the way you do, and that's why you and I have a problem."

"Then we should talk about it while you're here. Get things back on track."

"It's too late for that, Bill. Way too late."

"Meaning?"

"You're in breach of our agreement."

"No, I'm not."

"Yes, you are."

"How am I in breach?" Bill knew he was in breach, but he wasn't about to admit it.

"You're in breach because you're offering products from mills Kiplock Inc are not doing business with. Two Finnish mills and one in Sweden, if you want to get more specific. And you can't do that without written agreement from me. Don't bother trying to deny it, Bill, because I know it for a fact."

Maureen walked in with the coffee.

Bill glared at her. "Is this another piece of your treachery?"

Maureen had no idea what he was talking about and she opened her mouth to tell him so, but Kiplock beat her to it. "It wasn't Maureen who told me."

Maureen put the coffee on the table and quickly withdrew. She closed the door behind her.

"So who told you?"

"It doesn't matter who told me. What does matter is that I can't trust you anymore."

"You're a fine one to talk about trust," Bill said, his blood pressure rising. "You don't know the meaning of the word. You steal my business, you steal my commission, and you refuse to pay me commission you owe me. What the hell is it with you?"

Kiplock shrugged.

"So where do we go from here, Gerry?"

"Where we go is you have thirty days to remedy the breach, otherwise our agreement becomes null and void. And I don't have to remind you that if you don't remedy the breach, you have to pay me back the $150,000 I paid you for your shares, and the $75,000 I put into the company when Patrick came on board."

"And who pays me for the $75,000 I put into the company when Patrick came on board?"

"Not my problem."

"And who reimburses me for the salary I've paid Patrick since he came on board? The salary that you, in your infinite wisdom, offered him at twice what the job was worth."

"And he's proved himself worth every penny."

"Not to mention his car and travel expenses. He's cost me a small fortune."

"We've all had our crosses to bear, Bill."

"Jesus Christ, Gerry, you're something else. But hang on, if I remember rightly it states in the agreement that you are to pay me commission on what we sell for you. So you're in breach of contract, because you haven't paid me any commission."

Kiplock smiled. "I'm not in breach. Oscar sees to that. What it doesn't say in the agreement is when I have to pay you."

"So when will you pay me?"

"I haven't decided yet."

Bill could see there was no use trying to reason with him. "So I have to give up the business I've been developing with Finland, otherwise you declare our partnership agreement null and void. Is that how it is?"

Kiplock nodded. "Got it in one." He tilted his chair back and put his foot on the corner of Bill's desk, showing Bill the sole of his shoe. It was the ultimate sign of dominance.

Angela had been right; Kiplock had been teaching him a lesson. And he achieved his goal. He had won, and he knew it. The smirk on his face proved it. He had trapped Bill like a fly in a spider's web, and he was loving every minute of it.

Bill's anger turned to a feeling of loathing. He wanted to get up and pound some sense into the

American. And he could have; he was bigger and heavier than Kiplock. But that wouldn't achieve anything except getting him into trouble with the police.

Keeping a tight rein on his emotions, Bill tried to reason with him. "Gerry, haven't I done everything I promised to do? Haven't I given you a presence here in the UK, got the business started, and made you money? What more do you expect of me?"

"If you haven't figured that out after all that's been said, buddy, I'm not about to enlighten you. Perhaps we should just put it down to us being incompatible."

There were no sounds coming from Maureen's office. Usually, Bill could hear her moving about, or at least shuffling her feet. She always shuffled her feet when she was working at her desk. But there was nothing. Just silence. He knew she was in there. She was probably standing behind the door, listening. And taking notes, to be handed later to the man whom she was convinced loved her.

Something came to mind. "Correct me if I'm wrong, Gerry, but doesn't it say in the agreement that if either party is in breach, the other party has to notify them in writing, and give them thirty days to remedy the breach?"

"It sure does," Kiplock reached into the inside pocket of his jacket and withdrew a sealed envelope. He handed it to Bill. "This is official notification that you're in breach. I'll be in Patrick's office." He got up and walked out, taking his coffee with him.

Bill swung his chair round and stared out onto the street. Out there, normal people were doing normal things. He felt so far removed from them and their world that they might have been on another planet. He felt lost, adrift, disconnected.

He heard the door to the street close and then heavy male footsteps on the stairs. Then he heard a knock on Maureen's door.

"Come in," he heard Maureen call.

"Good morning," a cheerful cockney voice said. "You must be Maureen."

Bill immediately knew who it was. He hadn't known Trevor Kingsley was coming, or why. He felt his hackles rise.

He heard Maureen's feet shuffle and then the scrape of her chair as she pushed it back and no doubt stood up to greet her visitor. "Yes, I'm Maureen. You must be Trevor."

"One and the same. Trevor Kingsley. Large as life and twice as ugly."

You got that right, Bill thought.

"Nice to meet you, Trevor. Gerry's expecting you. He's in Patrick's office. I'll walk you down there."

Bill heard footsteps along the corridor, and Kingsley say, "That's a humdinger of a dress, Maureen."

"Why, thank you, Trevor. It came from Harrods."

"I don't doubt it."

Their voices trailed off down the corridor.

Fifteen minutes later, Patrick burst in. Bill was sitting with his back to his desk, staring gloomily through his French windows. "Do you know what's going on in there, Bill?" Patrick said to the back of Bill's head.

Bill swung his chair round. "No, I don't, Patrick. But I'm sure you're going to enlighten me."

Patrick's face was flushed. "I've just been told I'll be reporting to Trevor Kingsley from now on."

"Have you, Patrick?"

Patrick looked at Bill with concern. "Are you all right, Bill? You don't look very well."

"I'm fine, Patrick. But I've had some bad news of my own this morning. Pull up a chair."

"I can't. I'm supposed to be using the men's room. I can't stand the man, Bill. I'm seriously thinking of resigning."

"You and me both, Patrick. But I can hardly resign from my own company."

Patrick was so concerned with his own woes that Bill's comment went straight over his head. "What should I do, Bill?"

"You must do whatever you think you should do, Patrick. All things considered, I'm not really in a position to advise you."

"Bill, you're still the boss. Well you are as far as I'm concerned."

"That's not how it looks from my perspective, Patrick." Bill shrugged. "But, anyway."

"I can't report to him, Bill. I can't stand the man. Neither can most of the buyers. I don't know what Gerry's playing at."

"Tell me about it."

"I'd better get back," Patrick said. "They'll wonder where I am."

"We'll talk later, Patrick," Bill said.

Bill's head was still a million miles away when Angela walked in. Tall, slim and elegant in her wool dress, she looked sensational. "Not late, am I?" she said.

Bill smiled. "No, sweetheart, you're not late."

"Will I do?" She gave him a little twirl.

"You'll do just fine."

"That's not what you said the first time I wore the dress. You wanted to take me straight to bed."

232

He remembered and smiled. "I did, didn't I?"

"Hey, what happened to the successful businessman who breezed out of the house ready for anything just a few hours ago?"

"You might well ask. You'd better sit down."

Angela sat on the chair Kiplock had sat on and listened intently as Bill explained what had happened.

"And then he gave me this," he said. He handed Angela the official notification that he was in breach of the agreement.

Angela read it, and then read it again. "So he's found out what you were doing with Heikki."

Bill nodded. "I'm afraid so. There was always the chance he would. But I had to do something. He'd taken everything else away from me."

"Do you think Maureen told him?"

"He says not. And I can't see how she could have known. I've been extremely careful."

"Who else could have told him?"

"It could have been one of a few people. It could have been somebody at one of the mills Heikki and I have been working with. Gerry was in Finland recently. He probably found out then. And it could have been Trevor Kingsley, who, by the way, is sitting in Patrick's office with Gerry as we speak."

"What's he doing here?"

"You tell me. I don't know what's going on. Patrick came in out of their meeting half an hour ago and told me that Gerry has told him he'll be reporting to him from now on. So as far as Gerry's concerned, I seem to be well and truly out."

"Can he do that, Bill?"

233

"He's already done it. I'm effectively shut out of my own company, or I will be in a month. It looks like it's all over bar the shouting."

"Don't say that, Bill. There's always a way."

"Is there?"

"Can you remedy the breach, Bill?"

"Only by selling the house." He explained about having to pay back the money Kiplock paid him for his shares. "And I'd have to pay him back the $75,000 he put into the company when Patrick came on board."

"But that's $225,000, Bill."

"Correct."

"Dear God."

"And that's not the end of it. Gerry told me this morning that he still hasn't decided when he's going to give the $130,000 commission he owes me on the business Patrick has generated. He could stall literally forever."

"But he owes you that money, Bill."

"Which means nothing to Gerry. I don't think he has a scruple in his entire body. I'd probably have to take him to court to get it, and that would cost a fortune because he would fight it. And he still hasn't paid back the commission I earned on the Finnish business I did before he even came on the scene; the commission he had diverted to New York. It's impossible. I don't know which way to turn."

"If we did sell the house, Bill, would we have enough to clear the breach and get Gerry out of our hair? Make a fresh start."

Bill shook his head. "No, I don't believe we would. I think I would have to declare bankruptcy. And then we'd have no money, no house, we'd lose the cars, and we'd have to take the children out of school. We'd …"

Angela put up a hand to stop him. Her face had lost its colour. "Bill, I don't feel well. I'm going home."

"But Gerry's expecting us to join him for lunch, sweetheart. Could you at least manage that, if only to keep up appearances?"

"I don't think so, Bill. I couldn't be civil to him." Angela got to her feet. "What time will you be home this evening?"

"I don't know. I've got a feeling Patrick and I will be in need of a stiff drink, or three, when Gerry's gone, and we'll probably head for the boozer. So expect me when you see me."

Angela headed for the door. "Well don't overdo it. Remember what the doctor said."

Ten minutes after Angela left, Kiplock walked in. "Angela not here yet?"

"She came, but she wasn't feeling well and she went home again. She sends her apologies and says she hopes you have a good visit."

"Pity, I was looking forward to seeing her."

Trevor Kingsley was holding the door open and Patrick was standing in the corridor behind him.

"Hey, Bill," Kingsley said. "How's tricks?"

To keep up appearances, Bill replied, "Fine, thank you, Trevor. And you?"

"Yeah, just fine. Great set up you've got here. I'm looking forward to being a part of it."

"I feel a thirst coming on," Kiplock said. "You ready for lunch, Bill?"

"As ready as I'll ever be," Bill said.

Kiplock called towards the inter-connecting door, "You ready, Mo?"

"Be right there, Gerry."

They went to the same restaurant they had gone to when Kiplock was over for the first board meeting, and, as always, Kiplock insisted on ordering champagne.

Bill went along with it, but over lunch he only spoke when he was spoken to. He was trying to get his head round how he was going to get himself out of the impossible situation he found himself in. There was no way he could countenance carrying on working with Kiplock now, even if Kiplock had a change of heart and withdrew his claim for breach of contract. It had gone way too far for that.

Kiplock, on the other hand, was in fine form. He was quaffing champagne in copious amounts and regaling them with anecdotes and stories of funny things that had happened to him during his years in business.

Bill tried to involve himself in the conversation, but his heart wasn't in it. At one stage Maureen asked him if he wasn't feeling well. He assured her he was feeling fine.

She was in her element. Gerry was paying her a lot of attention, as was Trevor Kingsley, and she was lapping it all up.

Patrick was laughing at Kiplock's jokes, occasionally telling a joke himself, but Bill sensed that, like himself, he would rather not have been there.

As for Trevor Kingsley, whenever Kiplock said something even remotely funny, he would throw his head back and laugh uproariously. It got to be so obvious that he was sucking up to the American, that at one stage, after he had laughed uproariously at something Kiplock had not meant as a joke, Kiplock asked him what he was laughing at.

For Bill, the lunch dragged on almost interminably. When it was finally over and he had paid the bill, they all went back to the office.

Half an hour later, Kiplock headed off to the station to go back to London. Maureen went with him, as did Trevor Kingsley.

Bill and Patrick spent the rest of the afternoon talking in Bill's office.

They were both so shell-shocked by what had happened that they shut up shop a little after 5.30pm. and headed for the nearest bar.

A taxi dropped Bill off at home just before 11pm. Patrick had checked into a B&B.

Angela had not heard from Bill since she had left the office that morning, and she was shocked at the state of him. He was unable to stand unaided, and his speech was incoherent. The taxi driver helped her get him upstairs, and she gave him a healthy tip for his trouble when she paid Bill's fare.

That night, Angela did not go to bed until after 4am. She stayed downstairs, still fully dressed. As dawn began to break, the idea that had been germinating in her mind began to take shape.

Chapter 23

Bill needed time to think, and for several days after Gerry Kiplock's visit he went home for lunch. Angela went home with him.

On the Thursday, which was four days after Kiplock's visit, he was sitting at the breakfast bar watching Angela make his sandwiches.

She had been quiet for a while, but as she buttered his bread, she said, "Bill …"

"Yes…"

"It might not be a good time to ask this, but … would you mind if I went away for a few days?"

"To do what, sweetheart?"

"To have a break, to take a holiday. The thing is, Bill, that watching you drink yourself into oblivion every evening and then pace the house until the early hours is taking its toll on me. I've been stressed before, but never like this. If I don't take a break, I think I might crack up."

Bill strode across the kitchen and wrapped his arms round her and kissed her gently on the neck. "I'm so sorry, darling. Why didn't you tell me you had a problem? You always seem to be coping so well."

"You have more than enough on your plate without me adding to your problems." Angela gently disengaged herself. "If I can get away for a few days, I think it will make all the difference. Then I can be of use to you. I can't be of any use to you the way I feel now."

"Then of course you can go," Bill said. "I can't have you feeling like that." He walked back to the breakfast bar and sat down again.

Angela continued buttering the bread.

"Did you have somewhere in mind?" he asked.

Angela put a slice of ham on each of two of the four pieces of bread she had buttered, and then opened a jar of Coleman's English mustard. "I wanted to make sure it was all right for me to go, before I started thinking about where to go."

"What about the children?" Bill asked. "I don't think I could manage them on my own, especially with all the things I have on my plate at the moment. And, as you know, I have to go to Finland the week after next. If I don't get this thing with Heikki off the ground, I'll end up with less than I had before, in which case, as sure as eggs are eggs, the bank will pull the plug on me."

"I'm sure my mother will be happy to look after the children," Angela said. "She's always complaining she doesn't see enough of them. And she's over the problem with her heart, now."

"How will they get to Torquay?" Bill asked. "I don't have time to drive them down there. It's a day's drive."

"They are old enough to be put on a train unsupervised. My parents will meet them at the other end."

A movement on the lawn caught Bill's attention and he looked through the window. A fox was stalking a magpie. The magpie saw it and flew away. The fox slunk away with its tail between its legs. "What about the children's schooling?"

"The summer holidays begin at the end of next week."

Bill hadn't realised. "Time flies," he said. "How long would you plan to be away?"

"A week should be enough."

"Then why don't you take the week I'll be in Finland?"

"I will," Angela said. "Thank you, Bill. I'll set it up."

She cut his sandwiches in half, put them on a plate together with a sliced tomato, and handed the plate to him.

He thanked her and picked up a sandwich and bit into it.

"Bill, there is one more thing."

Bill waited until he had swallowed what was in his mouth before answering. "What's that, sweetheart?"

"Well, don't take this the wrong way, but would you mind not asking me where I'm going? And not trying to phone me while I'm away? I need to be left alone. I need some me time."

"All right, sweetheart, I can live with that. I would just ask one thing, and that is that you go easy on the credit card while you're away. I wouldn't ask, but … well you don't need me to explain. You know how things are."

"I'll be careful," Angela promised.

Over breakfast the next day, Angela asked him if he would mind her not coming in today, explaining that she had to get some things for her holiday.

He said he wouldn't mind at all, and asked her how her plans for the holiday were coming along.

"They're coming along fine," she said.

"Are you going somewhere nice?"

"Bill," she chided gently, "you agreed not to ask."

He pulled a face. "Sorry, I forgot. Can I do anything to help?"

"There is one thing you can do, you can drive me to catch my plane."

"Of course I will. When are you going?"

"The morning of Sunday week. The day before you go to Finland."

"Right, then everything seems to be sorted." He looked at his watch. "I'd better get back to the office. Although why I'm bothering beats me. With Trevor Kingsley throwing his weight about trying to impress everybody, and Maureen behaving as if she owns the place, I think I'd rather be digging ditches."

After Angela had dropped the children off at school, she drove to Welwyn Garden City station, parked the car, and took a train to King's Cross. From there she took the tube to Knightsbridge, where she left the station and made her way to Harvey Nicholls.

She took the lift to the ladies' clothes department, where she spent an inordinate amount of time looking at dresses. She found what she was looking for in a slim-fitting Nichole Farhi cocktail dress, in black, with a neckline that revealed a lot more than she usually revealed. The sales assistant assured her it was an original and that there would not be another one like it.

When Angela told her she would take the dress, the sales assistant asked her, "Who's the lucky man?"

Angela's eyes twinkled. "That would be telling."

When the sales assistant swiped her credit card, Angela could have sworn she heard it groan.

Next, Angela headed for the lingerie department where she spent almost as much time as she had spent looking at dresses. She was looking for a bra that would give her uplift without making her look tarty. She found one in black lace, and bought a pair of panties to match.

Then, she headed for the shoe department, where she bought herself an expensive pair of high-heeled Italian-made shoes, and a matching clutch bag.

Next, she headed for the perfume department where, after sampling at least a dozen fragrances, she found one she liked. Like her shoes and clutch bag, the miniscule bottle of perfume cost a small fortune. She also bought herself two pairs of skin-coloured tights.

She walked out of the store laden with bags and headed for a nearby hairdresser.

She was home in time to pick up the children from school, and since Bill never used her car, she decided to leave her purchases in the boot until she packed for her trip.

Bill's efforts to extricate himself from his breach of contract were being singularly unsuccessful. He had twice called New York and asked to speak to his partner, and on both occasions his partner had declined to take his call. He had also spoken to Oscar Blackman. But this, too, proved to be a dead end. Blackman, while sympathetic, said there was nothing he could do. His boss had dug his heels in, and wouldn't be shifted.

Things were looking dire, and every evening Bill was polishing off half a bottle of scotch. As a result, he was sleeping badly and getting more and more stressed and more and more bad tempered.

Patrick was being as supportive as he could, while Maureen and Trevor Kingsley were doing their best to keep out of Bill's way.

On the morning he dropped Angela off at Gatwick airport, Bill looked dreadful. His eyes were bloodshot and his face was the colour of chalk. He parked by the kerb at the drop-off zone and got Angela's luggage out of the boot.

"I'll be back before you know it," she said, giving him a hug. "In the meantime, try not to worry. Everything will work out fine, you'll see. And look after yourself, and don't drink too much when you're in Finland. Okay?"

"I won't," he promised. "You enjoy your holiday, and don't worry about me. I'll be fine. And let me know when you're coming back and I'll pick you up."

Angela stood on the pavement next to her luggage and waved him off. As he drove away, she wondered if things between them would ever be the same again. It was a risk she was going to have to take.

Chapter 24

The wide-bodied jet was packed to capacity, mostly with families heading to Walt Disney World and the numerous other attractions the Orlando area had to offer, and Angela's flight was cramped, noisy, and uncomfortable.

She was travelling economy, and because she had booked at the last moment and looked for the cheapest seat available, she was at the back of the plane near the toilets. In fact, she was so close to the toilets that she could hear the hiss whenever one was flushed. With three hundred and fifty people on the plane, the toilets were in constant use.

To add to her discomfort, a girl of five or six in the seat in front of her kept her seat fully reclined throughout the flight, even eating her meals with the seat back. With the back of the seat nine inches from her face, Angela found eating her meals nigh on impossible. And the eight or nine-year old boy in the seat behind her kept kicking the back of her seat. She couldn't move to another seat, because all the seats were taken. She tried to reason with the mothers, one of whom told her to 'For God's sake lighten up woman, we're on holiday!' She breathed a huge sigh of relief when the plane finally touched down at the Orlando International Airport.

Angela had booked herself a room at the Hilton Hotel on Hotel Boulevard next to the Disney Village at Lake Buena Vista, and she took a taxi from the airport.

When she stepped out of the taxi, it was if she had opened the door of an oven after baking a cake. The temperature was close to 100°F. The humidity was such that her blouse was instantly sticking to her back, and her hair to her face.

A bellboy hurried out to collect her luggage from the taxi. He told her to check in and he would bring her luggage to her room. She needed no second bidding. She hurried into the air-conditioned bliss of the four-star hotel.

When the bellboy arrived at her room with her luggage, Angela asked him how close to the hotel the Hyatt Regency Grand Cypress was.

"As the crow flies, ma'am, it's no more than a couple of hundred yards," the pleasant young man said. "But to get there, you need to hang a right out of the hotel, hang a left on Apopke-Vineland, and take the first left off of Apopke-Vineland. The Grand Cypress is a short way down the road on the left. You can't miss it. It's a huge place, set in its own grounds. There's a security guard at the entrance to the property."

For the next three days, Angela stayed within the confines of the hotel and its grounds, taking her breakfast and her evening meals in her room. The rest of the time she spent in a bikini soaking up the sun by the hotel pool. On several occasions, men approached her and tried to engage her in conversation, but she made it clear from the outset that she wasn't interested and they soon got the message.

If she had been in Europe, Angela would have removed her bikini top, to give herself an all-over tan, but she knew that here in the States this was not the done thing.

She used copious amounts of oil. It was tantamount to basting herself like a turkey. To tan her back, she enlisted the help of one or other of the waiters from the poolside bar. There was no shortage of offers to rub the oil on her back, and legs.

Angela tanned easily and, after two days by the pool, the blazing Florida sun had turned her skin the colour of mahogany. It had also bleached her hair, turning it from blonde to almost white.

At around 3pm on the Wednesday afternoon, she climbed off her poolside lounger, wrapped the hotel's cotton robe around her, collected her things and made her way to her room, where she closed the curtains and lay on the bed and tried to take a nap. But sleep wouldn't come. She had far too much on her mind to sleep.

At 4.30pm she started to get herself ready. First, she took a shower. To keep her hair dry, she wore one of the disposable shower caps the hotel had provided.

Apart from walking between her room and the pool, Angela had had no exercise since she arrived in Florida and lying in the sun all day had left her feeling tired and lethargic, so she turned the temperature control on the shower to cold, to try and wake herself up. And wake herself up it did. It took her breath away. She stood the cold for as long as she could, and then turned the water off. Feeling thoroughly invigorated, she stepped out of the shower and dried herself.

She padded, naked, into the bedroom and checked the time on the radio/alarm clock by the bed. It was 5.10pm.

She put on her new underwear and then sat at the dressing table and began to fix her hair. She fixed it the way she knew Bill liked; combed back at the sides and tied at the back with a black velvet bow. It had become a habit, and she liked it that way, too.

She kept her make-up simple, just eye shadow and lipstick. Then, she dabbed her new perfume on the inside of her wrist, rubbing her wrists together. She dabbed some behind her ears, and some between her breasts.

She put on her watch and earrings; the only jewellery she was planning to wear apart from her wedding and engagement rings, and then she slipped into her new dress. She stepped into her new shoes and then stood in front of a full-length mirror and took a long and critical look at herself.

She had brought with her a lightweight summer coat, and when she was satisfied there was nothing more she could do to improve her appearance, she put this on and buttoned it up. She picked up her new clutch bag and headed for the door.

She had not bothered to change the time on her watch since she arrived in Florida, and it was still on UK time. She had used the poolside bar clock when she wanted to know the time by the pool, and the radio alarm clock by the bed when she was in her room. When she got down to the lobby, she looked for a clock.

On the wall behind the reception desk were five clocks. One gave the local time; the second gave the time in London, which coincided within a minute to the time on her watch; the third gave the time in Paris; the fourth in Hong Kong; and the fifth gave the time in San Francisco. The local time was 5.50pm.

She walked to the desk and asked the female receptionist if it would be safe for her to walk to the Grand Cypress.

The receptionist took one look at her and reached for the phone. "Let me call you a taxi."

247

Forgetting where she was, Angela stepped outside to get a breath of fresh air while she waited for her taxi. She soon realised her mistake. The air was hot and humid. But she didn't mind because there was the smell of Jasmine from plants on the property, and she loved the smell of Jasmine. A Walt Disney World tour-bus soon put paid to that, arriving at the hotel with a hiss of brakes and a strong smell of diesel. It stopped right in front of her and began to disgorge noisy tourists.

When her taxi arrived, Angela apologised to the driver for only wanting to go round the corner, and she promised to compensate him for the brevity of her journey.

The huge black driver seemed unperturbed. "No problem, ma'am," he said, giving her a friendly smile.

The journey took all of six minutes. When the driver stopped at the guardhouse to the entrance of the grounds of the Grand Cypress, a uniformed guard came out and indicated with a circular motion of his hand that he wanted Angela to let the window down, which she did.

"Good evening, ma'am," he said, touching his cap. "Are you a guest at the hotel?"

"No," she replied, "I'm not a guest. But I'm joining one of your guests for dinner."

The guard touched his cap again. "Have a pleasant evening, ma'am." He waved them through.

The driver drove slowly through grounds planted with exotic bushes and shrubs, past signs indicating walkways and cycle paths, and up the ramp to the entrance to the hotel which some might see as Orlando's version of the Taj Mahal.

A uniformed commissionaire stepped smartly from his post and opened the door for her. Angela got out of the car and gave the driver a large tip, on account of how short a ride it had been.

The commissionaire welcomed her to the hotel and asked if he could direct her. She told him she was meeting a friend in the Atrium bar.

"That's at the far end of the lobby, ma'am," he said. He set the revolving door moving, waited until Angela was inside, and then turned his attention to a stretch Cadillac limousine that had just pulled up.

The lounge lobby was a large, open area, illuminated by natural light from an eighteen-storey atrium in which two banks of high-speed glass-walled lifts sped guests to and from their floors. On the ground floor was a patch of what appeared to be natural jungle, through which a stream ran over strategically placed pebbles. Two brightly coloured macaws sat, unfettered, on the branches of one of the trees and squawked at people as they passed. Two restaurants were visible, one behind the jungle, and one on the floor below. In the bar area, a man in a white tuxedo was playing *Smoke Gets In Your Eyes*.

Sitting at a table next to the piano, was the man she had come all this way to see. When he saw her, he smiled and got to his feet.

Dressed in a dark-blue double-breasted blazer, button-down shirt and grey slacks with razor-sharp creases, he looked every inch the successful businessman. She had forgotten how good-looking he was, and her heart skipped a beat.

His eyes crinkled in a smile. "So," he said, "you came. I didn't think you would."

Chapter 25

When Angela took off her coat, Kiplock's eyes opened like saucers. "That's some dress, Angela," he said.

"I'm glad you like it," Angela said. "Because I wore it for your eyes only."

The implication of what she had said was not lost on Kiplock, and he grinned. "That sounds like cause for celebration to me." He took Angela's coat and laid it over the back of a chair, and then raised his hand and called, "More champagne, waiter."

He held out a chair for her.

There was a practically empty champagne bottle in an ice bucket on the table. Beside it stood two flutes, both of which were empty, and one of which looked clean.

"Champagne, Angela?" He reached for the bottle.

Champagne was the last thing on Angela's mind. Tonight, she needed a clear head. "Gerry, if you don't mind, I'd rather have a glass of dry white wine."

"White wine it is." He emptied the contents of the bottle into his glass, and upended the bottle in the ice bucket, before draining his glass. "How's Bill?"

After the way he had been treating Bill, and especially after the bombshell he had dropped on Bill about being in breach of contract, Angela couldn't believe he had asked such a question. "How would you be if someone had dumped on you what you've dumped on him, Gerry? He's drinking heavily, he's not sleeping, and he's extremely bad tempered. Everyone's trying to keep out of his way."

A waiter arrived with an unopened bottle of champagne on a silver tray. He took the empty bottle out of the ice bucket and undid the wire and the wrapping on the neck of the bottle, before popping the cork. "Shall I pour, sir?"

Kiplock shook his head. "Just put it in the bucket, I'll pour. And bring a dry white wine for the lady. A large one."

"Right away, sir." The waiter walked away.

Kiplock filled his flute with champagne, and half-emptied it in a swallow. "I take it Bill doesn't know you're here."

Angela shook her head. "No, he doesn't. And he mustn't know. If he knew I was sitting here with you now, I doubt he would be responsible for his actions."

"And why did you come, Angela?"

"I came because of my children, Gerry. I can see it all falling apart, and if it does I'm not sure Bill's capable of putting it all together again. My children and I could be destitute, and I can't have that."

"I was surprised when you told me you were thinking of leaving him. You always struck me as being very happy together."

"We were happy," Angela said, "but we've been arguing a lot recently. Gerry, one thing I've been meaning to ask you is, why have you been treating Bill so badly? What's he done to offend you?"

"He's never done anything to offend me, Angela, but he wouldn't do as he was told. I made it clear from the beginning that I expected people on my team to do as they were told, and he wouldn't. He always wanted to do things his way. I had to teach him a lesson."

"But surely, Gerry," Angela reasoned, "he's entitled to have his say. He is your partner when all's said and done."

"Well, for the moment he is."

"If you wanted someone to agree with everything you said, you picked the wrong man. In all the years I've known him, Bill has never been a yes-man."

"You're right about that, Angela. I did pick the wrong man. And that's because I listened to Oscar. He talked me into taking Bill on. Trevor Kingsley's more my style."

"But why do you feel the need to put Bill out of business, Gerry? Why can't you just pay him what you owe him, and then you go your way and he goes his way. Revert to how things were before you got together, and then both of you get on with your lives again."

Kiplock thought for a moment before he answered. "I guess that's because I don't want to have to compete with him in the future."

Angela was surprised and dismayed by his remark. Surprised he had admitted it, and dismayed because it meant Bill didn't have a chance. She kept up the pretext. "Which is probably the nearest Bill will ever get to getting a compliment out of you."

"Yeah, it probably is."

"So you're not going to pay him what you owe him?"

"Hell no. Let him sue me for it."

"Gerry, you should be grateful to Bill, rather than trying to put him out of business."

Kiplock eyed her suspiciously. "Are you sure he doesn't know you're here? You're sure you're not here as his mouthpiece."

The waiter arrived with her wine. He took it off the tray and put it on the table in front of her. Angela smiled her thanks at him.

Kiplock raised his glass to her. "What shall we drink to?"

"A fresh start," Angela suggested.

"A fresh start it is."

They touched glasses.

The pianist finished playing *If It Takes Forever I Will Wait For You*, and leaned over and asked Kiplock if he would like him to play something for the lady.

"What would you like him to play, Angela?"

"Would you play April in Paris for me?" she said. "I love that."

"April in Paris, it is," the pianist said. He started to play.

They sat quietly listening to the music for a while, Angela sipping her wine, Kiplock doing his level best to polish off the champagne.

And then Angela asked, "Gerry, could you see my children and I destitute?"

"No, of course I couldn't," he said. "I'm sure we can come to some arrangement."

"You mean something along the lines that you will keep me in the style to which I have become accustomed, in return for certain, shall we say, favours?"

"Something like that."

"Well be warned, Gerry, Finsbury Park might work for Maureen, but it wouldn't work for me. If you want me, you'll need to be looking at the high-rent district."

Kiplock smiled. "Does that mean you're available?"

"I could be," Angela said. "Under the right conditions."

"Do you still love him?"

253

Angela put on a fake look of annoyance. "What's love got to do with anything? As I told you, I have my children to think of."

Kiplock emptied the bottle into his flute, and waved the bottle in the air. The waiter hurried over. "Another bottle, my man."

Angela caught his arm. "Gerry, I'm sorry, but I need to eat. I'm really hungry."

"Okay," Kiplock said. "Then we'll eat. I've booked a table at Hemingway's, so I hope you like fish." He drained his glass. "Forget the champagne, waiter. Just bring me the check."

Kiplock billed the charge to his room and left a $20 bill for the waiter. He slipped the pianist another one.

There were signs pointing the way to Hemingway's restaurant, named, Kiplock informed her, in honour of Ernest Hemingway the author. From the bar, they walked into a wide carpeted corridor, along each side of which were displayed what appeared to be priceless antiques and objets d'art.

Kiplock was carrying her coat over one arm, and he slipped his other arm through hers. The back of his hand touched her breast.

Angela had no way of knowing whether this was deliberate, or accidental, but she smiled at him and moved closer.

Halfway along the corridor, her courage deserted her and she felt a panic attack coming on. There was a ladies' room a few yards ahead. She slipped her arm out of his and excused herself, saying she needed to use the restroom.

Her heart was pounding. In the sanctity of the restroom, she leaned against a wall until her heart stopped racing. Her cheeks felt hot and she patted cold water on them. To help her cool down, she ran cold water on the insides of her wrists. She began to feel better. She dried her hands, checked herself in the mirror, and stepped back into the corridor.

Kiplock asked her if she was okay. "You were gone some time, and you look flushed," he said.

Angela slipped her arm through his and snuggled up against him. "I was feeling a little faint," she said. "It's probably because I'm hungry. I'm fine now."

The restaurant, which was accessed by a short wisteria-covered walkway from the corridor, was contained within its own building in the grounds at the rear of the hotel. And it was busy. It was so busy that, even though Kiplock had made a reservation, they had to wait several minutes before a waitress was available to show them to their table.

Their table overlooked a large kidney-shaped swimming pool with its own waterfall, tunnels, and caves. Some people were swimming, while others were standing by the poolside bar dressed for the evening and drinking cocktails from plastic glasses.

Almost before he had sat down, Kiplock was into his third bottle of champagne of the evening and it was beginning to show. Angela who drank only sparingly, watched his condition deteriorate as he finished one bottle, and started on another. The more inebriated he became, the more obnoxious he became, saying loudly at one stage, "Did I ever tell you you have great tits, Angela?"

"Gerry, please," she hissed. "Keep your voice down. People can hear you. They're beginning to stare."

There were two couples on the next table and they were all looking at him.

"What the fuck are you looking at?" he growled.

When the waitress came to take their main course plates away, she asked if they would like to see dessert menus.

Kiplock was away with the fairies and couldn't have cared less.

Angela told her thanks, but they should probably be going, and asked her to bring the bill.

While Kiplock was trying to focus on where to sign the bill, the waitress quietly asked Angela if she was going to be all right.

Angela smiled at her. "I'll be fine. He's my husband's partner and I'll just get him to his room and let him sleep it off. There's nothing to worry about."

Angela walked round the table and helped Kiplock to his feet. He put his arm round her, cupped her breast in his hand and grinned. "Been wanting to do that for a long time."

"Gerry, for God's sake!" She removed his hand.

The four people on the next table had been watching. The two men in the group were oilmen from Texas, in Orlando with their wives for a convention. In typical Texas fashion they wore string ties, jeans and cowboy boots. Even sitting down it was obvious that they were big men, but one of them was huge. He uncoiled his huge frame and got to his feet. "Sir, if you don't treat this little lady with a bit more respect, I'm gonna have to take you outside and teach you some manners."

Kiplock's response was to tell him to go to hell.

The big Texan shook his head in disgust. "Never could stand a man who couldn't hold his drink. Ma'am, I'll be happy to help you get him to his room. He sure don't look like he can make it under his own steam."

Angela thanked him and assured him she would manage.

The coat-check girl was equally concerned. Angela told her what she had told the waitress, that he was her husband's partner, etc.

Between the restaurant and the lifts in the lobby of the hotel, several concerned onlookers offered to help. Angela told them word for word what she had told the waitress and the coat-check girl.

When she finally got him to the lifts, she propped him against the wall and pushed the call-button to summon one. "What's your room number, Gerry?"

"Shit, I don't know," he mumbled. "Key's in my pants pocket." Angela put her hand in his right-hand trouser pocket and found the key.

"Watch what you're doing down there," he mumbled, grinning innately.

Angela ignored him. The fob attached to the key told her it was room 509. When a lift arrived, she manhandled him into it and pressed five

At the fifth floor, she found to her relief that his room was only four doors from the lift. She held him against the wall while she opened the door. She got him into the room and across to a king-size bed, where she let go of him and he collapsed in a heap. He was snoring almost immediately.

Her chest heaving from her exertions, Angela stood there trying to decide whether she should take his jacket and his shoes off. She decided against it, in case she woke him up. For what she had in mind, she needed him to be a lot less drunk

She found the remote for the TV, and took off her coat and shoes and settled down on the bed to wait for him to wake up. She turned the volume on the TV down low, so she could hear it but it wasn't likely to wake him.

It was just after 1.30am and Angela was watching the old black and white movie Casablanca with Humphrey Bogart and Ingrid Bergman on the TV. Bogart had just asked the pianist to Play it again, Sam, when a voice in the darkness growled, "If it's an apartment in the best part of town you want, now's the time to start earning it."

He sounded wide-awake, and Angela had the uneasy feeling he had been laying there watching her.

He sat up and switched on a bedside lamp.

Angela clicked the on/off switch on the remote to switch the TV off. "All right, Gerry," she said. "But I need to use the bathroom first."

He lurched over and grabbed her breasts. She made no effort to remove his hands, even though he was hurting her. "Take your clothes off." His voice was thick.

"Don't be ridiculous, Gerry. If I need to use the bathroom, I need to use the bathroom."

He let go of her. "All right, but be quick about it. And don't try to leave."

"Why would I try to leave when I've been sitting here waiting for you to wake up?" She had left her clutch bag on the nightstand beside her. She picked it up, rolled off the bed and headed for the bathroom, where she switched on the light and locked the door.

Kiplock yelled, "Don't lock the door."

"Shut up, you stupid man," she muttered.

In her clutch bag was a slim plastic container of about three inches' diameter. In it was a diaphragm. She took out the diaphragm, lifted her dress, fitted the diaphragm, and pulled her dress down again. Her dress had become badly creased after lying on the bed for four and a half hours, and she tried, unsuccessfully, to smooth out the creases. She took a quick look in the mirror, unlocked the door, switched off the bathroom light, and walked back into the bedroom.

She almost burst out laughing, because Kiplock was standing in the middle of the bedroom naked, not to mention fully erect, and he was trying to take a condom out of its foil package. He was clearly still very drunk because he was making a complete hash of it. And when she saw the size of the protuberance between his legs, she realised it was not only his millions that Maureen was interested in.

She took the foil package from him. "I think we can dispense with that," she said, tossing it in the waste paper basket. "I didn't come all this way to have one of those get in the way."

A thoughtful look crossed Kiplock's face. "It seems I might have underestimated Bill. He evidently knew what he was doing when he married you."

Angela said, "Gerry, can we please stop talking about Bill. It's you I came to see." She pressed herself against him.

Kiplock threw his arms around her and tried to undo the zipper on her dress.

She let him fumble with it for a moment or two, and then she backed away from him and looked him in the eye. "Are you going to take all night?"

"The zipper's stuck."

"The zipper is not stuck, Gerry. There's a little hook you have to undo first."

He tried to find the hook.

She backed away from him again. "For God's sake, Gerry" she tut-tutted. "Are you going to take all night?"

"I can't find the hook."

"Then rip my dress off."

This time it was he who backed away; suspicion written all over his face. "What are you up to, Angela? I know an expensive dress when I see one."

"Gerry, haven't you figured out yet that it's the rough stuff I like? Just stop talking, and rip it off."

"Anything to oblige a lady," Kiplock said. He grabbed the front of Angela's dress and ripped it off. It fell in a heap on the floor. "Now what?" he said. "You seem to be in charge here."

"I'll tell you what, Gerry, Bill isn't half as slow on the uptake as you are."

Kiplock's eyes narrowed. "If it's rough stuff you like, lady, it's rough stuff you shall have." He ripped off her bra and threw her on the bed. He ripped off her panties and climbed on to the bed. He forced his knee between her legs.

As he prepared to enter her, Angela looked deep into his eyes. "You're not going to disappoint me, Gerry, are you?"

Chapter 26

Angela bit back a scream. She dug her heels in his back, and gasped, "Is that the best you can do?"

With his brain befuddled by alcohol, Kiplock associated Angela with Bill and the grief Bill had caused him. And fuelled also by Angela's goading, not to mention good old-fashioned lust, he set about her with a vengeance.

He violated Angela in every way it is possible for a man to violate a woman. There was nothing he didn't do to her, and Angela just lay there and took it. She submitted to everything he did to her, which only served to further infuriate him.

The onslaught, which had begun a few minutes shy of 1.30am ended when he lost interest in her, and rolled off her and fell asleep at 3.15am. Angela knew exactly what time it had begun and what time it had ended, because to try and take her mind off what he was doing to her, she had focused on the illuminated dial of the radio alarm clock on the nightstand. She had watched the minutes tick by, minute after minute after minute. At times, it had seemed like the onslaught would never end.

She waited until she was certain he was asleep, and then climbed off the bed, wincing as she got to her feet. She was in a lot of pain.

By the light from the bedside lamp Kiplock had switched on earlier, she made her way to the bathroom. She didn't close the door, because when she had used the bathroom earlier, she had noticed that when she switched on the light it had started a rather noisy extractor fan, and she didn't want to disturb him. Working by the glimmer of light reaching the bathroom from the bedside lamp, she removed the diaphragm, rinsed it under the tap, and put it back in its container. She limped back into the bedroom and put on her dress. It was torn from the breastbone almost to the hemline. She stuffed her underwear into her clutch bag, stepped into her shoes, and put on her coat. Holding her coat together at the front, she let herself out of the room, making as little noise as possible.

She limped along the deserted landing, and pressed the button to call a lift. She felt faint and leaned against a wall for support while she waited for a lift to come. As the lift descended, she looked down through the glass. Apart from a young lady in a red jacket on duty at the reception desk, the lobby was deserted.

The young lady at the reception desk saw and heard a lift coming down, and she was pleased at the thought that she might have someone to talk to, if only briefly. The graveyard shift, as it was referred to, was the loneliest of all the shifts. The lift door opened and her smile turned to a look of horror when Angela hobbled out and limped across the lobby towards her, in obvious pain and with her open coat revealing a naked breast. The receptionist hurried round the desk to see what she could do to help.

Before collapsing into her arms, Angela pleaded, "Please help me, I've just been raped."

From then on, Angela lost all track of time. She was aware of being lifted onto a stretcher and being wheeled briefly out into the cool night air; of riding in the back of an ambulance with its sirens wailing and its red lights flashing; of being briefly out in the night air again; of being wheeled down a corridor with people walking alongside asking rapid and urgent questions, none of which she was in a fit state to answer; and of being wheeled into a room with blindingly bright lights.

When she was finally able to understand what was going on, her feet were in some kind of stirrups and she could feel gentle probing hands as the medical team examined her. When she winced, she heard a murmured, "Sorry, but we need to know where you're hurting."

A man's deep and kindly voice said, "This is one of the worst cases of rape I've ever seen. Whoever did this to her should be locked up for the rest of his life."

When the medical team had finished examining her, Angela was wheeled down a corridor and into a small private ward.

A nurse walked in with a glass of water and a pill. "This will help you sleep," she said.

"Has he done much damage?" Angela asked anxiously.

"We think it's mostly severe bruising. You're going to be sore for a while."

When Angela woke up, it was broad daylight. She fumbled on the nightstand for her watch. It wasn't there. In a panic, she yanked on the emergency cord that hung over the head of the bed, and a nurse hurried in.

"What time is it?" Angela asked breathlessly.

The nurse checked the watch pinned upside down on her uniform. "It's ten-fifteen."

"Oh, God! He'll be checking out."

"Are you talking about the man who raped you?"

"Yes. He told me he was booked on a twelve-thirty flight."

"To where?"

263

"To New York. La Guardia, I think he said."

"Well, we'll see about that!" the nurse said. She hurried out. She came back almost immediately with two police officers in uniforms bearing the badge of the Orlando Police Department. One of them, a sergeant judging by the three chevrons on his sleeve, had the look of a man who had seen it all, and still cared.

"These gentlemen have been waiting to talk to you," the nurse said. "Now you're awake, I'll organise you some breakfast." Before leaving, she glanced up at the two policemen. "You take it easy with her, you hear? She's had a rough time."

"Don't worry," the sergeant said. "We will."

They stood at the foot of the bed.

"Don't let him get away, please," Angela implored. "He can't be allowed to get away with what he did to me."

"We don't plan to, ma'am," the sergeant said. "We need to know his name, or, if you don't know his name, which room he was in."

"His name's Gerry Kiplock," Angela said. "I know that because he's my husband's partner."

The two policemen looked at each other.

"And he's in room 509. Or he was last night. Please, hurry. He'll be on his way to the airport."

"Use the phone, ma'am?" the sergeant asked the nurse.

"Right this way," the nurse said. She hurried out of the room with the policeman hot on her heels.

The officer who stayed was a tall, broad-shouldered man who looked to be in his late thirties. He had a careworn face and prematurely grey hair, which probably made him look older than he actually was.

"How can a man do this to his partner's wife?" Angela said.

The policeman shook his head. "Beats me, ma'am. Does your husband know?"

"No, and he mustn't know. I don't want anyone to know."

"Any reason for that?"

"There's a very good reason. My husband would kill him if he knew."

"Is your husband here, in Orlando?"

"No, he's back home in England. We'd been having problems with the business and I needed to get away for a break. He didn't come with me."

"Do you plan to press charges?"

"After what he did to me? I most certainly do."

The sergeant stepped back into the room. "Let's go," he told his colleague. He looked down at Angela. "You leave this guy to us, ma'am. We'll take real good care of him."

Angela heard their heavy footsteps marching purposefully down the corridor.

A nurse brought her some breakfast, together with a pill and a glass of water. She asked Angela if there was any chance she had been pregnant before she was raped.

Angela shook her head. "No, I wasn't pregnant. Why do you ask?"

The nurse handed her the pill. "Since he obviously didn't wear a condom, you'd better take this."

"What is it?"

"It's a morning-after pill."

Angela had never heard of a morning after pill. It certainly wasn't available in England. She asked the nurse if it was safe.

"It's perfectly safe," the nurse assured her. "We've been prescribing it since 1977."

Angela took the pill and popped it in her mouth, washing it down with water from the glass the nurse handed her. She ate her breakfast and spent most of the rest of the day sleeping.

That evening, she was sitting up in bed watching a chat show on TV when there was a knock on the door.

"Come in," she called.

Oscar Blackman put his head round the door. "Mind if I come in?"

Angela was not at all surprised to see him. Knowing how Gerry Kiplock relied on his in-house attorney, she had been expecting him. "Not at all, Oscar. Come in.

Blackman walked in and stood by the bed. "How are you feeling?"

"Sore, if you must know. Do you know what he did to me?"

Blackman nodded. "I've talked to the police, and the hospital staff, and I've seen the medical notes."

"Where is he, Oscar?"

"In a police cell, in downtown Orlando."

"Good!" Angela exclaimed. "That's just where he belongs."

"He's claiming you led him on, Angela."

"He would, wouldn't he?"

Blackman walked to the window and looked out. Speaking with his back to her, he said, "Angela, why did you come to Orlando?"

Angela could see the reflection of his eyes in the window. "I came to ask Gerry not to put Bill out of business. I came because I didn't think I'd get anywhere with him by phoning him. Someone had to talk to him, Oscar. Bill could be forced into bankruptcy by what

266

Gerry's insisting on, which could mean us losing our home, having to take the children out of their private school, and losing everything we've worked for. I couldn't let that happen without coming over and trying to make Gerry see sense. Bill wasn't getting anywhere."

"But why Florida, Angela? Wouldn't it have been simpler, and more business-like, to fly to New York and meet Gerry in the office?'

"Oscar, if I'd gone to New York and talked to Gerry in the office, it would have got back to Bill. And what do you think Bill would have said if he'd known?"

"He wouldn't have let you come if he'd known beforehand. And he would have hit the roof if he'd known while you were still here."

"That's putting it mildly. The police asked me if there was someone they could call, my husband, for example. I told them I didn't want anyone to know, least of all my husband, because if he found out, he hates Gerry so much he would probably kill him. So I had to come on the quiet."

"What did you say to Bill, to persuade him to let you go away?"

"I told him the stress was getting to me, and I needed to get away for a while. I asked him not to ask me where I was going. He has no idea where I am. And he mustn't know. Promise me you won't tell him, Oscar."

Blackman turned to face her. He leaned with his back against the windowsill and folded his arms across his chest. "Gerry said you told him you were leaving Bill."

"Oscar, do I sound to you as if I'm thinking of leaving Bill? Nothing is further from my mind. I love Bill. I always have, and I always will.

Blackman sighed. "Do you mind talking about what happened?"

"I don't mind talking to you about it. I'd probably mind talking to anybody else, aside from hospital staff, or the police, of course."

"Thank you for that. He said you told him to tear your dress off."

Angela's eyes filled with tears. "He was drunk, Oscar. We had dinner and I took him to his room to let him sleep it off. I almost had to carry him from the restaurant."

"So I've heard. There seems to be no shortage of witnesses. Do you plan to press charges?"

"I most certainly do. What he did to me was unspeakable." A tear rolled down her cheek. She brushed it angrily away.

Blackman sighed. "I know, Angela. I know." He got to his feet. "I have to go. I haven't seen Gerry yet. I've only spoken to him on the phone, and I came straight here from the airport. Okay if I drop in again in the morning?"

"Yes, of course it is."

The next morning, Blackman arrived as Angela's breakfast dishes were being cleared away. He put his head round the door. "Am I too early?"

"No, you're not too early," Angela said. "Come in. Oscar, you look terrible. You look as if you haven't slept."

"I haven't." He stifled a yawn. "I've been up all night. I've never seen Gerry so angry." He walked to the window and back. "He's saying you set him up, Angela."

"To be honest with you, Oscar, I don't much care what Gerry says. All I care about is what he did to me."

Blackman sat in the only chair in the room. He sat forward in the chair with his elbows on his knees and spoke earnestly. "Angela, if you press charges, he will be finished. I probably shouldn't tell you this, in fact I know I shouldn't, but I'm appealing to the woman I think I know you to be. Gerry was accused of rape eight years ago, but he got away with it because the woman didn't press charges. With all the evidence against him, if you press charges, there's no way on God's earth he'll get away with it. Do you have any idea what kind of prison term they hand to rapists in this country?"

"What do you want, Oscar? Sympathy? Considering what he did to me, don't you think I'm the one who should be getting the sympathy?"

"And his wife won't take it this time either. She's taken a lot from Gerry over the years, but she won't take this. She'll divorce him, and take him to the cleaners financially. And when the industry learns he raped his partner's wife, it will turn its back on him. He'll be finished. Gone. Kaput. Do you really want that, Angela?"

"He should have thought of all that before he did what he did to me, Oscar."

Blackman got to his feet and paced the room. He walked to the window and stared out, not seeing anything. "Is there any way you'll let him off the hook, Angela?"

"Such as?"

There was a pause. "He's a very wealthy man."

"You bastard!" There was a tumbler of water on her nightstand and Angela picked it up and hurled it at him. It missed him and smashed against the wall. Pieces of glass flew everywhere, and water ran down the wall.

"Angela, I'm sorry. Gerry just thought …"

Angela looked round for something else to throw.

"Angela, be reasonable," Blackman cried.

Hearing the commotion, a nurse hurried in. She took one look at Angela, halfway out of bed with a demented look on her face, and turned on the lawyer. "I don't know what's going on in here, but I think you'd better leave." She helped Angela back into bed.

Blackman walked to the door. "Don't close the door on him, Angela. Please. I beg you."

"Get out," Angela screamed.

Blackman returned early that evening with a huge bunch of yellow roses. He put his head round the door and waggled them at her. "Peace offering."

He had such a comical look on his face that Angela burst out laughing. "You idiot."

"Can I come in?"

"Of course you can."

He handed her the roses.

"Oscar, that's really sweet of you. Thank you. They're lovely." Angela put the flowers to her face and sniffed them.

"They're from Gerry."

Angela's face changed. She drew her arm back, preparing to throw the flowers at him.

"Angela, please."

She took pity on him and laid the roses on the nightstand.

"He just wants to say he's sorry."

"And a handful of flowers will make up for what he did to me, will it? Can you possibly imagine how what he did is likely to affect me in the future? I could be carrying the scars, mentally, and physically, for the rest of my life. Do you have any idea what it means to a woman, to be raped, Oscar?"

Blackman sat down in the chair by the bed and shook his head. "I couldn't possibly imagine. Being a man, how could I? Look, Angela, Gerry can't undo what he did to you. The only way he can make restitution, and please, don't throw anything at me ... the only way is financially."

Angela sighed. "Everything comes down to money with Gerry, doesn't it, Oscar?"

"Angela, let me finish. Gerry's prepared to send Bill a cheque for the commission on the business Patrick's done, and the commission on Bill's Finnish business that he diverted into one of his own accounts. That would amount to $300,000, give or take."

"But Gerry owes him that money."

"You didn't let me finish. He's also prepared to give you, personally, $500,000 if you'll drop the charges and sign an agreement that you will never, ever, tell a soul, beyond who knows already, what happened."

"Is that it?"

"That's it."

"After what he's put Bill through, and what he's done to me?"

"Isn't it enough?"

"It isn't anywhere near enough. He can rot in hell as far as I'm concerned!" Angela picked up the roses and flung them in the direction of the open door. "And he can take his flowers with him."

Chapter 27

The hospital told Angela they would be discharging her the next day, which left her with a problem. The police had taken her clothes and her shoes, and apart from the hospital gown she was wearing and her lightweight summer coat, she had no clothes available. She needed somebody to collect some clothes from the hotel for her. The question was, who?

The only person she could think of was the young lady who had been on duty at the Grand Cypress, whom, at the insistence of the hotel's general manager, who had been raised from his bed, had accompanied her to the hospital in the ambulance. In the ambulance, she had introduced herself as Mary Lou and she had told Angela she was born and raised in Charleston, South Carolina, and had been working at the hotel for just over a year. She had seemed like a caring and trustworthy person, and Angela asked a nurse to get her the number of the hotel.

The nurse got her the number, and brought a phone on a trolley so Angela could make the call from her room.

The operator at the Grand Cypress informed Angela that Mary Lou was off duty, and she asked her if someone else could help. Angela said not really, and when she told the operator who she was and why she was calling, the operator asked her to please hold. When she came back on the line a couple of minutes later, she apologised profusely for keeping Angela waiting, and gave her Mary Lou's home number.

Angela dialled Mary Lou's number, and got a busy signal. She tried again five minutes later, and this time Mary Lou answered.

"Well hi," she said, in her warm southern accent. "How are y'all feeling?"

"I'm sore, but I'll live," Angela replied.

"I think I know why y'all are calling."

"You do?" Angela said.

"Y'all are calling to ask me to pick up clothes for y'all."

"Are you psychic?"

Mary Lou laughed. "I just got a call from my boss. He said y'all had just phoned, and I'd be real happy to pick up some clothes for y'all."

"That's brilliant, Mary Lou. Thank you very much."

"You're welcome. Say, Angela, do you have any plans for when you get out of hospital?"

"I can't say I'd given it much thought," Angela said. "Did you have something in mind?"

"Sure do. The general manager thought I should spend some time with you, and I thought ..."

"What's the general manager got to do with anything?" Angela said. "Why is he involved?"

There was a pause, then Mary Lou said, "I haven't told y'all this, you understand, but the hotel are afraid y'all are going to sue them."

The thought had never crossed Angela's mind. The hotel was not responsible for what happened, she was. "Why would I want to sue them?" she said.

"Because it happened in the hotel," Mary Lou said. "And most people would sue if that had happened to them in the hotel."

"Well I'm not most people," Angela said. "I wouldn't dream of it."

"Okay with y'all if I tell the general manager? He probably hasn't slept since it happened. They take this kind of thing real seriously."

"Yes, by all mean tell him."

"He'll be real happy about that," Mary Lou said. "So where are y'all staying, and what's y'all's room number?"

The following morning, Saturday, Angela was sitting in her room in her hospital gown when Oscar Blackman walked in. He looked like he hadn't slept for a week, and his suit was in dire need of pressing.

"Oscar, for God's sake, what are you doing to yourself? You look awful."

"So would you if you'd been through what I've been through," the lawyer said. "You gotta help me out here, Angela, because Gerry's threatening to fire my ass."

Angela bridled. "Oh, is he, now? Well, you can go right back to your precious boss, and you can tell him ..."

"Angela, please." The lawyer looked close to desperation. "One of you has to cut me some slack." He looked so weary that Angela got up, wincing, and offered him her chair. She sat on the edge of the bed.

The lawyer eased himself into the chair. "Thank you," he said, gratefully. "Tell you what, Angela, I wish Gerry was half as civilised as you are. He's behaving like a madman. I'm going to sleep for a week when I get back to New York."

"So what's the latest offer?"

274

"A million dollars, payable to you personally, and payable into an account of your choice, anywhere in the world."

"And the money he owes Bill?"

"He pays him what owes him."

"And what happens when the dust has settled, Oscar? There's no way Bill would work with Gerry after the way he's been treated. And, quite frankly, I wouldn't want him to."

"Not a problem," the lawyer said. "Gerry wants the partnership winding up. And by the way, his offer is contingent on agreement being reached by 5:00 p.m. today. Otherwise, the message is that he'll take his chances with a judge and jury."

"That's nonsense, and you know it," Angela said. "All right, Oscar, give me a minute to think about it."

It was crunch time and Angela knew she had to make a decision. She limped to the window. Her room was on the third floor overlooking the hospital car park and she watched ambulances leaving and arriving and cars coming and going for a while. Finally, she turned to face him. "What about the money he paid Bill for his shares?"

"Bill doesn't have to pay it back."

"And since Bill put into the company the same amount of money Gerry put in when Patrick started, I don't see why Bill should pay Gerry's money back.

Sensing he was finally getting somewhere, Blackman felt his energy returning. "Take it he doesn't have to pay that back, either. So what do you think, Angela? Do we have a deal?"

"Hold your horses, Oscar, I'm still thinking about it. So what we're taking about is winding back the clock and Bill reverting to where he was before you guys came on the scene. Right?"

"Except that you and Bill would be a whole lot better off financially than you were before. Not to mention you get to keep your business, you get to keep your house, and you get to keep your kids in private school."

"All of which I'm aware of, Oscar, but that about the Finnish business Gerry took from under Bill's nose. I want Bill to have that back."

"Gerry won't like that," the lawyer said.

"Then he'll have to lump it, won't he. And Bill must be allowed to operate freely in any market he chooses, without hindrance from Gerry."

"With the exception of the US," the lawyer said. "Gerry won't agree to Bill competing with him on his own his home turf."

Angela knew that Bill had no interest in getting into the US market. He had always said it was too far away. His main focus had always been the UK, and Europe. "Agreed," she said. "There are two more things, Oscar."

The lawyer sighed. "All right, Angela. Go on."

"I want it all in writing."

The lawyer brightened. "No problem. As a lawyer, I wouldn't have it any other way. You said there were two things. What was the second thing?"

"The second thing is that I want you to take down a letter, addressed to Bill and marked private and confidential and signed by Gerry, as if it had been written by him."

"Which I imagine you'll want typed on Kiplock stationery," the lawyer said.

"No flies on you, I see, Oscar."

The lawyer smiled at the compliment. "Consider it done."

"And I want it to reach Bill's office by courier by 9:00 a.m. on the morning of Wednesday of next week."

"I'll see to it personally," the lawyer said.

"Let me make one thing clear, Oscar; Bill must never, ever, learn what happened. If he ever found out what Gerry did to me …"

"Have no fear, Angela, this will be buried here and now. There would be no mileage in anyone knowing about it, let alone Bill."

"All right, Oscar, thank you for that. With respect to the million dollars…"

"Yes?"

"Will it be paid by cheque?"

"Sure, if you want it paid by check. You can have it any way you like."

"Would it be possible to let me have a cheque tomorrow morning?"

"I don't see why not."

"Then I'd like a cheque, made payable to me personally, delivered to my room at the Hilton Hotel at Lake Buena Vista tomorrow, Sunday, morning at 10:00 a.m. precisely." She gave him her room number.

He made a note of it. "Is that it, Angela?" he asked hopefully. "Are we done negotiating now?

"Yes, we're done, Oscar."

She felt as relieved as he looked.

He actually looked like he wanted to dance a jig. He took a folded document from the inside pocket of the jacket, and explained to Angela that it was a statement confirming everything they had agreed, the detail of which he would now fill in. He also explained that it was an undertaking on her part never to discuss with any third party what had happened, or seek to raise the charges against his boss again at any time in the future.

"I take it you have no objection to signing such a document," he said.

"None whatsoever," Angela said.

Blackman entered the details on the document and had Angela initial each and every one item. He then had her sign the document. He then repeated the procedure himself, following which he excused himself and took the document to the hospital's administration department to get it photocopied. He came back and handed a copy to Angela.

"Now," he said, sitting down again, "about this letter you want Gerry to sign."

Angela had expected to get everything she wanted, and had not planned to leave Florida until she did, and she had made some notes. She referred to these as she dictated the letter.

Blackman had suspected from day one that Angela had engineered the whole thing, and he now realised he had been right. He gave her a wry smile.

She knew that he knew. She spread her hands in a gesture conveying but what's a girl to do? And he chuckled.

He wrote down, word for word, everything Angela dictated to him. When she had finished, he read it all back to her. Then, to be on the safe side, he had her read it aloud to him. He had just finished reading it, when Mary Lou walked in carrying a small suitcase.

"Oh, sorry," she said, "I didn't know y'all were busy."

"Give me a few minutes, Mary Lou," Angela said. "We're almost done."

Mary Lou said she would wait in the visitor's room at the end of the corridor.

"Who was that?" Blackman asked, frowning.

"Don't get your knickers in a twist, Oscar. She's just the receptionist from the Grand Cypress. She's brought me some clothes."

Angela read the letter, and handed it to him. "That looks fine. Don't forget, Oscar, 9:00 a.m. next Wednesday morning."

"Trust me, Angela, I won't forget." Blackman got to his feet and extended his hand. "A pleasure doing business with you."

"For me, too," Angela said.

They shook hands.

"You gave him quite a scare."

"Serves him right," Angela said. "One last question, Oscar; whose side have you been on through all this?"

A ghost of a smile appeared on the lawyer's lips. "Whose side do you think I've been on?"

Angela nodded. "I thought as much." There was a manila envelope on the nightstand and she picked it up. "Then you'd better have this." She handed it to him.

He looked at it, puzzled. "What is it?"

"It's my hospital bill. You can pay it on your way out."

Chapter 28

After Oscar Blackman had left, Angela limped down the corridor to find Mary Lou. She found her speaking sympathetically to a young couple with a little girl whose head was swathed in bandages. They walked slowly back to her room, where she changed into the clothes Mary Lou had brought for her. Before leaving the hospital, Angela made a point of thanking individually the members of staff who had looked after her, and before she left the building, she checked that her bill had been paid. It had.

Out in the hospital car park in the scorching heat, Mary Lou led the way to a battered old Chevrolet Bel Air that banged and smoked when she started it. "Where to?" she asked, putting the car in gear.

"Just my hotel, if you don't mind," Angela said. "I have things to do today. But if you're free tomorrow, perhaps we could spend the day together."

"Sure thing," Mary Lou said. "I'm at y'all's disposal."

As they drove through Kissimmee, Mary Lou told Angela that the president of the Japanese company that owned the Grand Cypress was flying over from Tokyo to apologise to her personally. "They're taking it real seriously," she said.

Angela groaned. "I do wish they'd let it drop. None of it was their fault. There's been enough fuss already."

"Too late to do anything about that now," Mary Lou said. "He's arriving later today."

When she had booked her ticket out, Angela had no real idea of how long she would have to stay in Florida and she had left her return ticket open. There was a travel agent in the lobby of the Hilton and when Mary Lou dropped her off at the hotel, she made a beeline for it.

Her plan was to get to Welwyn Garden City on the morning Bill got his letter, because she knew there were going to be repercussions and she wanted to get them out of the way as quickly as possible so they could get on with their lives. There was a seat available on a flight leaving late evening on Tuesday next and getting into Gatwick at 7.15am on the Wednesday morning, and this should work perfectly. The letter wouldn't be delivered to Bill's office until 9am on the Wednesday, which meant he could pick her up at Gatwick, drive her home, and he would get the letter when he got to the office. She was on the point of telling the travel agent to book the seat for her, when the thought occurred to her that at 10am tomorrow she would become a dollar millionaire, and that there was absolutely no reason why she had to suffer the indignity and discomfort she had suffered on the way out, when she could now easily afford to travel first class. Bill would never know. The travel agent confirmed that there was a seat in first class available, and Angela had her book it for her, putting the additional cost on her credit card.

When she went to the reception desk to get the key to her room, the receptionist who had been on duty the night she had met Gerry Kiplock was on duty, and keeping her voice low because people were checking in and checking out beside them, she said, "A woman by the name of Mary Lou dropped in yesterday asking for the key to your room. She said you were indisposed and had asked her to pick up some clothes for you. I'm guessing you're the lady who was attacked, and you've just got out of hospital."

The cat seemed to be out of the bag, and Angela saw no point in denying it. She nodded and said quietly, "For my sins, yes I am."

The receptionist shook her head in dismay. "You come all this way, just to get attacked. That's not supposed to happen in Florida. This is supposed to be a happy, fun place. Is there anything I, or the hotel, can do to help?"

"I can't think of anything," Angela said. "But it's kind of you to offer. Oh by the way, I'm booked on a flight back to England on Tuesday evening, so I'll need to check out that day. What time is check-out time?"

"Normally, it's 11am, but in your case we'll make an exception. Keep the room until you need to leave for the airport, and we'll have a limo take you, at our expense, of course. We can't have you leaving the country harbouring bad thoughts about Florida.

When Angela got to her room, she ordered a Caesar salad and a bottle of sparkling mineral water for lunch from room service. After she had eaten, she put a call through to Bill.

"I was wondering when I might hear from you," he said. "Are you feeling less stressed?"

He sounded as if he had been drinking.

"I'm feeling absolutely fine," Angela said. "I'm feeling much less stressed. And how are you, Bill? You sound tired."

"Which is hardly surprising since Gerry's about to pull the plug on me."

"Has nothing come up?"

"Not a thing, and I've tried everything."

"I'm so sorry, Bill."

"Yeah well, as they say, shit happens."

"I'm missing you."

"I'm missing you too, darling. When are you coming home?"

"I'll be home Wednesday morning. My flight gets into Gatwick at 7:15 a.m. If it's too early for you, I can take a taxi."

"I'll pick you up. No sense spending that kind of money on a taxi."

"How are the children, Bill? Are they having a good time at my mother's?"

"They seem to be," Bill said. "Your parents seem to be taking them everywhere. They went to Dartmouth yesterday, and Plymouth the day before. I've spoken to them every couple of days."

"Good, I'm glad you have. Give them my love, Bill. And tell them I miss them and I look forward to seeing them next week."

"I will."

"How are things at the office?"

"Pretty much the same as they were when you left. Maureen's still behaving as if she owns the place, and Trevor's behaving like the idiot that he is."

"And Patrick?"

"Patrick's fine. He's been my rock while you've been away. He's travelling most of the time, but he phones in at least twice a day, mostly to check that I'm all right."

"I must remember to thank him for looking after you." Angela paused. "Bill, if there's nothing else, I should probably hang up because this call must be costing a small fortune. I love you, Bill."

"And I love you, too, sweetheart."

The next morning, Sunday, at precisely one minute to 10am there was a knock on the door of Angela's room. She had been sitting waiting for this, and her pulse quickened. She got up and limped to the door. Through the spy-hole she saw a man in a brown uniform. To be on the safe side, she called, "Who is it?"

"DHL. I have a parcel for Mrs Angela Smith."

"Give me a minute," Angela called. She got two one-dollar bills from her purse and limped back and opened the door. "Good morning, I'm Angela Smith."

"Good morning, ma'am." The courier handed her a small, slim package and asked her to sign for it.

Angela signed for it, and handed him his tip. "Thank you," she said. "Thank you very much."

"You're welcome, ma'am." The courier touched his cap. "Have a good day."

"You too," Angela said, and closed the door.

By now, her heart was racing, and she limped across the room to a chair at a table by the window and sat down. Her hands shaking, she tore off the strip that sealed the package and took out a white envelope. Her name was written on the front of the envelope in a stylish script she recognised as Oscar Blackman's.

Angela had never seen a cheque for a million dollars before, and she had lain awake in the night visualising this moment. But instead of a seven-figure sum, she found a six-figure sum - $996,750. She felt angry and cheated, but on reflection she thought there must be some explanation for this and in the envelope she found a folded note. It was handwritten, and it read, 'Angela, I never agreed to pay your hospital bill. Have a safe trip home, Gerry.'

Angela saw the funny side and laughed until she cried. She locked the cheque in the room's safe, together with her passport, and her air ticket.

A weather forecast on TV had said it was going to be another scorcher, with temperatures reaching the mid to upper 90s, and she had taken the decision to wear shorts and flat-heeled shoes for her visit to Winter Park with Mary Lou. With her hair combed back and tied at the back in a black velvet bow, as she had worn it to meet Gerry Kiplock, and her sunglasses nestled in the hair on the top of her head, casual she might be, but she was nonetheless elegant. A female friend had once told her she would look elegant in a bin bag.

She was still sore, but her limping was less pronounced. She was hoping her soreness would have gone by the time she got home, because she didn't want to have to explain to Bill why she was limping. She hated lying to him.

She got her things together and went down to the lobby to wait for Mary Lou.

From the hotel, Mary Lou turned right on to Hotel Boulevard, then right on Apopke-Vineland. A couple of minutes later, they were heading up the on-ramp on to Interstate Highway 4. I4, as it was known. Traffic was heavy in both directions, and many of the cars had rental car stickers on their bumpers.

Twenty minutes later, they were driving past a handful of smallish high rises that constituted downtown Orlando. At the next exit, they left I4 and followed the signs to Winter Park.

Within a mile or so of leaving the interstate highway, they came upon a scene that could have been plucked straight from the movie *Gone With The Wind*: towering oaks and hornbeams, with the obligatory Spanish moss; magnificent two-storey plantation-style mansions with flagpoles flying the stars and stripes, although these hung limply today on account of the heat and humidity. Where horse-drawn landaus would have been the order of the day in the era of *Gone With The Wind*, gleaming Rolls Royce, Bentley, Cadillac, Jaguar, Mercedes and BMW cars now stood in their driveways.

A speed limit of 20mph was posted at the town line, and Mary Lou observed it to the letter, explaining to Angela, "Judges and magistrates live here, and the cops are real hard on people breaking the speed limit."

They drove into town and Mary Lou parked in the car park behind Jacobsen's Department store. A sign on the store proclaimed, 'Purveyors of Ladies' and Children's Fine Clothing'. Her battered old Chevrolet looked about as much at home among the late model luxury vehicles as a naked man at a garden party.

Mary Lou had told Angela that Winter Park was the nearest thing Florida had to old world England, and as she limped along Park Avenue, the main thoroughfare, Angela could see what Mary Lou had been talking about.

Off Park Avenue were narrow wisteria-clad alleyways with musty old book shops, purveyors of rare coins, purveyors of rare stamps and other collectibles, antique shops, curiosity shops, boutiques, and elegant little tea shops and coffee shops. One delightful little shop was offering what they claimed to be Genuine English Cream Teas, and had it been mid-afternoon rather than lunchtime, Angela would have been tempted to give it a try.

Many of the shop fronts had been designed to look Dickensian, with small-pained bottle-glass windows, and had it not been for the heat and the American accents, Angela would have been halfway towards believing she was walking through a genuinely Dickensian part of London, if there was such a thing now. She marvelled at how they had managed to create such an atmosphere right here in the heart of central Florida.

Angela had never had money of her own; she had always to rely on Bill for it. When he asked her to be director and company secretary of his company, she had suggested he put her on a salary, but he had put her off, saying he would give her money when she needed it. Admittedly they enjoyed a good lifestyle, but she had always had to watch the pennies. She had never in her entire life been in a position to buy something just for her, but now she was. The problem was, if she did buy something, she would have to explain to Bill why she had bought it when he had asked her to be careful how much she spent, so she ended up buying herself nothing.

For the same reason, she couldn't buy anything of significance for Bill, or for the children. But she wanted to buy them something, and she ended up buying Jason, who was interested in stamp collecting, a book on American stamps and two packets of stamps; Melanie, a pair of moccasins made by American Indians; and Bill, a bottle of bourbon produced, so the label said, by an old-established family distillery in Kentucky.

Frustrated because she had not been able to spend much, and because she was hungry, Angela told Mary Lou she was taking her to lunch. "And I'm taking you to the best place in town," she said. "So where is it?"

"That would be the Garden Restaurant," Mary-Lou said. "But you have to book a month in advance to get a table."

"Who says you do?" Angela said. "Where is it?"

"It's just up the street," Mary Lou said.

The entrance to the restaurant was uninspiring to say the least. To get to it, they had to walk through a dark and unprepossessing bar in which two drunks were propping each other up. But when they got through the bar and into the restaurant, it was another story altogether.

A string quartet in full evening dress played the music of Ivor Novello in a room that looked to have been created from the space between two buildings. The walls were white-painted brick, the floor was stone, and a striped awning formed the roof. It actually gave the impression of walking into a marquee. The tables and chairs were white wrought iron, and there was a lighted candle on each table.

What with the Dickensian atmosphere in the alleyways, and this, it was like stepping back in time, and Angela was loving it.

There were nine tables in the room, and eight of them were occupied by chic and obviously well-heeled people.

Angela nodded towards the empty table and whispered to Mary Lou, "we'll have that one. Watch and learn."

Mary Lou giggled.

A maître d' was in attendance and he, like the string quartet, was in evening dress. He wore the expression of someone living with a perpetual bad smell under his nose. He stepped forward. "Can I help you?" he said snootily.

Angela had met people like him before and, for just such occasions, she had perfected a superior upper class British accent, and she laid it on thick.

"I say, my good man, your restaurant is famous far and wide, and I couldn't possibly go back to jolly old England without eating here. My friend and I are remiss in not having booked a table, but I wonder if we might have the spare table in the corner."

Convinced he was in the presence of English aristocracy, the maître d' picked up two menus. "If you'd like to follow me."

"Sure wish I could talk like you," Mary-Lou whispered.

As they ate, Mary-Lou discreetly pointed out several famous people, and a couple of local TV personalities.

Angela sipped her glass of crisp dry Californian chardonnay and looked around her. "You know something, Mary Lou," she said. "I could get used to this. I could get used to this very easily indeed."

Chapter 29

The meeting at the Grand Cyprus had been set for 10.30am on the Monday morning, and at 10.15am a stretch Lincoln limousine arrived at the Hilton to collect her.

In a simple white cotton dress and low heels, today Angela was every sensible mother's idea of the girl she would like her son to bring home. A far cry from the woman who had walked into the hotel five days ago, hell bent on getting justice, no matter what the cost.

The general manager, Ishiri Ishido, greeted her in the lobby with a bow. "Mrs Smith, I'm so pleased to be finally able to meet you and to apologise personally for what happened."

"Please," Angela said, "it wasn't your fault. And please call me Angela."

He bowed again. "If I may, I'll call you Angela-san?"

"Of course you may. And what may I call you?"

"My first name is Ishiri. And you may, if you wish, call me Ishiri-san. May I ask if you are recovering from the … unfortunate incident?"

An interesting choice of words, Angela thought. "Yes, thank you," she said, "I'm feeling very much better. A few more days and I'll be as right as rain."

Being in the Atrium lobby again brought back the memories of the night of the unfortunate incident, and Angela shuddered at the thought of what Gerry Kiplock had done to her. They travelled up to Ishido's ninth floor office in the same lift in which she had helped the drunken Kiplock to his room.

Ishido's office was a large, square, well-appointed room, overlooking: to one elevation, the hotel's two championship courses, and to another, the golf-ball shaped dome of Planet Earth at Walt Disney World's EPCOT Centre.

Standing at one of the windows was a diminutive Japanese gentleman who looked to be in his mid to late seventies. He had a thick head of pure white hair and he was dressed in black tails and grey pinstripe trousers.

Ishido introduced them and Yukohito Yamamoto bowed deeply. He then said something in quiet but rapid Japanese to his general manager.

"Hai!" Ishido barked. He translated. "Angela-san, Yamamoto-san asks me to apologise that he speaks no English, and asks if you would like something to drink. Green tea, perhaps?"

Angela smiled at Yamamoto. "Please tell Yamamoto-san that I don't need a drink, thank you. And please tell him his not speaking English is not a problem, because I don't speak Japanese."

Ishido translated and Yamamoto's eyes twinkled. He bowed slightly and indicated a chair by a coffee table.

Angela sat down and Yamamoto followed suit. Angela noticed that his legs were so short his feet didn't touch the floor. She also noticed that he had tiny feet, like those of a five or six-year old child.

Mary Lou had told Angela over lunch in Winter Park, that Yamamoto was one of the old-school Japanese who had never ventured out of Japan, had never shaken hands, and had never used a knife and fork. She had also told her that when Gerry Kiplock came down from his room to check out, the police were waiting for him and he was arrested and handcuffed. Struggling violently and loudly protesting his innocence, he made such a scene that the police called for reinforcements and he was forcibly restrained and carted off unceremoniously in a police van.

Unfortunately, the scene was witnessed by a large group of golfers who had just flown in from Tokyo and, being Japanese-owned, the hotel was as much concerned about loss of face and damage to their reputation as they were about what had happened to Angela.

So Ishido was in double trouble. He was not invited to sit. He stood ramrod straight, as if on parade.

Yamamoto never once raised his voice, but it was clear to Angela that he was giving his general manager the mother of all dressings down. Ishido stood there bowing and barking 'Hai!' whenever his boss paused, and she knew that getting a dressing down like this in front of her was causing Ishido huge loss of face. His face was the colour of beetroot and there was sheen of perspiration on his top lip and his brow.

When the tirade was finally over, Yamamoto said something in a more moderate tone of voice and nodded towards Angela.

Ishido barked, "Hai!" He turned to Angela. "Angela-san, Yamamoto-san instructs me to tell you that the company apologises for my stupidity in allowing this unfortunate incident to happen."

"But, Ishido-san," Angela protested. "None of this was your fault."

"Please, Angela-san, allow me to continue. Yamamoto-san instructs me to tell you that you and your family are welcome to stay at the hotel, as our guests, for any two weeks convenient to you. And Yamamoto-san wishes to present you with a small token of the hotel's regrets, for this unfortunate incident." Ishido being Japanese, 'regrets' came across as 'leglets'.

He strode across the room and took a white envelope off his desk and handed it to his boss.

Yamamoto got to his feet and stepped across to Angela. Bowing, and using both hands as if he were offering her a piece of priceless jade, he handed her the envelope. Then, in faltering English, he said, "Please to accept this humble token of my leglets." He bowed again, turned, and was gone.

The interview was over. It had lasted less than ten minutes.

Angela wasn't sure if she should open the envelope now, or later, and she looked to Ishido for guidance.

"Please," he said, indicating she should open it now.

Angela opened the envelope to find a cheque for $5,000, made payable to her. Ironically, it would have more than covered her hospital bill. Now she had two cheques to take care of. She needed to open a bank account and she had no idea how or where to begin. Again, she looked to Ishido for guidance.

Ishido recommended the downtown Orlando bank that the hotel banked with and offered to phone his friend whom, he said, was senior vice president.

"That would be brilliant," Angela said. "And since I'm flying home tomorrow evening, perhaps you could ask him if he could see me this afternoon."

Ishido phoned his friend and made Angela an appointment for 2pm. "You'll need to take your passport for ID," he said. He wrote down the name and address of the bank, and the name of his friend, and handed the slip of paper to her.

Ishido saw Angela to the stretch limousine, which was waiting to take her back to the Hilton, and told her that he had been very impressed with the way she had handled herself through what must have been a very traumatic experience for her, and he told her that, if she was ever looking for a job, to let him know.

Angela thought this might have been just a platitude, and she asked him if he was serious.

"I'm very serious," he said. "And so was Yamamoto-san. He was very impressed with you."

Ishiro Ishido's friend, Michael Dowding, or Mike as he introduced himself, greeted Angela warmly and took her to his office overlooking a lake on which there was a preponderance of birdlife, including swans, pelicans, ducks and coots.

"I understand you have a cheque to deposit," he said, sitting her down on the other side of his desk.

"I have two to deposit, actually," Angela said. She took the cheques from her handbag and handed them to him.

Mike glanced at the cheques, before laying them on his desk. If he was surprised by the size of Gerry Kiplock's cheque, he didn't show it. "What kind of account did you have in mind, Angela?"

"Ishiro-san told me you have current accounts, or checking accounts as he called them, which pay interest on the balance."

"We certainly do."

"Well I think one of those would work for me."

The banker opened the top drawer of his desk, took out a form and began completing it. "I see you wear a wedding ring, Angela," he said, looking up. "Is the account to be in your name, or the joint names of you and your husband?"

"It's to be in my name, Mike."

"Which is?"

"Angela Penelope Smith."

The banker smiled. "My god-daughter's called Penelope." He wrote Angela's full name on the form. "I'll need to see some ID, Angela. Did you happen to bring your passport with you?"

Angela handed him her passport.

He opened it up and checked the details, and then glanced at her, and then her photograph. "I'll need to get this photocopied," he said. He called his secretary in and asked her to photocopy the passport. Then he got back to completing the form.

"What's your home address, Angela?"

"Mike, would it be a problem if I said I didn't want anything to go to my home address?"

"No reason why it should be. Do you have a local address you could use?"

"No, I'm afraid not."

"Then I suggest you open a post office box here in Orlando. The main post office is just down the street. When you leave the bank, hang a right, and it's two blocks down the street on the right-hand side. And when you're done with that, let Rosita on reception downstairs have the details. I'll have a word with her, so she will be expecting them. And if you need to redirect your mail from your post office box, all you have to do is ask them to give you a form."

"I wish it was as easy getting things done in England," Angela said.

"We aim to please," the banker said. His secretary came back and handed Angela her passport.

Mike entered the details of the two cheques on a deposit slip and handed the carbon copy to Angela. Then he asked her for a specimen signature, before handing her a temporary chequebook. "The cheque drawn on the bank in the Bahamas could take up to ten days to clear, but you can use the $5,000 immediately. And feel free to overdraw. I'll make sure it's covered. Well, apart from your post office box address, I think we're about done." He got to his feet and put out his hand. "Thank you for your business, Angela. We really appreciate it."

Chapter 30

The limousine that the Hilton had arranged for her turned up earlier than expected, which meant that after Angela had got to the airport and checked in, apart from two members of staff, one of whom served her a coffee, the first-class lounge was deserted.

She took her time drinking her coffee, and then, still having almost two hours to kill, she wandered around the terminal. Unfortunately, as she walked past the gate from which her flight would ultimately depart, she spotted a woman she had known for years, and didn't much care for, in the distance. And she was walking towards her.

"Cooee, Angela. Cooee." Rachel Robinson was waving at her like someone demented.

Pretending she hadn't seen her, Angela turned on her heel and began to walk rapidly in the direction from which she had come. But the woman was not about to be put off. She hurried after her. "Angela, cooee. It's Rachel. Rachel Robinson. Cooee."

Angela could hear the woman running after her and she knew she had no choice. She stopped and turned. "Rachel! Good gracious, fancy meeting you here."

Rachel grabbed Angela's arm and dragged her to the ever-increasing crowd by the departure gate, where her husband and two children were sitting.

"Henry, look who I've found."

Her husband was a loud and uncouth man with a beer belly, a florid complexion, and enough broken veins in his nose to create a road map of Hertfordshire. They knew he and his wife because their children attended the same school as Jason and Melanie. He looked ridiculous in the way only some English people on holiday can look; old khaki shorts, flip-flops, and a safari hat.

He lumbered to his feet.

Angela could smell alcohol on his breath, and she took a step back in case he gave her a hug, which he had a nasty habit of doing when meeting attractive women. "Hello, Henry." She desperately wondered how she could get away.

Rachel's face suddenly lit up and she clapped her hands excitedly. "Why don't we try and get the airline to put us together. It's been ages since we had a good natter."

Angela couldn't remember ever having a good natter with the woman. She avoided her like the plague when she saw her at the school, as did many of the other mothers. And she didn't natter at the best of times. She wasn't the nattering type.

"I don't think they would do that, Rachel," she said. "The plane's probably full. It certainly was on the way out."

"Well let's at least try," Rachel said. "We're in row 47. What's your seat number?"

Angela's heart sank. If she had known she would bump into someone she knew, she would have travelled home in economy. Now, there was every chance Bill would find out she had travelled first class.

She knew she had no choice. "I'm in 3C."

Rachel frowned. "But that's in first-class, isn't it?"

"I'm sorry," Angela said, "you'll have to excuse me." She patted her stomach. "Something I ate, I think." She turned and fled.

So there would be no chance of bumping into the Robinsons again before the flight, Angela hung around in the first-class lounge for so long that when she finally got to the gate the ground staff were about to close the flight. "Thank goodness," they said. "We thought we'd lost you."

Once she had settled into her seat, she began to relax. She knew the Robinsons wouldn't be able to get at her in here.

Angela had never flown first class before and she decided to enjoy the experience. She accepted a glass of champagne before the plane took off, and another one after the seat belt sign had been turned off. Dinner was a culinary delight, and she ate every morsel they put in front of her. She had a Chateau-bottled French Chablis with her smoked salmon starter and her sole bonne femme main course, and a five-star Remy Martin cognac with her cheese platter.

Her dinner things had just been taken away and she was about to settle down and watch a film, when she heard Henry Robinson's strident voice.

"But she's a friend of ours. I only wanted to ask her if she wants to join us for a drink."

"Well, I'm sorry, sir. You can't go in there. It's first class."

"I know it's first class, I'm not blind. All I want to do is ask her if she'll join us for a drink."

A voice exhibiting some degree of control said, "What's her seat number, sir?"

"She's in 3C. Jesus, anybody would think I was trying to get a free upgrade."

Angela closed her eyes and lay still. She was in an aisle seat and she sensed a movement beside her. And then she heard, "I'm sorry, sir. She's sleeping. And now I'm going to have to ask you to return to your seat, sir, because people are trying to sleep and you're disturbing them."

Try as she might, there was no way Angela could sleep. She had far too much on her mind. She ended up watching movies all night long, without a clue what she was watching.

She had known before she phoned Gerry Kiplock and told him she wanted to meet him that she was taking a huge risk, but she had not been able to think of another way of bringing him to heel. She had known he wouldn't listen to reason, and she had been right about that. Now, the second part of the equation came into play, which was how Bill would react when he realised she had slept with Kiplock. And realise he would as soon as he read the letter.

When they had boarded the plane in Orlando, the temperature had been a balmy 86°F. When the captain announced just before breakfast was served that the weather at Gatwick was rain, with squally winds and a temperature of 44°F, a collective groan ran through the plane.

When they taxied to the terminal, Angela waited until the seat belt sign had been switched off, and then she jumped to her feet and started getting her stuff together. She then made her way to the rear of the cabin to wait for the crew to open the door. The moment the door was open, she was off the plane and into the jet way like a scalded rabbit.

She virtually ran through the airport and was second in line at passport control, where she was waved through with a nod and a cursory glance at her photograph. She hurried over to a bank of monitors advising on which carousel passenger's bags would be arriving, found her flight number, checked the number of the carousel, and raced down the escalator. In the baggage hall, she grabbed a trolley, found the carousel, and stood by it urging it to start up.

Her suitcase arrived on the carousel at the exact same moment the Robinsons walked into the baggage hall.

Rachel spotted her and threw her arm in the air and waved. "Cooee, Angela. Angela, cooeee."

Angela grabbed her suitcase and dragged it on to the trolley. She hurried through the nothing-to-declare section of customs and excise and into the crowded arrivals hall.

Bill was standing behind the rail between two large Asian families and Angela spotted him immediately. He looked dreadful. He looked like Oscar Blackman had looked after shuttling between herself and Gerry Kiplock for three days with virtually no sleep. And, while she had only been away for ten days, he looked to have lost weight. His face looked gaunt, which made him look much older than he actually was.

He spotted her, and his face lit up. He made his way through the crowd and threw his arms round her neck and buried his face in her hair.

"God, I've missed you," he said.

"I've missed you too, Bill."

They kissed long and hard.

"Now then, you two. We'll have a bit less of that if you don't mind. This is a public place."

Angela's heart sank.

Robinson guffawed, as if he thought he had just made a great joke. It made him sound like a braying donkey.

"Well this is a small world," Bill said. "Hello, Henry. Hello, Rachel. Have you come off Angela's flight?"

"Oh, yes," Robinson sniffed, "we've come off the same flight, but we travelled coach. We can't afford to travel first-class."

Bill looked at Angela. "But I thought …"

Angela said, "I'll explain later. Bill, can we go home? Please, I'm really tired." She nodded to the Robinsons. "Rachel, Henry, children." She headed for the exit.

Bill had a quick word with the Robinsons and then excused himself and hurried after her.

They walked to the multi-storey car park in silence. She could feel him smouldering. He didn't even offer to push her trolley for her. When they were on the floor on which his car was parked, he spoke for the first time since they had left the Robinsons. "Why are you limping?"

"It's nothing," she said. There was a cold wind blowing through the car park, and she was really cold. She was wearing what she had been wearing in Florida. Not expecting it to be so cold when she got back, since it was still August, she had packed her lightweight summer coat in her suitcase. When they got to Bill's car, she got it out of her suitcase and put it on.

Bill tossed her suitcase in the boot, and slammed the lid. He shoved the trolley out of the way, letting it bang into a wall, and then climbed into the driver's seat.

For the first time since Angela couldn't remember when, he didn't open the car door for her.

The interior of the car was uncomfortably cold, but Bill didn't seem to notice. He sat staring through the windscreen with the ignition key in his hand. Finally, he turned to her. "Angela, I'm just about to go under, and you're swanning around the bloody world flying first-class. I thought we had an agreement. What the hell are you playing at?"

"Bill, there is an explanation, but I haven't slept and I'm really tired. Can we talk about this later? And I'm cold, Bill. In fact, I'm freezing. Would you please turn the heater on?"

Bill started the car, and turned the heater up to full. He then turned the fan speed up to full.

Angela endured the cold air battering her face without a word.

By the time they had got to the M25, the interior of the car had become comfortably warm and Angela let her seat back and tried to take a nap.

But Bill was not playing loving husband this morning. He knew what first-class air tickets cost and he was so angry with Angela that he tried to make the journey as uncomfortable for her as he possibly could. When he came up behind another vehicle, he jammed on the brakes, and then he swerved around the other vehicle and accelerated away, hard. And this went on for some time.

Angela was thrown around like a rag doll. She rarely had a problem with motion sickness, but on two occasions she was on the point of asking him to pull over because she felt sick and thought she might throw up.

Twice, he looked down at her, his eyes blazing, and demanded, "How could you, Angela? We had an agreement. How could you?"

When they got home, he skidded to a stop outside the front door, and yanked on the handbrake. He leapt out of the car, leaving the engine running, and marched round to the boot. He got Angela's suitcase out of the boot and dumped it on the drive.

Angela got out of the car and picked up her suitcase. "Thank you for picking me up," she said.

"You're welcome. I'll be in my office." He jumped back in the car and roared off down the lane.

The house was cold and Angela switched on the heating and turned up the thermostat. She walked into the kitchen and put the kettle on. She put a teabag in a mug and sat at the breakfast bar to wait for the water to boil.

The house felt cheerless and unwelcoming, as if somehow conveying to her the message that she no longer had any right to be there. What with that, and the way Bill had treated her after what she had put herself through for him …

"Welcome home, Angela," she murmured.

The water in the kettle began to boil.

Chapter 31

Bill drove to the office, muttering darkly about disloyalty and not being able to trust anyone including your wife. But angry as he was with her, he was glad Angela was back. He had missed her. Rattling around in that big house with nothing but a bottle of malt scotch for company was a downhill slope to nowhere.

As he drove, his anger began to dissipate and he began to think more clearly. What Angela had done had been completely out of character. She had always been the one to count the pennies, instilling in the children, and in him from time to time, the age-old mantra that, if you look after the pennies, the pounds will look after themselves. He felt sure there was a rational explanation for her spending all that money on a first-class ticket, but the main thing was that she was back safe and sound.

He got to the office a few minutes after 10am. Maureen was not at her desk, but she had evidently been in because the mail and the overnight faxes from New York were on his desk.

He read the faxes first. They were all from New York, and they were the usual stuff: vessel nominations, answers to Patrick and Trevor's queries, making suggestions as to where a certain grade of paper or board might fit, etc.

In addition to sending overnight faxes, at close-of-play each day New York also sent a package containing copies of original bills of lading and original invoices for onward transmission to forwarding agents, with copies to the buyers, and Maureen had, as usual, opened last night's package and put everything in a pile. In the middle of the pile was a cream-coloured envelope addressed to him and marked private and confidential.

There had been a time when Maureen would have put an envelope addressed to him and marked Private and Confidential, at the top of the pile, and there had been a time when her putting it in the middle of the pile would have hacked him off. But at this stage, there was no point in getting hacked off. Two days from now, Friday, his world would collapse like a pack of cards and nothing would matter.

He slit the envelope with his pearl-handled paper knife, and withdrew the letter it contained. He unfolded it to read it and, to his astonishment, two cheques fell out.

The cheques, which were drawn on a Manhattan back, were from Kiplock Inc and they were made out in favour of his, Bill's, original company. One was for the exact amount of the commission Patrick had earned on business he had brought in since he had joined the company, and the other one was for the exact amount of the commission that he, himself, had earned on the business he had concluded with Heikki Pentilla's company before the joint venture had been created, and which Gerry Kiplock had snatched, entirely illegally, from under his nose.

Mystified as to why these cheques had been sent to him, he picked up the letter. It was a one-page letter typed on Kiplock Inc stationery and signed by Gerry Kiplock. It began, 'Dear Bill, I have no doubt you will be surprised to be getting this letter and these two cheques, but all things considered I feel it would be in the best interests of both parties if we were to wind up the joint venture.'

"What in hell is going on?" Bill muttered.

Under normal circumstances, he would have jumped for joy, but his immediate reaction was to question why Kiplock was letting him off the hook.

As he read on, it made less and less sense. Kiplock was saying it wasn't necessary for him to pay back the $150,000 he had paid him for his shares in his company, which made no sense at all, because it was clearly stated in the partnership agreement that in the event of the partnership being wound up, this money had to be paid back. The same applied to the $75,000 Kiplock had stumped up to help the company's cash flow when Patrick came on board. This had been covered by a codicil to the effect that this also would have to be repaid. None of it made any sense. Gerry Kiplock was known as a hard-headed businessman, not a philanthropist.

The rest of the letter was about releasing him from all and any present or future obligations towards Kiplock Inc, and informing him that he was free to trade without encumbrance or restriction in the UK and any other market in which he chose to trade, America excepted. The letter wished him well in the future.

Bill put the letter down and sat back in his chair, flummoxed. What on earth could have prompted this seismic about turn?

The more he thought about it, the more the penny began to drop. Angela had had something to do with it. She must have. She must have met up with Kiplock while she was away. There was no other explanation.

He knew from the quick word he had had with Henry and Rachel Robinson earlier that morning that Angela had come from Orlando. All right, so she hadn't gone to New York, but Orlando, to a man who travelled the world as much as Gerry Kiplock did, was a mere hop, skip, and a jump. He would make a trip like that as easily as someone else might get into a taxi to go across town in Manhattan.

But as to how she had persuaded Kiplock to do what he had done, that didn't bear thinking about. Bill knew with a cast-iron one-hundred-percent degree of certainty that his partner would not have let Angela sweet-talk him into letting him off the hook, it had to be something more. She had to have slept with him.

But there had to be more to it than that, because Kiplock was turning his back on a lot of money, and he was certainly not naive when it came to money. Could she have blackmailed him? Yes, blackmail would do it. But what could she have threatened him with? It would have to be something serious, like threatening his future, or his liberty.

By now, Bill's imagination was running wild. His thoughts went back to her asking him not to ask her where she was going, and not to try and contact her while she was away. What else had she been up to? And why had she travelled first class on the way back? He had a pretty good idea how much that must have cost. Was she suddenly feeling rich for some reason? He wasn't surprised she had been so keen to get away from the Robinsons. If they hadn't told him she had travelled first class, he would never have known. It must have been quite a shock to her to realise they were on her flight.

This was a side to Angela he hadn't known existed, and he began to wonder what else he didn't know about her.

Just then, Maureen walked in.

"Morning, Bill. Did Angela get back safely?"

He nodded. "Yes, she got back safely."

"Are you all right, Bill? You're as white as a sheet. Would a coffee help?"

Bill had a sudden thought. "Maureen, do you happen to remember if you spoke to Gerry last week?"

"Which part of the week were you thinking of, because he was away from Wednesday onwards and I couldn't make contact with him. Why do you ask?"

It all fitted together. The thought of Angela in bed with Gerry Kiplock made him feel physically sick.

"No reason. I'm going out for a while. If there are any calls, take a message."

Bill spent the next two hours driving round the Hertfordshire countryside. He was in a daze, and he was oblivious to other traffic, or to where he was. He began to realise he had been doing a lot of surmising and that he could have got a lot of it wrong. The only way to get at the truth was to talk to Angela, and he drove home.

In the house, there was no sound other than the ticking of the clock on the wall in the kitchen. Angela's unopened suitcase was in the hall and he assumed she was asleep in bed. He was tempted to open it to see if he could find some incriminating evidence. He went into the kitchen and started to make himself a cup of tea.

A voice from upstairs called, "That you, Bill?'

"Yes, it's me. I'm making myself a cup of tea. Do you want one?"

"I might as well. I've been trying to sleep, but I can't."

Bill made two mugs of tea and carried them upstairs. Angela was sitting up in bed in her pyjamas with the curtains drawn. "You might as well open the curtains," she said. "I'm obviously not going to be able to sleep."

Bill put the tea down and drew back the curtains, flooding the bedroom with light. He handed Angela her tea.

"What are you doing home?" she said, taking a sip and warming her hands on the mug.

He put his tea down and took the letter and the two cheques from the inside pocket of his jacket and handed them to her.

"I don't suppose you know anything about these?" he asked sarcastically.

"What are they?" Angela said, feigning ignorance.

"I would have thought that was obvious. One of them is a letter from Gerry, and the other two are cheques. They came in with the overnight courier bag."

Angela made a show of reading a letter she had dictated verbatim, and then looking at the cheques. She put the letter and the cheques on the duvet in front of her, and looked up at him.

"But this is brilliant, Bill," she enthused. "It means you have nothing more to worry about."

"Angela, do you seriously expect me to believe you know nothing about this?"

"Perhaps he just had a change of heart."

"Yes, and pigs might fly. You met him while you were away, didn't you, Angela?"

Angela saw no point in denying it, or dragging it out. The sooner it was brought out into the open and dealt with, the sooner they could move on.

"Yes, I met him," she admitted. "I couldn't see everything you and I had worked for, for all these years, go down the drain."

"And you slept with him, didn't you?" Bill demanded, his blood pressure rising and his face reddening. "There's no other way he would have done what he's done."

His attitude was beginning to annoy her. He couldn't see beyond the end of his male pride, and after all she had done for him.

"Hang on a second, Bill. You've gone from the depths of despair, from staring bankruptcy in the face. Your debts have been wiped out; you've got your business back, and you've got Gerry Kiplock off your back. What's a little sacrifice on my part compared to all that? You should be over the moon."

"Ah," Bill said gleefully, knowing he had been right, "so you did sleep with him?"

"Yes, Bill, I slept with him."

"Tell me, Angela, was he as good in bed as me? Or was he better?"

Her temper rising, Angela said, "What do want Bill, a blow-by-blow account? You shouldn't ask a question like that; you might get an answer you don't like. Drop it, for God's sake! I slept with him. Get used to it."

"And what if I can't get used to it?"

"Then we have a problem."

Chapter 32

Gerry Kiplock was at his desk working on a report when his phone rang. He picked up. "What is it, Marcia?"

"Your stockbroker's on the line."

"Put him through."

"It's not a him, it's a her."

He recognised her voice immediately. "Marcia said it was my stockbroker."

"I didn't say it was your stockbroker, I told her it was about an investment you made about a year ago."

He chuckled. "How are you, Angela?"

"I'm fine, Gerry. How are you?"

"Hang on, let me shut the door. My wife's in the office." There was a pause. "I wondered if I might hear from you."

"Are you angry with me?"

"Hell, no. I'm not as rich as I used to be, but I respect a worthy adversary."

"I'll take that as a compliment."

"It was meant as one. What can I do for you, Angela?"

"I thought it was time I touched base. I've left Bill."

"I heard. So what are you up to?"

"I've moved to Orlando."

"That figures. Since that was where you banked the cheque."

"I've found myself an apartment in Winter Park, and I've got the children into a really good school. And I've

312

accepted the post of vice president public relations at the Grand Cypress, with responsibility for taking care of celebrities and high-profile people."

"Good for you. Did you and Bill part on good terms?"

"Anything but. I left because he wouldn't stop calling me a bitch and a whore. It got so bad that the children were begging me to leave him."

"And after what you did for him."

"He didn't see it that way."

"Good thing you kept the million dollars."

"Correction, the million dollars less my hospital bill."

Kiplock chuckled.

"Actually, Gerry, your deducting my hospital costs gave me the first real laugh I'd had in ages. I didn't tell Bill about the money because I didn't know how he would react when he found out what I'd done."

"More fool him."

"If only he had tried to understand that I did it primarily for him. I couldn't stand to see him under all that stress."

"So he knows nothing about the money."

"Not a thing. But all credit to him; when I left he put the house on the market and he's promised me half the proceeds when it's been sold. There's a buyer in the offing as we speak."

"Was it in joint names?"

"Yes, it was."

"So you were entitled to half the proceeds, anyway."

"Yes, but he could have been difficult about it. And he helps towards the cost of the children, even though we are living three thousand miles away."

"Does he keep in touch?"

"Not with me. I sent him a card at Christmas and on his birthday, but he doesn't send me cards. He sends them to the children, and he calls them from time to time. And they've been back to England to see him. Apparently he was looking well. And he's found himself a girlfriend, which I'm very pleased about."

"And what about you, Angela? Have you found yourself somebody?"

"Actually, I have met someone. He's vice president of Imagineering at Disney. His wife was killed in a skiing accident in Colorado two years ago, and he has a boy and a girl of similar ages to my two. The kids all get on really well together."

"I hope it works out for you."

"Thank you."

"Will you and Bill get a divorce?"

"I expect so, at some point. Do you still see Maureen when you're in London?"

"Maureen who? You're beginning to sound like an American, Angela. You're picking up the lingo."

"You should hear the children. They sound as if they've been here all their lives."

"Are they enjoying Florida?"

"They're loving it. They have lots of friends, and Jason's taken up golf. By all accounts he could be very good at it."

"That's great."

"And how are things with you, Gerry?"

"Same old, same old. I have offices in Germany, Italy, and Spain now."

"Is Patrick still working for you?"

"Yes, he is. He's one of my best people. I fired Trevor Kingsley. I should have listened to Bill. He was right about him."

314

"Do you ever see Bill, I mean in the course of business?"

"I saw him about a month ago, at a trade dinner in London."

"How was he?"

"He seemed fine. We chatted for a while. He told me his business was doing well."

"Interesting he'll talk to you and not to me. Gerry, I have to go. We have some bigwigs flying in from Washington DC, and I have to make sure everything's ready for them."

"You sound as if you're enjoying life."

"I am. Are you planning a trip to Florida at any time in the foreseeable future?"

"I've no immediate plans, but I'm sure I'll be in Florida at some point. We do have business down there. Did you want to get together?"

"For a drink, for old time's sake, perhaps. Nothing more."

Kiplock raised his voice. "Be right there, hon. Just talking to my stockbroker. I gotta go, Angela." He hung up.

Angela smiled as she put the phone down. "Goodbye, Gerry."